U0092382

Critical Inquiry into English Language Teachers' Minds

解構英語教師

楊文賢　著

封面設計：實踐大學教務處出版組

出版心語

近年來，全球數位出版蓄勢待發，美國從事數位出版的業者超過百家，亞洲數位出版的新勢力也正在起飛，諸如日本、中國大陸都方興未艾，而台灣卻被視為數位出版的處女地，有極大的開發拓展空間。植基於此，本組自民國 93 年 9 月起，即醞釀規劃以數位出版模式，協助本校專任教師致力於學術出版，以激勵本校研究風氣，提昇教學品質及學術水準。

在規劃初期，調查得知秀威資訊科技股份有限公司是採行數位印刷模式並做數位少量隨需出版〔POD＝Print on Demand〕（含編印銷售發行）的科技公司，亦為中華民國政府出版品正式授權的 POD 數位處理中心，尤其該公司可提供「免費學術出版」形式，相當符合本組推展數位出版的立意。隨即與秀威公司密集接洽，出版部李協理坤城數度親至本組開會討論，雙方就數位出版服務要點、數位出版申請作業流程、出版發行合約書以及出版合作備忘錄等相關事宜逐一審慎研擬，歷時 9 個月，至民國 94 年 6 月始告順利簽核公布。

這段期間，承蒙本校謝前校長孟雄、謝副校長宗興、王教務長又鵬、藍教授秀璋以及秀威公司宋總經理政坤等多位長官給予本組全力的支持與指導，本校多位教師亦不時從旁鼓勵與祝福，在此一併致上最誠摯的謝意。本校新任校長張博士光正甫上任（民國 94 年 8 月），獲知本組推出全國大專院校首創的數位出版服務，深表肯定與期許。諸般溫馨滿溢，將是挹注本組持續推展數位出版的最大動力。

本出版團隊由葉立誠組長、王雯珊老師、賴怡勳老師三人為組合，以極其有限的人力，充分發揮高效能的團隊精神，合作無間，各司統籌策劃、協商研擬、視覺設計等職掌，在精益求精的前提下，至望弘揚本校實踐大學的校譽，具體落實出版機能。

實踐大學教務處出版組　謹識

2006 年 7 月

自序

台灣目前正興起一股「英文學習」熱潮，全民學英文的盛況可說是空前激烈，孕育而生的是學術界對於英語學習各種教學法與相關議題的研究、探討和創新。然而，對於「英語師資」課題的探討，相較之下卻顯得異常冷清，一方面是因「流浪教師」的議題發酵、教師員額過剩、和英語師資不致匱乏的問題掩蓋了對研究英語師資培育問題的熱情；另一方面，則是因為英語學習者似乎非常熱中追求所謂的英語神速學習法，而對於英語師資的議題也就顯得不是那麼關心。事實上，要達到成功的英語教育，「老師」絕對是一個重要的關鍵因素。在英語學習的領域之中，我們大部分關心的是學生要學什麼、學生在想什麼；可是，「英語老師在想什麼」卻似乎得不到相同的關愛眼神。

老師不是與生俱來就會教書，他們必須不斷接受專業訓練、教學刺激、學習者的回饋和自我的專業成長，才能逐漸形成出一套屬於自己恆久的教學哲學、教育理念、教學態度和方法，而這些個人化的信仰卻深深地決定老師們在課室裡的教學表現，進而影響到學習者的學習。本書的目的即在將英語教學研究的焦點轉到英文老師們的身上，藉由一篇篇的研究專文論述來探討台灣的英文老師心中對於自己的專業到底作如何的詮釋和思考，來幫助老師和旁人更了解我們的英語老師心中到底如何看待「英語教學」這份專業。因此，本書的各章節大部分都是以現職的英文教師做為研究對象，探討的議題包括了：英語教師的特質、好的英語教學、外籍英語與本籍英師的比較、職前教師培訓、教師評鑑等等議題。茲將各章之重點扼述如下。

第一章為本書其餘各章節奠定研究理論哲學的框架。在教育研究的範疇之中，長久以來存著研究法的「典範之爭」，量化研究和質性研究實各有所長，但亦各有所缺，孰優孰劣的爭論一直困擾著教育研究者。本章即將兩種不同的研究法做了一系列的比較和對照，最終目的在於鼓勵研究者根據自己所抱持的哲學論和知識論選擇最適合的研究方法。因筆者深信教育研究的對象幾乎都是以「人」為主，而人的處理與非生命性資料的處理本質上是不同的，因此本書所進行的各項研究幾乎都是以質性研究方法的理論做為一系列研究的框架。

第二章探討了目前在台灣的全民運動－英語學習熱潮。本章分為兩部分，第一部分討論了英語如何影響我們的生活層面，包括中文的使用、文化習慣的養成和自我認知等等。第二部分則著重在探討台灣目前的英語學習熱潮所帶出來的一連串值得我們重新省思的議題，比如學習資源的分布不均、英語能力的城鄉差距、或被普遍接受和推崇的英語教學方法等等議題。此章在鼓勵英語教師對現存的英語教育做一批判性的反思。

在第三章裡，我們調查了英語學習者和未來的英語老師們對於現今台灣英語教育的態度和認知。雖然大部分的參與者都認同學習英文在現今社會的重要性和急迫性，但是，職前英語教師的態度卻相較保守許多，其對於英語學習的成效和急迫性似乎沒有比其他組別來得樂觀。第四章中將探討目前台灣許多英語學習者和他們的家長的一種普遍迷思－金髮碧眼的外籍老師教英語一定比台灣籍的老師教得更「血統純正」。本章在第一部分中首先比較了這兩種英語教師在教學上先天的教學優劣，並嘗試破除對外師過度崇拜的迷戀情節；在第二部分中，我們提供了自己的英語教學和與外籍老師共事的經驗來佐證前半章中所提出的論點。

第五章則研究了所謂「好的英文老師」所應具備的特質。雖然我們通常可透過一些評量工具來評鑑一位英語老師是否稱職，包括其教學技巧與策略、英語教學的學科知識、或個人的教學信仰等等，但多數的這些評量工具都是由歐、美所謂的英語系國家或學者所研發的，換句話說，也就是缺乏了融入在地化的教學特色。本研究即顯示台灣的英語學習者對於所謂好的英語老師所要求的條件和能力比重可能與他國有所不同，此項發現對於有心在台灣從事英語教學的台灣或外籍老師應該有啟發的作用。

本書的第六、第七章都在探討英語教師的職前訓練等議題。師資培育者對於英語實習老師的評鑑除了臨床視導外，另一項被視為評量實習老師實習過程的另類評量工具即是「實習檔案」。藉由實習檔案的建立，大學指導教授、實習學校輔導老師和英語實習老師能清楚的檢視實習中的成長過程和教學脈絡，也希望透過教學檔案的建立能培養出實習老師時時省思教學的能力，進而達到專業成長。然而，本研究卻發現缺乏師資培育機構職前的導入教育、和實習學校的輔導與督促，實習教師所整備的檔案會過度流於表面化甚至綜藝化、缺乏深度的教學省思、無法體認現今的教育方針和政策等等，因此最終導致流於形式而已。而在第七章中，我們探討了現今台灣師資過剩的問題，即如何提升職前教師未來的競爭力。本章採用了「藍海策略」中所提倡的四大行動模式－即去除、降低、提升和創造，來幫助英語職前教師創造出屬於自己的個人價值曲線，使得其他競爭者變得不相干，進而開創出無人能取代、不易模仿的新個人價值。本章發現，現今職前英語教師的同質性過高，且選擇從事英語教學的原因多屬於外部驅動，也因此造成老師們普遍缺乏內部省思、和自我能力強弱分析的能力。

本書的最後一章，第八章主要在研究現職英語教師對於「教師評鑑」的知覺和態度，並試圖從社會文化的層面來探討台灣中等學校實施教師評鑑的可行性。台灣在成功進入世界貿易組織與世界經濟接軌之後，「追求卓越、競爭世界」的教育政策是政府在全球化下的另一個教育目標，而實施「教師評鑑」便是達成卓越教育中的一項重要政策。然而，在移植西方社會的教育政策過程中，往往台灣的社會文化因素會被輕忽而嚴重影響到政策的推行。本章便研究了任職於台灣國、高中的二十三位英文教師對於「教師評鑑」的認知和態度，且檢視台灣的社會文化因素在實施教師評鑑中可能所扮演的影響角色。文中亦回顧了文獻中有關「教育改革」和「教育進步」的不適連結的課題、全球化中所忽略的個別情境、教育改革中的跨文化和多元面向的檢視，及提出了曾經實施過「教師評鑑」的國家所面臨的難題和窘境。此研究發現，參與的英語老師易將實施教師評鑑的可行性與台灣社會中普遍存在的「關係」文化及其他文化考量產生連結，進而懷疑其實施的可行性和公正性。研究亦提出下列建議：體認「教改」的複雜性及不確定因素、改革須融入地域特色、考量文化性的反彈、教師的角色須重新定位及賦予權責、和比較教育範疇中的兩地文化。

綜上所述，本書中的大部分章節在於探討英語教師對於其專業的各種可能議題的看法及意見為何。我們深信唯有培育出一個能時時刻刻將自己專業做一番省思的英語教師，才能不斷地促使自我追求專業上的成長，鞭策其在英語教學上的不斷創新，進而維持其全心全意投入英語教學的熱忱。「英語老師到底在想什麼？」著實應該也是研究台灣英語教育中不可或缺的一個重要環節。

最後，我想感謝下列人士的鼎力幫助促使本書能順利完成。感謝所有參與本書中各研究的英語老師與學生，你們的熱情參與和真實回饋激發我能不斷地研究英語師資培育的相關議題。也要對於曾經對於各文章從事匿名審查及提供意見的專家學者們致上誠摯的謝意。當然，最重要的是要感謝實踐大學和教務處出版組的同仁，你們無私的支持和嚴謹的校正工作使得此書能夠順利付梓。也歡迎各位前輩先進能對於本書不吝給予指正。

作者
楊文賢
2006 年 7 月

Preface

This book collected eight research papers which mainly examined English language teachers' perceptions and attitudes towards a number of critical issues about English language education in Taiwan, such as the underlying problems of the heat-wave of English learning island-wide, English language teacher education, and the evaluation of (English) teaching.

For the past few years, English learning has become a whole-people-campaign in Taiwan; thus, the research interests in English language education would largely focus on discussing, investigating or innovating English teaching methods. However, it cannot be ignored that successful English teaching relies much on English language teachers themselves. These English teachers, indeed, have very different teaching philosophies, perceptions, beliefs or attitudes towards their profession which are shaped and refined during the stages of pre-service and in-service teacher education in a very large extent, and would definitely affect their latter performance in a language classroom. What English teachers believe about their quality, training education, and professionalism precisely reflect their teaching philosophies. Hence, reading their minds about the above issues becomes indispensable during the process of developing and ensuring qualified, responsible, reflective, effective, and then successful English teachers. This book is divided into eight chapters, most of which examine a number of critical issues about English teachers' perceptions of their profession. The followings are the abstracts of each chapter.

Chapter 1 establishes the research framework for the following chapters i.e. the appropriate research paradigm for researching human's minds. First, it discusses the issue of paradigms war between scientific research and interpretative research. For many years, these two research paradigms have been regarded miscible, because they are greatly diverse in their assumptions of ontology and epistemology. Nevertheless, this chapter addresses the danger of drawing a clear boundary between the two paradigms, and thus proposes an agreement of armistice. First of all, in order to provide researchers and teachers a basic but clear idea of the characteristics of each paradigm, on the one hand, the paper makes an essential and objective comparison between these two research paradigms in the following areas: assumptions about reality and knowledge, research topics, relationship between the researcher and participants, methodologies, research methods, process and methods of verification, application of research results, and criteria for assessing interpretative and scientific research. In the issue of criteria of evaluating research, the concerns of validity and reliability are discussed together with some personal contributions. However, on the other hand, this chapter also argues that in the domain of education interpretative paradigm or an integrated method can be more desirable and applicable in identifying education problems, especially when the issue of teachers' doing action research in a language classroom is greatly advocated currently. The reasons are firstly, interpretative research emphasises the process of teachers' and students' decision making and interpretation of their own world rather than the objective description of an event. The meaning of each action taken in a language room is equally significant. Secondly, to understand the causality of any event in classroom, teachers' and learners' intentions, reasons, and purposes need to be located, which is exactly valued by interpretative research paradigm. Thirdly, due to the diversities and uniqueness of an educational context, 'particularisation' should be educators' or teachers' major concern instead of 'generalisation'. It is very rare to locate two identical teaching contexts in education and thus one solution cannot be applied to all contexts indiscreetly. Finally, this chapter concludes that there is no golden rule to any paradigm; contrarily, what is of concern should lie in the researcher's flexibility and adjustment to his/her research contexts. It also suggests researchers and teachers liberate themselves from prejudice or exclusion of any research paradigm, and receive any peculiarities and differences for it is believed that knowledge is constructed and multi-dimensional.

Chapter 2 mainly examines the impacts of Englishlisation in Taiwan. For the past few years, due to the deliberate promotion of English learning, status, and value from the Taiwanese government, English seemingly has exercised its overwhelming impacts in the Taiwanese society to an influential degree. The chapter is divided into two major parts to explore these influences of Englishlisation. First, these impacts are examined from three different aspects, namely linguistic area, social area, and cultural area. Linguistically, English language has influenced the morphology of Mandarin in the increasing frequencies of using bi-syllabuses and multi-syllabuses, and of using suffixes. Furthermore, at syntax level English also affect the length of phrases, the use of passive verb together with the use of numeral modifier in Mandarin. In the perspective of social impacts, English has apparently intruded its values on the job market, the media, education, and technology in Taiwan society. In addition, in the aspects of cultural shocks English, indeed, has greatly changed the ethnic identity, the gourmet culture, and traditional values of Taiwan in an invisible but rapid speed. Second, this chapter also argues that though the prevalence of Englishlisation in Taiwan seems irresistible and inevitable presently, it is urgently indispensable to re-examine some critical issues about English language teaching situations and assumptions from now on. English language teaching policies, power, and inequality has lead to the abnormal phenomenon of two peaks distribution in learners' English proficiency. Furthermore, the effectiveness and appropriateness of native ELT methods, especially CLT, and materials also need to be re-considered cautiously for a large number of them are not culture-sensitive enough and neglect to take localised context into consideration. These issues aim to raising language teachers' awareness and reflection on rethinking the English status, impacts, cultures, teaching methods, and learners in their own peculiar teaching contexts. In the end, this chapter concludes that English will still openly and aboveboard exercise its linguistic, social, and cultural power on the Taiwanese society; however, the critical issues of many localised factors need to be addressed in order to achieve productive and culture-sensitive English language teaching. After all, talking about globalisation of English language teaching is impractical and unilateral if without the critical consideration of localisation.

Chapter 3 investigates university students' and English teachers' perceptions and beliefs about English language education in Taiwan. The participants involved in this research are divided into four different groups, including 77 English-majors, 89 non-English majors, 44 prospective English teachers, and 14 in-service English teachers. The revised Foreign Language Education Questionnaire was adopted as the measuring instrument for this study in the first stage. The follow-up interviews were also used as the data of the second stage. These participants' responses reveal that many of them have a very positive attitude towards English language education in Taiwan; however, the four groups also express different degrees of beliefs and concerns in a number of areas of current English learning in Taiwan. The findings indicate that firstly the deliberate promotion of English status from the Taiwanese government has greatly increased the value and importance of English for language learners. Yet secondly, the in-service teacher group comparatively holds a more realistic and cautious view towards English learning. This chapter in the end, suggests that learners' perceptions of English language education may not share a single entity with English teachers in Taiwan, and this perception gap should be came into notice by those prospective, non-native in-service, and newly-introduced native English teachers.

Chapter 4 aims to provide a critical discussion on the value of the native speaker teachers in Taiwan, who have long been presumed to be the authentic and best model of English language instruction. In the first part of the paper, the authors review some significant claims concerning the comparison between the native English-speaking teachers (NESTs) and non-native English-speaking teachers (non-NESTs) and the advantages they can offer to their students respectively. In the second part, the authors refer to an authentic experience in their teaching context to give a further insight into the notion whether native teachers are bound to be superior to their non-native colleagues. In the end, this chapter suggests that students can benefit most from an appropriate form of a collaborative model between the native teachers and their non-native colleagues, and can enjoy the pleasure of learning English.

Chapter 5 explores English language learners' perceptions of qualities and competences of a good English teacher in Taiwan. To achieve a successful practice, English teachers are usually supposed to possess different knowledge and skills. These include practical knowledge about techniques and strategies, content knowledge about ELT, contextual knowledge about the institution, pedagogical knowledge about the restructure of content knowledge, personal knowledge about teaching beliefs, and reflective knowledge. However, the examination of learners' perceptions of what makes a good language teacher can provide teachers and educators another perspective on good teaching. This questionnaire-based research studies university students' opinions about qualities and competencies of a good English teacher from three different positions i.e. ELT competencies, general teaching competencies, and knowledge and attitudes. The results indicate that these learners' concerns about good English teachers are culture-oriented and contextualised. This finding can be helpful for native speakers who plan to teach English in Taiwan.

Chapter 6 and Chapter 7 place the concern on the pre-service English language teacher education in Taiwan. In Chapter 6, it studies the effectiveness of assessing pre-service English teachers' practicum by using the portfolios. In terms of assessment, close-ended testing types have been traditionally preferred by language teachers to adopt on their learners for the consideration of their assumed high reliability and easy execution. However, the current new trends of assessment, in fact, have been regarded to be novel, multiple, alterative, performance-based, communicative, and flexible. The types of these assessments can be represented by task, project, or portfolio for they can evaluate appraisee's performance in a holistic and humanistic perspective. This chapter argues that the means of assessing pre-service English teachers' performance should be based on the above rationale and consequently the adoption of portfolio can be an alternative. This research collected twenty-two pre-service English teachers' practicum portfolios and self reports for data analysis. It is found that most of the participants agree with the claimed advantages of teacher portfolios; however, they also hold a cautious attitude towards the application of its use. Furthermore, most of the data collected are in paper format at a surface level, and data about one-through-nine curriculum are critically lacked. This implies the insufficient preparation of this area for the practice teachers.

Chapter 7 probes pre-service English teachers' perceptions of their current internal strength, internal weaknesses, external opportunities, and external threats of becoming English teachers, and to discuss how to maximise their chances for being English teachers successfully in the future by applying the "blue ocean strategy." Due to the excessive number of prospective English teachers "wandering" over Taiwan presently, forthcoming joiners i.e. pre-service English teachers cannot help but try hard to add extra values in order to increase their chances in job competitions. This competition-based strategy is grounded from the theory of beating others in existing contest space. Thus, they would rather make great effort to create new strength than convert their innate threats into innovative values. Nevertheless, such a red ocean strategy generates more competitions and merely exploits existing demand instead. What a pre-service English teacher needs is to create uncontested opportunities and thus to make his/her competitors irrelevant. This research adopts the method of self-reports to analyse the participants' perceptions of their own existing strength and weaknesses, and their foreseen opportunities and threats for success. The data collected are categorised into several perspectives for further discussion i.e. English language education policy, socio-economic influences, cultural concerns, career planning, and language teacher professionalism. It is found that firstly these pre-service English teachers tend to pessimistically de-value themselves in terms of personal characteristics and secondly they perceive that the way to future success lies mainly on improving their present shortcomings and weaknesses. In other words, they are unable to see the importance of creating innovative values and capturing new demands for English teachers in the 21st century. They simply follow others rather than making others followers. This chapter ends with arguing the application of blue ocean strategy to re-transform this situation.

The final chapter, Chapter 8 is the longest article in the book, which talks about a very popular issue in Taiwan currently i.e. teacher appraisal. This chapter investigates the potential problems of introducing teacher appraisal in secondary schools in Taiwan and discusses the desired leadership and management in education for implementing this new change from the perspective of societal culture concerns. After Taiwanese government's successful entry into WTO (World Trade Organisation), the authorities concerned, mainly MOE (Ministry of Education) also try to link their educational policies with world globalisation in order to pursue excellence and compete with other nations. One change among these is teacher appraisal. However, cultural issues on implementing this westernised educational change are always neglected, which may greatly influences the success of change in the end. This research examines twenty-three Taiwanese secondary English teachers' perceptions and attitudes towards teacher appraisal, and the roles of culture playing in administering teacher appraisal by conducting two-staged procedures i.e. open-ended questionnaire and following-up semi-structured phone interviews. This chapter also briefly reviews the literature on the issues of inappropriate connection between educational change and educational progress, the lacks of considering individual societal context while pursuing educational globalisation, and cross-dimensions and cross-cultural examination of educational change. Furthermore, the practical difficulties a number of countries i.e. the US, the UK, Korea, Japan, and Hong Kong have met while implementing teacher appraisal are discussed as well. This research finds that the participants' responses to the introduction of teacher appraisal are highly linked with the influences of cultural dimensions in Confucianism Taiwan. The participants do not strongly reject teacher appraisal but highly doubt the effectiveness and fairness of its administration in Taiwanese society, where "*guanxi*" may play an important part in influencing the fairness of appraisal results. The findings of this research suggest that firstly, due to the huge misunderstanding in associating educational change with educational progress, we need to recognise the complexity of a change such as types of leadership, destabilisation, or uncertainty. Secondly, a critical reshape of globalisation to fix local context is required in implementing educational change because 'globalisation' and 'accountability' mainly come from economy or commerce, and thirdly, cultural resistance or worries towards the fairness of change should be taken into account. Fourthly, in order to achieve long-term professional development, the final objective of teacher appraisal, an educational leader should help teachers to transform themselves to be empowered leaders as well as changing agents, and finally the government is advised to compare what are the gaps in existing in the educational systems between western societies and Taiwanese society before it implements a borrowed educational change.

Most of the above chapters are written and organised around one central theme i.e. how English language teachers perceive their profession. It is argued that without helping these teachers raise their own concerns, perceptions, and reflections about themselves and their profession, successful language teaching is hardly attainable. It is our hope in this book to educate and develop reflective teachers in an English language classroom by challenging them to keep asking and reflecting on their profession and to achieve professional growth in the end.

This book is the product of my several years of teaching English and training English teachers in Taiwan. The participants' contribution did teach and inspire me a lot. Their positive supports stimulated and affirmed me researching these issues constantly. I am very grateful to all the participants who got involved with the studies in this book. In addition, I appreciate a lot for many unknown reviewers who spent much time and efforts reading the papers and offering me invaluable advice to make the papers more solid. Finally, my gratitude also extends to my colleagues in Shih-Chien University, especially the Publishing Division. Without their generous help in editing, this book cannot be finished.

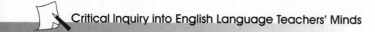

Table of Contents

目次

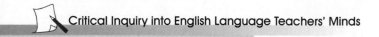

Chapter1

The Appropriate Paradigm for Educational Research

The most important thing is not where we are
but where we are going to

-----by myself

INTRODUCTION

"Paradigms War" is a commonly used term to vividly describe the opposite of two main different research paradigms i.e. scientific paradigm versus interpretive paradigm. Are these two paradigms thoroughly opposite or could they be compatible to some extent? Trying to answer this complicated question would perhaps lead to another "war".

Lincoln and Guba (1988) consider these two paradigms "miscible", just as oil is infusible with water. The basic distinction of the two is deeply rooted in their different assumptions of ontology and epistemology. If we try hard to fuse them together reluctantly, then both of them will be fakes.

As Belleck's (in Gou, 1994) illustration, the relationship between two paradigms are based on three arguments. The first one is "subjective interpretation" versus "objective description." The former one emphasises teachers' and students' making their own sense in any classroom event subjectively while the latter focuses on researchers' describing the teaching objectively. In other words, interpretivism tries to understand the meaning of action toward actors but empiricism tries to understand the meaning of action toward researchers. Secondly, it is the relationship between "quality" and "quantity". Some interpretivists believe if social phenomena can be "measured", then they have already lost the originalitities. However, to empiricism, "numbers" or "statistics" do possess great scientific and inner values. The third argument is about reason/intention and causality. Interpretivists put stress on the reasons, intentions and purposes from teachers and students in order to understand the causality of any event in classroom; however, empiricists ignore the reasons and intentions while only describing the causality of any classroom event objectively.

Moreover, Schulman (1986) also proposes that the main difference between social science and natural science lies in that social science can embrace many different competing paradigms in order to obtain a clearer view about events. An event can be made sense from different paradigms, from different theories, from different angles, from different concepts and even from different levels. With embracing so many different paradigms, we could have a panoramic view of an event. Therefore, Schulman (1986) asserts that to develop social science soundly, the combination of different research designs seems to be necessary. Despite that, we also should bear in mind that this different knowledge, deriving from different designs, would definitely serve different needs. Failing to realise this would bring about chaos in the educational research.

Furthermore, when taking about teaching, Erickson (1986) believes some phenomena in teaching are absolutely identical across cultures and countries. Some are the same under the identical history and culture while the others are totally unique to participants. What interpretivists really concern is "particularisation" rather than "generalisation".

In fact, there are still numerous disputes about the compatibility of two different paradigms; however, is it the right time to cease the "paradigm war" now? As discussed earlier, my purpose of doing research should determine my choice of a paradigm and there is no right or wrong (good or poor) in-between, I believe. The choice totally depends on our own assumptions of reality and knowledge; however, if we could have a clearer idea about more differences between these two paradigms, then it would be of help for us to make a right decision more easily in doing research. Hence, in the following section, I try to make some comparisons between interpretive paradigm and scientific paradigm from some different aspects.

THE DIFFERENCES BETWEEN TWO PARADIGMS

In this part, I would like to discuss briefly about some potential differences between scientific paradigm and interpretive paradigm.

In the assumptions about the ontology/reality and epistemology/knowledge

First of all, we need to look at the philosophical underpinnings of two paradigms. Perhaps talking about ontology and epistemology would be all Greek to researchers or teachers, yet I believe that "without the light of an articulated philosophical perspective, one is likely to stumble over objects and to misunderstand the nature of rooms within which one is stumbling around" (Maykut & Morehouse, 1994: 22). Moreover, practically speaking, philosophic concepts are also fairly crucial in determining which research methodology we would apply and then what criteria we need to assess our research.

In the beginning, we would like to ask: "What is the nature of the world?" and "What is real?" These questions are exactly what ontology concerns: what is the nature of reality? In the scientific viewpoint, there is merely one reality. "By carefully dividing and studying its parts, the whole can be understood" (Lincoln & Guba, 1985). It means only one truth exists in the world, no matter who tests it, when and where s/he tests it. On the contrary, to interpretivism realities are multiple, constructed and interconnected. That is reality exists only when we make sense of the world and is "the product of processes by which social actors (human beings) together negotiate the meanings for actions and situations" (Crotty, 1998:11). Thus, we can assert reality is always changing in different forms. Accordingly, our different views about reality would directly affect us how we see ourselves in relation to knowledge. Then, this is indeed what "epistemology" concerns: "How do we know what we know?" "What is the relationship between the knower and the known?" In scientific paradigm, knowledge is obtained by studying the objects in the right way, and then we can discover the objective truth i.e. knowledge is created out of nothing. Knowledge can be divided into several parts and examined individually. The knower keeps a distance from who or what s/he is examining (Crotty, 1998; Lincoln & Guba, 1985). However, for an interpretivist, s/he cannot separate herself/himself from what is known. For him/her, there is no objective truth waiting for being discovered. Knowledge is not discovered but constructed and only exists when we engage realities in our world. Knowledge is constructed out of our minds and obviously different minds interpret different meanings even about the same phenomenon (Crotty, 1998).

Also, Erickson(1986) points out clearly that the basic distinction between a scientific research and an interpretive research lies is their separate assumptions about the causality. Under the insistence of scientific paradigm, any causality existing between two individual objects in the natural world could be described with a mechanical, chemical, biological term.

"One event comes before another event and can be said to cause that event" (Lincoln & Guba, 1985). Causality is definitely fixed and identical. When this concept is applied by the empiricists to explain the causality between each human being, it is the researcher that defines the meaning of the "observed behaviour", not the action-giver himself/herself (Gou, 1994). However, based on Erickson's (1986) view toward the causality, "behaviour" is totally different from "action" for an interpretive researcher. The former refers to the object's movement while the latter means not only "behaviour" but the interpretation of it between an action-giver and an action-receiver. It is because interpretive researchers recognise

> *the existence of structural conditions and within these conditions the way that people interpret the meaning of the process and practices as they appear to them in the situations that confront them and how they construct new forms of action as a result of that interpretation. The individual is at the forefront, interacting, negotiating and having influence on the groups and the organization of s/he is a part (Radnor, 2000 : 19).*

And, it is this interpretation that reveals clearly the reality of human's interpreting the causality in a social world i.e. causality is in multi-directional relationship and shaped mutually.

In the research topics

In scientific research, a researcher usually already has a clear idea of what s/he does not know in the beginning and therefore s/he would design some certain kind of research instrument then in hope of digging the "truth" out. Contrarily, a researcher conducting interpretive research does not know what s/he does not know before carrying out the research (Guba & Lincoln, 1988). In other words, what s/he really concerns is "What happens here and now?" and "What does this mean for the researcher and the participants actually?" Usually, the scientific research is closely related to the studies of psychology, sociology, economics and politics while the interpretive ones would mostly establish an intimate relationship with the studies of sociology, history and anthropology (Bogdan & Biklen, 1982; Lincoln & Guba, 1985).

In the relationship between the researcher and participants

Owing to the pursuit of the claiming "objectivity" by scientific researchers, a researcher's relationship with the participants (or" the researched"—a term would mostly used in a scientific research in replace of the word "participants"; however, I prefer to use the term "participants" because human beings should not be viewed as animals, waiting for being elicited some data.) is totally "distant." Here, I mean their relationship is supposed to be independent mutually. The distance between two are clearly drawn. Conversely, in interpretive research, their relationship can be described as "inter-subjectivity." Because a researcher himself/herself is used as the research tool, the relationship between them is "interactive", which would help the researcher look at the whole context or questions more closely and deeply from the point of being one of the participants.

In the methodologies

Methodology refers to "the frames of references, models, concepts, and ideas which shape the selection of a particular set of data-gathering techniques" (Hitchcock & Hughes, 1989:14). This means a researcher will choose his/her most suitable or appropriate methodology based on his/her assumptions of reality and knowledge; therefore, usually the methodology a researcher adopts for his study can reflect which paradigm s/he stands for.

Though some researchers would propose that the different objectivities of researches should need different methodologies, Schulman (1986) suggests that different realities in research determine different applications of methodologies. This means the researcher's attitude toward the concepts of learning and teaching would influence his/her choice among different methodologies. As a whole, scientific and interpretive researchers tend to use different research methodologies naturally.

According to Gou's (1994) categorisation, the using of experiments, survey, and structured-observation would be adopted in scientific-based research. Scientific research mainly is verified through statistical methods; therefore, the number of participants is usually large enough to be "representative" and thus the results of the research could be hopefully generalisable to other contexts. In this way, the research tools are supposed to be quite objective i.e. the research items and contents had been set in advance; then whoever uses the tool later would be satisfied with the consistent results.

Contrastingly, an interpretive researcher would mainly use what s/he already has in hand now (Guba & Lincoln, 1988). The methodology in interpretive paradigm may include ethnography, participant observation, naturalistic inquiry, case study and field study. Under the shield of an interpretive methodology, the research herself/himself is the best ready-made research tool here and now. Hence, the most common characteristics are communicating, longitude-observing or reviewing the related literature through exchanging the sensitive senses and empathetic feelings between a researcher and participants. It is because an interpretivist will not usually make an assumption of what will happen in advance, i.e. none of fixed or advance-designed procedure or testing items will be set up; in other words, the researcher simply keeps on participating, discovering, adjusting and verifying the procedures and answers by continuous observations and interactions between two parties.

As a whole, the characteristics of interpretivism methodology can be concluded as follows, compared with that in scientific paradigm (Huang, 1991). It is

(1) descriptive: The data are descriptive and soft; each phenomena is equally important. What it is concerned about is the research process instead of the products.

(2) holistic: The researcher will conduct the study in a holistic view rather than treating place and participants as separate variables.

(3) naturalistic: The researcher focuses on the natural context, not designed context to conduct the study. S/He interacts, observes, listens and reviews with their participants to obtain first-hand knowledge.

(4) participant perspectives: The researcher explores the knowledge or reality as an insider instead of an outsider. In other words, s/he thoroughly involves herself/himself with the research as a participant to embed the meaning to the research.

(5) inductive: The researcher is continuously developing or re-shaping his/her ideas, theories or perspectives through data collection instead of verifying the assumption by collecting data.

(6) flexible: The researcher is flexible, filed-based, not controlled by variables. Not until the researcher enters the field does s/he gradually discover the problems, clarify them and then negotiate meaning.

(7) non-judgmental: Each perspective is equally valuable. What the researcher looks for is not making the judgment of the

truth or moral standard, but respects for the perspectives of each participant.

(8) humanistic: Everything in the society happens for its first time and is researchable for an interpretivist. S/He learns and appreciates human's inner life, efforts, success and failures through interacting with people.

(9) the process of learning: An interpretive researcher learn how to view his/her world from the participants and raises new perceptions about his/her values.

In the research methods

As discussed in the previous section, different methodologies result from different assumptions of knowledge, which cannot be changed easily for a researcher. However, research methods can exist across different methodologies. Thus, different methods cannot be categorised exclusively. It means it is nearly impossible to allocate each method to either a scientific or an interpretive methodology absolutely and exclusively. Sometimes, a scientific methodology may adopt a method from an interpretive aspect in our presumption and so does an interpretive methodology. Even sometimes, a method will be classified into different areas on the basis on researcher's viewpoints. For example, the method of a case study would be classified into the interpretive methodology for the most part; however, data collecting and data analysis in a case study are still strongly influenced by researchers' academic areas. It is obvious that the means of collecting and analysing data are distinguished between a case study in psychology and a case study in ethnology (Gou, 1994).

Usually, it is very easy to categorise mistakenly all quantitative methods into scientific paradigm narrowly and all qualitative methods into interpretive paradigm. However, the truth is that by using a qualitative method, a researcher could conduct his/her study either qualitatively or quantitatively. Similarly, a quantitative method could also be used in either qualitative or quantitative research studies. "Research methods are techniques which taken on a specific meaning according to the methodology in which they are used" (Sliverman, 2001) and it is the overall of a research methodology that shapes how each method is applied.

However, generally observation, analysing texts and documents, interviews are the examples of methods used in a qualitative research. In interpretive paradigm, the researcher himself/herself is the tool of collecting data and analysing them. This 'humanistic tool' enters its researching filed, where is filled with ideas, thoughts and emotions in a society, with its own emotions, ideas, and thoughts. It means the process of collecting data in interpretive paradigm is the process of learning— learning how to communicate ideas and learning how to establish trustworthy relationship.

On the contrary, in scientific paradigm the researcher usually adopts the methods of experiments, tests or questionnaires. Usually, these 'tools' are ready-made and used to elicit many numbers or data to testify the original assumption, develop a generalised theory or establish one truth or standard from a large sample.

As discussed earlier, we need to clarify that a method could be quantitative or qualitative depending on its nature of research methodology. Then, now we can clearly understand why a quantitative method will be used in qualitative-based research in order to enhance its reliability, and similarly a qualitative method will be administrated as well in quantitative-based research in order to test its validity. (e.g. an open-ended questionnaire will be used for piloting before the final close-ended one is settled down.)

In the processes and methods of verification

Before I explain this difference, it would be helpful if we can identify the characteristics of the processes and verifications between two paradigms with the following words, "Ongoing data, modes, theories, concepts, induction, analytic induction and constant comparisons" are for interpretive paradigm while "gathered data, statistics and deduction" belong to the scientific paradigm (Lincoln & Guba, 1985).

In scientific research, data are always analysed after the complete collection and then verified. However, in interpretive research, data are emerging continuously on the spot and then collected, verified in a circle way through the ongoing interaction between the researcher and participants. Guba and Lincoln (1988) use the Chinese Tai-chi-tou (Yin-Yang) to describe this phenomenon i.e. the stages of discovering data and verifying them are not only mixed but continuous, and cannot be drawn a clear line in-between.

Verification is another potential difference between scientific paradigm and interpretive paradigm. In the scientific research, a researcher will make a hypothesis first and then confirm or falsify it through the statistical methods Therefore, the consideration of validity and reliability are fairly necessary and crucial at each stage. However, though "validity" and "reliability" are taken into account in an interpretive research as well, yet some researchers like Guba and Lincoln (1981) would regard "validity" and "reliability" as unsuitable terms for the interpretive research and thus they replace them with other terms. "Internal Validity" is replaced with "Credibility", "External Validity" is replaced with "Fittingness" and "Reliability" is replaced by "Auditability".

In fact, the interpretive research would be sometimes criticised as being too "soft" just because "validity" and "reliability" are not emphasised so often. Usually, in the interpretive research, the researcher would begin at analysing data, then induct phenomena and finally draw the conclusion without verifying clearly at each stage. This is the main reason why the interpretive research would be thought "weak" (Erickson, 1986). However, this does not mean "verification" is not emphasised at all but just because what the interpretive research concerns is different from a scientific research. In fact, the interpretive research has its own distinct verifications of "validity" and "reliability". This topic will be discussed in detail in the later section, criteria for assessing research.

In the application of research results

According to what Erickson (1986) asserts, the scientific research is searching for "abstract universals" while "concrete universals" is the pursuit of the interpretive research. In other words, the former is trying to conclude a "generalisation", which can be applied to the whatever, whenever and wherever. Explanations from one time and place can be generalised to other times and places, and ambitiously the results can be applied to the largest populations and experiments (Lincoln & Guba, 1985).

But contrarily, interpretivism is looking for a particular phenomenon, which would change accordingly based on different participants, time, places and contexts i.e. "case by case". Only temporary explanations from one time and place are possible (Lincoln & Guba, 1985). In other words, what an interpretivist concerns is "particularisability" while an empiricist is looking for "generalisation" instead (Gou, 1994).

In an educational context, the claims of scientific research seem quite attractive to teachers because it proposes that applying what suggests in the research can lead to a predicted and controlled future. However, is this a truth? "Definitely not." Otherwise, teaching would become a mechanic and easy job. As Radnor (2001: 20) acutely points out, "people in society as one of active agents participating in a dynamic changing network of interaction framed within structural conditions," and very obviously, the school life is changing all the time and it is nearly impossible to "predict" what will happen next to our active students and find out certain solutions to manipulate in advance.

Very realistically, when a teacher is coming across a problem from his/her students, s/he should be endowed with more possibilities to consider, more choices to make, and more solutions to adopt finally. Although the teacher is in control of the setting yet s/he cannot plays the God. S/He should be democratic enough to be ready to negotiate and communicate with her/his participants (or students) instead of forcing her/his own way on them. In other words, s/he is flexible and open enough to re-shape the strategy again and again to satisfy both herself/himself and the participants (or students) (Radnor, 2000). And, this interactive transaction between a researcher and participants is exactly what interpretive research can offer us.

The Criteria for assessing interpretive and scientific research

Usually, we would mis-conceptualise that operating "mounts of" data in a complicated statistical method to get the result can make scientific research enjoy higher status in validity and reliability. In interpretive research, it is because 'human beings' are usually the main research instrument and thus research results mainly come from the researcher's own 'interpretation', which may make it look "soft" in validity and reliability.

However, what I need to clarify is that there is no "perfect" paradigm existing in the world to make its research thoroughly valid and reliable. Each paradigm itself incurs criticisms and what we can do is trying to make each 'better', to make it more 'valid' and 'reliable'. In this following section, I would discuss the general criticism about scientific research and interpretive research and then provide some commonly accepted viewpoints to enhance their validity and reliability.

Validity

Talking about the validity of research, usually those stages in research would be involved: "the study design used, the sampling strategy adopted, the conclusions drawn, the statistical procedures applied or the measurement procedures used" (Kumar, 1999: 137). It is firstly because an interpretive researcher usually verify her/his results from mounts of data from the "well-chosen" examples without applying any complicated statistics, and secondly it is also because "human" is always the only instrument in interpretive research without using any ready-made design from the "fast-bursting assessment market" so that interpretive research is criticised as lacking of validity. Indeed, how to convince researchers themselves (and their audience) that their findings are truly based on the critical investigation into all the collected data, not relying on a few "well-chosen samples" is a very critical problem (Silverman, 2000). Therefore, it appears that some interpretive researchers cannot help but to design some "technical" methods in order to defend their validity and reliability.

In fact, how to enhance validity and reliability has been a major concern for interpretive researchers and thus not surprisingly, many "corrective measures" have been emerging and adopted for the last few decades. As discussed earlier, usually 'human beings' are the only instrument in interpretive researches; therefore, human beings do play a fairly influential role in validity in the research. Then, the question, like "What are the desirable qualities for human instrument?" would rise inevitably. Guba and Lincoln (1981: 138) offer a "straight but unsatisfied" answer as such: "those who have conducted naturalistic inquiry [or interpretive research] over the years." Now, what kinds of qualities should those people be provided with to be considered that their research could have desirable validity? They are supposed to be empathetic, which can facilitate their understanding; they are good listeners and speakers as well, which helps them collect more sensitive data, personal stories and "truth" in a value-resonant social context (Gorden 1975; Wax, 1971; Guba & Lincoln, 1981).

Reliability

Regarding to the threats of internal reliability, referring to "the degree to which other researchers, given a set of previously generated constructs, would match them with data in the same way as did the original researcher," (LeCompte & Preissle, 1993: 323) in interpretive research, firstly it may come from researchers' biases (similar to filters or selective perceptions), which means researchers may filter some unwanted data, select well- representative samples or draw the conclusions in order to match their theories and knowledge in the research assumptions.

Since we cannot eliminate our own theories and knowledge, then the possible way to avoid biases is to become increasingly aware of them i.e. how they filter what we hear, how they interfere our reality and how they transfigure truth into falsify (Guba & Lincoln, 1981). At least, we should do our best to transfer our "biases" into the limitations of our research rather than the "attacked targets."

Secondly, the threat may come from misinterpretation or oversimplification of an interaction. The most common ways to solve this problem are:

- having multiple researchers involve with the same research site
- requiring research assistants (e.g. doing the job of translation) if needed
- manipulating the peer examination of the findings
- and recording data mechanically with tape recorders, photographs or videotapes, etc.

Next, with respect to how to enhance the external reliability, meaning if a researcher can discover the same phenomenon or generate the same findings under the identical or similar settings, of the data in interpretive research, here are some principles recognised and provided by ethnographers. First of all, a researcher should clearly states his/her role and status within the participants investigated.

Secondly, the researcher should clearly describe how s/he selected the participants in case the similar setting has to be replicated in the later research. Thirdly, the context of the participants should also be explicated in complete detail in order to avoid some unlikeness of the same or other researched groups for the later examinations.

Fourthly, if the researcher can outline the theoretical premises suitably in advance, define his/her constructs distinctly, and inform the audiences continuously whether the concepts are still intact or just newly-generated, then it would be more possible to facilitate replications. Finally, the researcher also has to clearly identify and fully discuss how to analyse the gathered data, and provide retrospective explanations of how data were checked and synthesised (LeCompte & Pressile, 1993).

Some distinctive viewpoints about validity and reliability

After introducing the above commonly-accepted methods, I would like to discuss, especially, two distinctive viewpoints about the criteria for assessing an interpretive research. One is from Smith and the other is from Radnor.

Smith (1984) is strongly opposed to talking about the validity and reliability in an interpretive research. He even claims, "we do not need do reliability and validity" (in LeCompte & Preissle, 1993: 324). Smith objects any conventional standards and any common criteria for assessing the research for he takes the position that "the philosophical assumptions of interpretive research prelude any common standards for evaluating qualitative studies" (LeCompte & Preissle, 1993: 324).

On the other hand, Radnor (2001) summarises her own criteria for assessing an interpretive research as follows. One is the researcher has to build his/her trust in the data collection and analysis. The other is that s/he embodies the interpretation validity. With regard to collecting and analysing data trustworthily, Radnor offers three "principles" (not "rules", there is no golden rule to assessing the interpretive research) explaining it. First of all, the researcher should engage reflexively in the process of data collecting and analysing, and be aware of his/her interpretive fieldwork, which requires confidence from his/her integrity while "trying to represent faithfully and accurately the social worlds or phenomena studied" (Radnor, 2001: 39).

Then, the researcher should convey a clear image to his/her participants that they would be listened without any prejudice during the interaction i.e. their relationship is based on trustworthiness. Thirdly, the participants should receive complete respect and this is exactly what the 'principles' of ethics-in-action focuses on.

Regarding with how to enhance the validity of findings, Radnor (2001) suggests that it would be of help if a researcher could separate a descriptive analysis from interpretation. Through a descriptive analysis, the audience obtains a clear idea of what the context truly is, which then could serve as a supportive evidence for the researcher's interpretation. "The interpretive process is an act of conceptualisation that informs the acts of the individuals and this unique situation is illuminated and at the same time insights are conveyed that exceed the limits of the situation from which they emerge" (Radnor, 2001: 40).

My own special criteria for assessing research

From the above discussion, we know that criteria in the legitimacy of an interpretive research has long been a key issue for debate and I believe this debate will continue without end. This situation is just similar to an Indian story: "Where does the elephant reset on? A turtle's back. Then, where does that turtle rest on? Another turtle. And how about that turtle?" The bottom cannot be touched ever. Frankly speaking, it is very clear that how could it be possible to create two exactly the same settings for increasing "reliability" in interpretive research. The world is changing; human behaviours are never static and even the interpretations are always refining and reshaping all the time during the research.

Then, is it still worthy for us to spend so much energy in pursuit of "criteria" just in order to "persuade" the audiences our research is valid and reliable? Is it absolutely necessary for a researcher to convince others of our "interpretations"? As far as I am concerned, criteria in interpretive research for me could be defined as "a kind of insistence to honesty." "Be HONEST to my belief/knowledge; be HONEST to my design; be

HONEST to my participants and be HONEST to my interpretation."

This is a chain of contributions of duties and rights from both the researcher and the participants. I believe these are all ethical concerns while conducting a research. In order to be honest ethically, I, as a researcher, have some compulsory duties and rights to obey during the research. Similarly, my participants also have ethical rights to claim. Table 1 shows what I mean by being honest in doing research.

In my interpretive world, trust exists not only between my participants and myself but also in any of my choice during the whole research. It seems to me that a researcher needs not be trapped by criteria in his/her mind; otherwise, s/he certainly will lost something insistent to his/her interpretive world. I agree that "all knowledge is based on assumptions and purposes and is a human construction" (Hammersley, 1992: 52). Everyone is making his/her sense of the world, and there seems no need to "test" whether a sense is valid or reliable, merely depending on some golden rules.

Table 1: Duties and Rights

Researcher's Duties:	*Participants' rights:*
- inform the purpose of the study	- ask for confidentiality
- be empathetic and patient	- withdraw at any point
- allow no cheating	- change/withdraw the responses
- explicate ethical positions	- have the right to say 'no' and the courage to say so
- have no bias-selection	

- conduct a bias-free observation	- know the results
- protect identity of participants	
- create appropriate atmosphere	
- be a reconstructor of reality	
- report the truth	

Researcher's rights	*Participant's duties:*
- terminate the research	-maintain integrity in the research
- have the access to the truth	-be responsible for their answers
	-create appropriate atmosphere
	-read carefully before signing

Source: Personal Reflection from Doing Research

CONCLUSION & REFLECTION

From the above discussions, we still can detect some potential problems, existing between two different paradigms. For example, interpretivism has always been criticised to be too subjective, lack of reliability in processing data and incapable of deducting from findings. In a word, interpretivism is too "soft" (Guba & Lincoln, 1988). However, interpretivts also rebut by arguing that they just use different terms and criteria to replace "validity" and "reliability" in assessing the research. The reason I made comparisons between two paradigms is not intending to intrigue more disputes but to have a clearer understanding about characteristics of each paradigm. Realising these characteristics can be helpful in choosing our own paradigm before we conduct research. As discussed in the introductory section, there is no definitely right or wrong/ good or poor paradigm in researches. What counts more is that we need to adopt a suitable paradigm to help us solve the problem; in other words, we should choose paradigms according to our research questions.

In the fields of social science, some phenomena are general, some are particular and even some are in-betweens when we explore human interactions. This means we, teachers, should be able to make good use of the different paradigms skilfully in order to obtain an non-fragmentary view of an event in classroom. Just as what Schulamn (1986) suggests, there is no golden key to any paradigm, and what a researcher (or a teacher) can do is always prepare for adjusting himself/herself flexibly based on his/her research topics and contexts. Different paradigms enable a reader to have a broader understanding about his/her world, and then s/he can be offered more choices in determining which action to take next. I believe different paradigms should not be examined oppositely but should be thought "compatible" to one another.

In conclusion, knowledge is defined by its contents, as these endow it with the forms we perceive the world. We create knowledge so that it exists. I believe the world of knowledge has attained the most power but could be in danger if any boundary is drawn in-betweens, such as paradigms. The world of knowledge we live is mutli-dimensional constructively and should celebrate its meaning without imposing any bias since that is where its truth lies. We, being researchers for knowledge, should open ourselves up to any possible knowledge in existence, receiving it with its peculiarities and differences, without prejudice or exclusion.

REFERENCES

Belleck, A. A. (1978). *Competing ideologies in research on teaching.* Sweden: Uppsala Reports on education 1.

Bodgan, R. C. & Biklen, S. K. (1982). *Qualitative research for education: An introduction to theory and methods.* Boston: Allyn and Bacon.

Crotty, M. (1998). *The Foundations of Social Research.* London: Falmer Press.

Erickson, F. (1986). Qualitative methods in research on teaching. In M. C. Wittrock (Ed.), *Handbook of research on teaching.* New York: Macmillan.

Gou, Y. S. (1994). Are interpritivism and scientific paradigms compatible or opposite on teaching? In Chang, F. D. (Ed.), *The symposium of research methodologies in education.* Taipei: NCU.

Gorden, R. L. (1975). *Interviewing: Strategy, Techniques, and Tactics.* (rev. Ed.) Homewood, Ill.: Dorsey Press.

Guba, E. G., & Lincoln, Y. S. (1988). Do inquiry paradigms imply inquiry methodologies? In D. M. Fettman (Ed.), *Qualitative approaches to evaluation in education.* New York: NY Greenwood Press.

Guba, E. G. & Lincoln, Y. S. (1985). *Naturalistic Inquiry.* Beverly Hill CA: Sage.

Guna, E. G. & Lincoln, Y. S. (1981). *Effective Evaluation.* CA: Jossey-Bass.

Hammersley, M. (1992). *What's Wrong with Ethnography: Methodological Explorations.* London: Routledge.

Hitchcock, G. & Hughes, D. (1989). *Research and the Teacher.* London: Routledge

Huang, R. C. (1999). *Methodology in Qualitative Research.* Taipei: Psychology Press.

Kumar, R. (1999). *Research Methodology: A step-by-step Guide for Beginners.* London: Sage.

LeCompte, M. & Preissle, J. (1993). *Ethnography and Qualitative Design in Educational Research.* London: Academic Press.

Maxwell, J. A. (1996). *Qualitative Research Design.* London: Sage.

Maykut, P. & Morehouse, R. (1994). *Beginning Qualitative Research.* London: Falmer Press.

Radnor, H. (2001). *Researching your Professional Practice: Doing Interpretive Research: To Know is to Interpret.* Buckingham: Open University Press.

Schulman, L. S. (1986). Paradigms and research paradigms for the study of teaching. In M. C. Wittrock (Ed.), *Handbook of research on teaching.* New York: Macmillan.

Scott, D. & Usher, R. (1999). *Research Education: Data, Methods and Theory in Educational Enquiry.* London: Institute of Education, University of London.

Silverman, D. (2001). *Interpreting Qualitative Data.* London: Sage.

Smith, J. K. (1984). The problem of criteria for judging interpretive inquiry. *Educational Evaluation and Policy Analysis, 6,* 379-391.

Wax, R. (1971). *Doing Fieldwork: Warnings and Advice.* Chicago: University of Chicago Press.

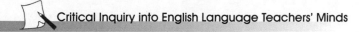

Chapter 2

Critical Issues under the Heat Wave of English Learning in Taiwan

INTRODUCTION

> *The non-native Englishes are the legacy of the colonial period, and have mainly developed in "unEnglish" cultural and linguistic contexts in various parts of the word, wherever the arm of the Western colonizers reached* (Kachru, 1981).

This chapter is going to examine English impacts on Taiwan from the perspectives of linguistics, society, and culture in the first half part; besides, the article also argues that though the prevalence of Englishlisation in Taiwan seems irresistible and inevitable presently, it is urgently indispensable to re-examine some critical issues about English language teaching situations and assumptions from now on English language teaching policies, power, and inequality has lead to the abnormal phenomenon of two peaks distribution in learners' English proficiency. Thus, this chapter will be divided into two major sections to explore these influences of Englishlisation, i.e. English impacts in linguistic area, social area, and cultural area, and the critical issues to ELT in Taiwan.

First of all, it would be helpful if we shall take a brief review of Taiwan history in advance. Historically, Taiwan was used to be a colonised country, which means it was occupied and governed by some foreign nations before. Portugueses discovered Taiwan and named it 'Formosa', a beautiful island in Portguese. Spaniards also had settled down in Northern Taiwan temporary in a short period of time. After their leaving, came the Hollanders. They built up castles and forts in both Northern and Southern Taiwan for their bases. This was the first time that Taiwanese exposed to Western culture indeed. Then, from 1895 to 1845, Taiwan had been under the control of Japan for nearly fifty years until the restoration to the KMT, the previous ruling government. However, there exists an interesting issue that Taiwan was never governed by an English-speaker country e.g. the U.S. or Britain, but why is it that in Taiwan English becomes the most dominant foreign language?

Theoretically speaking, Japanese should have been the most dominant foreign language in Taiwan for it was used as the only official language in Taiwan for the past fifty years. The reasons may be firstly, after the restoration of Taiwan, people were eager to get rid of the influence of Japan, and also the

KMT government took a negative and hostile attitude towards the Japanese government; therefore using Japanese was banned till the 1980. Secondly, from 1970s, Taiwan and the U.S. had maintained a strong relationship since U.S. government launched forces to protect Taiwan form the invasion of China. It was during the garrison of the U.S. forces that Taiwanese began to explore English and its culture. Finally, from an economic and political perspective, now Taiwan eagerly hopes to become an active member in the global village and thus realises that English is the most and only useful medium to help achieve this goal for English is currently the mostly used language worldwide.

According to the following statistical figures, in 1998 (Ministry of Education, 1999), there are nearly four million Taiwanese students take English as their required subject. Besides, in 1986 (Pennycook, 1994), over eighty thousand people took TOEFL exam, which ranked the first place in Asia; moreover, in 1998 (Ministry of Education 1999), there are more than forty-three thousand students in total choosing either the U.S. or the U.K. to conduct their further study. Taiwan is even ranked in the fourth place among overseas students in the U.S. These numbers imply that English has indeed became the most dominant and important foreign language in Taiwan. Accompanied by English, a number of its inevitable impacts and influences also have brought to the Taiwanese society. In the following sections, I will firstly investigate the different impacts of Englishlisation on Taiwan linguistically, socially and culturally, and secondly re-examine the critical issues these impacts lead to for ELT in Taiwan.

THE LINGUISTIC IMPACTS OF ENGLISH ON CHINESE IN TAIWAN

Morphology

Linguistically, according to Tsao (1993), English has influenced Chinese morphology in two aspects: (1) the frequency of using bi-syllables and multi-syllables phrases is increasing and (2) the frequency of using suffixes is mounting as well. These will be discussed respectively in details in the following sections.

The using of bi-syllable and multi-syllable phrases in Chinese

In the development of Chinese, the most noticeable trend is the increasing of bi-syllables phrases. It was especially after 1912 that a large amount of English words or phrases pouring into Chinese has made this current more perceptible (Tsao, 1993). In other words, two Chinese synonyms or nearly synonyms-like are put together to form a new phrase. For example, both "hisn 行" and "wei 為" mean "action"; however, we use "hsin-wei" to translate the word "action". Here is another example: both "yi 意" and "yi 義" imply "meaning" in Chinese but now the word "yi-yi" was bound together to mean "meaning". This change transforms Chinese into a non one-syllable language. Even now, in modern Chinese, except for the imperatives and some idioms, it is nearly unlikely to make a sentence with one-syllable subject and complement now. For example, the following sentences are both correct except the first one. (The symbol of * asterisk preceding a sentence indicates its ungrammatical usage.)

*1. Hua hong (花紅) (The flower red.)
2. Hua hen hong (花很紅) (The flower is very read.)
3. Hua bu hong (花不紅) (The flower is not red.)

In fact, according to Tsao (1993), the using of bi-syllables phrases in Chinese can be traced back to 1500 A.D.; however, not until a plenty of foreign words and phrases, especially English, are introduced into Chinese does this application become more and more evident.

The using of suffixes in Chinese

Based on Wong (1947), a number of certain Chinese writing characters, "hua 化", "hsin 性", "du 度", "chia 家" and "zhe 者", are often used to translate some suffixes of English. Below are some examples of this.

化 (*hua*) -ise	idealise (Li-shian-*hua*); modernise (Hsien-dei-*hua*)
性 (*hsin*) -ty, -ce, -ness	importance (zong-yia-*hsin*); necessity (Bi-zen-hsin)
度 (du) -th	depth (Hsun-du); width (koung-du)
家 (chia) -ist, -ian, -er,	linguist (Yu-yan-shiu-xiao-chia) chemist (Hu-xiao-chia)
者 (zhe) -er, -or	reader (du-zhe); owner (Suo-you-zhe)

Nowadays, these Chinese suffixes are extensively applied to form many new phrases. For instance, if a Chinese stem is followed by a hsin (性), then a new phrase will appear. Consequently, Duo 惰 (lazy) will become Duo-hsin 惰性 (laziness); Do 讀 (read) will become Ke-du-hsin 可讀性 (readability). Furthermore, 度 (du) was used to translate –th words of English but now it can imply a Chinese noun phrase containing the meaning of "at a certain degree." Wen-du 溫度 (temperature), and Shi-du 濕度 (moisture) are examples of this. Moreover, 者 (zhe) was used to be a very literature word but at present it is commonly applied to daily usage to indicate a person's identity e.g. Pao-zhe 跑者 (runner) and Da-zhe 打者 (hitter).

Another very remarkable morphological change is that there is a plural –s form (Men 們) in most English countable nouns but in Chinese only the class of human beings had the plural form in the past. However, the situation also has changed; thus, we can use Shu-mu-men 樹木們 (trees) and He-jia-men 禾嫁們 (corps) in Chinese, which were not acceptable at all before. Owing to the introduction of many English words and phrases, the traditional Chinese morphology has broadened its dimension.

Syntax

"At the syntactic level, the influence of English on Chinese can be exemplified by the length of phrases, the use of passive verb" (Cheng, 1992) and the use of numeral modifier (Tsao, 1993).

The length of phrases

In Chinese, the modified often comes before the modifying part, which is opposite to English; hence, Englishlised Chinese sentences "often contain long modifiers before the head noun to accommodate English subordinate clauses" (Cheng, 1992: 166). As the following, sentence (a) is English, (b) is Englishlised Chinese, and (c) is standard Chinese (Wong, 1955).

(a) People who regard literary taste simply as an accomplishment, and literature simply as a distraction, will…

(b) Naxie (those) ba (co-verb) wenxue (literary) renwei (regard) chunran (simply) yizhong (a kind) caiyi (accomplishment), ba (co-verb) wenxue (literature) renwei (regard) chunran (simply) yizhong (a kind) xiaoqianpin (distraction) de (possessive) renmen (people), jiang (will)…

(c) Yigern ruguo ba wenxue renwie chunran yizhong caiyi, ba wenxue renwei chunran yizhong xiaoqianpin, jiang…

The Englishlised Chinese like sentence (b) puts the subject, renmen (people), in the end of the long modifier. However, in traditional Chinese, a subject is normally placed in the beginning and "ruguo (if)" is used to qualify it.

The use of passive verb

In Chinese, bei 被 (passive voice) was always used only when expressing the subject's unhappy, unpleasant and unfortunate situations for its original meaning was Zao-shou (suffering). For example: Ta 他 (He) bei 被 (passive: was) che 車 (by a car) zhuang-le 撞了 (hit), and Wo 我 (I) bei 被 (passive: was) chi-diao-le 辭掉了(fired). Therefore, most of the usages of passive voice in Chinese were used to mean something bad or unfortunate. However, nowadays, bei 被 (passive voice) can usually be heard in describing a pleasant situation in Chinese. For instance, Ta 她 (She) bei 被 (passive: was) suo-ai-de-ren 所愛的人 (by her beloved) yong-bao-zhao 擁抱著 (embraced), which conveys a pleasant feeling and is generally acceptable now.

The use of numeral modifier

In traditional Chinese, a countable noun without using any article is acceptable; however, since articles play an important grammatical role in English, Chinese also begins to adopt this rule to almost "every" noun overly no matter whether the noun is countable or uncountable. In fact, the notion of 'countablity' and 'abstractness' in Chinese nouns are vague and sometimes undistinguished.

On the one hand, Chinese use "yi..." 一... (a/an) to express yi-ben-shu 一本書 (a book) or yi-zhi-bi 一支筆 (a pen) on the countable nouns. On the other hand, yi-zhong 一種 is used to modify the uncountable nouns. Examples like this are

Yi-zhong-ji –mo 一種寂寞 (loneliness), Yi-zhong-li-liang 一種力量 (strength), Yi-zhong-feng-zi 一種風姿 (grace) or Yi-zhong-yi-ran-zi-de 一種怡然自得 (self-satisfaction and ease). Chinese speakers use their imagination to embed the words with numerals even this application is ungrammatical in English. Therefore, due to this excessive overgeneralisation of this rule, many Chinese-speaking students will use "a kind of", equal to yi-zhong in Chinese, unconsciously before an uncountable English noun.

From what has been discussed above, it can be argued that English indeed has a strong impact on Chinese in linguistic aspect, which converts the habits of using Chinese words or phrases, and even encourages Chinese speakers to create more novel unexpected expressions.

THE SOCIAL IMPACTS OF ENGLISH ON CHINESE IN TAIWAN

Next, in this section, I will examine the impacts that English has brought to Taiwan society. These influences are so powerful that they affect Taiwanese people's daily life very directly. These influences will be divided into four main sub-headings: (1) the opportunity of job, (2) the media, (3) education, and (4) the technology and life.

Opportunity of job

Decades ago, standard Mandarin was the only required and official language when a person applied for a job; however, due to the branch-establishment of more and more joint-companies and foreign companies in Taiwan such as IBM, CITI Bank, Anthea Insurance, Boeing, etc, English-proficiency has become a required ability when those companies need new recruitment. The rapid changes in workplace globalisation and changing needs of English literacy have attracted job-seekers' considerable attention (Pennycook, 2001). Even applying for a position in a Taiwanese-run firm, candidates are also expected to be English-communicative, and those who are proficient at English always get higher pay and enjoy more promotions than those who are not capable of English. It is because that most bosses believe that "English have always been very pragmatic—better English equals better business" (Boyle, 1997: 6). In this way, it is not surprising that there is a very high percentage agreement on the importance of English for their careers. "Attitudes to English were quite pragmatic. English was necessary at the international level, and proficiency in English was the high road to a better job" (Boyle, 1997: 6). However, the connection between workplace demands of English language and relations of power in an institution also raises a critical issue, i.e. those whose English proficiency is not qualified are deprived of working opportunities, and their professional skills and values rather than English practices are marginalised at a social level (Pennycook, 2001).

The Media

As Crystal (1997) claims, during these days we cannot discuss language without taking the role of the media into consideration for the functions of media is so widespread and so powerful that we cannot neglect its influences in the 21st century. Taiwanese do not only "learn" English in the classroom but also "use" it in media presumably. Several examples will be used to illustrate English impacts on the different aspects of the media.

The Press

Though most of newspapers, journals and books are still printed in Chinese, yet more and more press start to emphasise the using of English in Taiwan. We can read many headlines of newspapers printed in English to attract readers' attention. Some journals will add the English translation of each article to appeal the international readers or make the journal more authoritative. It is not difficult to find English papers or magazines on the shelf in Taiwan e.g. English-country-imported ones like The Wall Street, U.S.A. Today, Newsweek or Times. Moreover, Taiwan has its own English papers such as China Post, Taiwan News and a newly published one, Taipei News. Not only does this satisfy the native speakers' need in Taiwan but also hope to covey the Taiwan voice to the world via English.

Entertainments

Most teenagers in Taiwan now prefer to watch English-speaking programs, because those programs represent for "fashion". Hence, Hollywood's motion pictures take up almost the whole movie theaters island-wide and even hardly can we watch a Chinese-speaking film. When referring to music, English released albums always reach a record high in the market, and furthermore it seems trendy that Taiwanese composers like using some English lyrics to make their Chinese work more popular and easier to be memorized. Whit regard to the television, the channels such as Discovery, Explore, National Geography Channel, Animal Planet, CNN, or BBC symbolise the high treasures for knowledge and update news. HBO, Cinema, Cartoon Network or ESPN channels stand for high quality movies and sports. To catch up with the times and fashion, people would rather watch English-pronounced programs than Chinese programs even some of them have great difficulties in understanding English. However, that if these English-speaking programs can facilitate English learning is still doubtful. More and more these English channels begin to speak Chinese with Chinese subtitles now.

Advertisements

Using English directly in the advertisements apparently makes the products more original and thus can arouse the interest of the customers. Because an English advertisement is so different form the others, this leads the customers easily follow to its purpose and memorise the name of the products. Therefore, many people of different ages in Taiwan including those who do not understand English at all can pronounce TV commercial's slogans like, "Trust me, you can make it!", "I'm loving it!" or even "Seven-Eleven." Nobody will try to translate it into Chinese for such an attempt will merely destroy its meaning and make customers forget what the commercial is about easily.

Education

According to a recent published research paper, there will be more than three billions of people speaking English and 2 billions of learners studying English within the next ten years (中廣新聞網，民 93). Learning English has become a whole-people-campaign in Taiwan recently. Owing to the government's great promotion of English education, Taiwan makes several unbelievable records of it. First, elementary school students now need to study English officially from the fifth grade since 2000, which has made nearly twenty thousand competitors seek the nine hundred openings of being an elementary English teacher (Ministry of Education, 1999). Moreover, some local educational authorities even require their pupils to learn English from the 2nd grade such as the Taipei City. In addition to the formal English classes in school, students "go to evening schools (cramming schools), take correspondence courses or spend much money seeking private English tutors, expecting to learn extra English" (Zhang, 1997:

139). So bilingualism, using both Chinese and Taiwanese to teach students, kindergartens always attract parents to send their children to attend. Besides, Taiwan becomes the country with the most examinees taking the TOEFL tests in Asia (Pennycook, 1994) and thus it also ranks the fourth place among the international students in the U.S. as well. In fact, due to the need to English proficiency certificates, there are many different types of English proficiency tests currently in Taiwan like American-based TOEFL, British-based IELTS, BULTA and Cambridge Main Suite, Taiwanese self-designed GEPT, FLPT-English, and computer-based NETPAW. Recently, the Ministry of Education (MOE) in Taiwan has always required each university to construct a well-designed plan or structure of improving its students' English proficiency. Thus, a number of universities would set a threshold of English proficiency test for their graduates like National Taiwan University. Statistically, there are nearly 140 English departments among Taiwanese universities. Furthermore, the Taiwanese MOE also begins to introduce native speakers to teach English in 2004, and is planning to endow English with an official status in Taiwan (蘇以文，民 93). All these efforts hopefully will ensure Taiwan to become a member of the global community under the shield of English. Hence, ELT becomes a profitable market and the profession of being an English teacher is more enviable than other professions now. However, we may worry about the quality of English language education with such rapid growth in Taiwan if there is no appropriate need and context analysis beforehand.

Technology and Life

In fact, English can influence our daily life in so many aspects. There area number of important reasons accounting for this. In this section, we will examine why English has become one part of our life in Taiwan. First of all, when a new English word or phrase is introduced into Chinese and if Chinese lacks the equivalents to meet this new term, then English is necessary to keep and will be used. Especially when some terms come into Taiwan too quickly to get the suitable or appropriate translations. Such words mostly belong to a technical field e.g. Excel, Internet, IE, Word, E-mail, ICQ or Google. Secondly, because these English terms sometimes are embedded with their concise effects and subtle denotations thus Taiwanese people would rather keep the original English forms than ask for a Chinese equivalent. For example, "many people know that CT is an effective way of diagnosing some illness, but few know that the name of the technology is an abbreviation of computerised tomography" (Kang, 1999: 47). Most people in Taiwan will use the form "TVBS" (the largest cable TV company in Taiwan) to name it instead of the complete expression for Television Broadcasting System, which has six characters in Chinese scripts; the English expression is short and occupies less space. Furthermore, teenagers would prefer saying "NBA" to calling Mei-guo-guo-chai-lan-chiu-shie-hui (National Basketball Association). Thirdly, as what we discussed above in the section of media, due to the variety and novelty of English letters, the designers of the advertisements will try to make the advertisement more effective by stressing the importance of visual effects. As a result, a shop may have an English advertisement page or poster. On the one hand, this can appeal native speakers' notice, and on the other hand, it makes this shop different form the ordinary others. Thus, an English advertisement page may attract more customers' attention than Chinese version does. In addition, some products will provide the customers with only English-version manuals or user guides because the manufacturers hope that the customers will believe these are imported goods to "satisfy their vanity of the moon in a foreign country being brighter" (Kang, 1999: 48).

Another interesting hybrid usage between Chinese and English has been extensively created among teenagers circles recently. They will use LKK (the acronym of lao-ko-ko,) to describe an aged or "slow-motioned" person or use SPP (the acronym of su-pi-pi) to name an old-fashioned person. This contextualised hybrid usage embeds the new energy to Taiwanese society and its languages.

THE CULTURAL IMPACTS OF ENGLISH ON CHINESE IN TAIWAN

Seldom can it be denied that language is a part of its culture and when English comes into Taiwan society, inevitably English also bring its values and cultures into Taiwanese society. Therefore, traditional Taiwanese cultures, traditions and values will be influenced and changed by some degree accordingly. We cannot say these impacts on Chinese cultures are negligible for the changes are indeed so significant that we need to take a cautious attitude towards it. This issue will be considered from three aspects: (1) the ethnic identity, (2) the gourmet culture, and (3) values.

The Ethnic Identity

In Confucianism countries or areas, Hong Kong could be the most Englishlised territory due to its previous colonial status. Lin (1999) proposes that English teaching in Hong Kong may lead to either the reproduction or the transformation of class-based inequality, which certainly influence their identities. The form of English and its popular cultures make learners start to identify with Anglo-Saxon values and cultures (Pennycook, 2001). It is very common that some Taiwanese parents are more willing to send their children to English-speaking countries to learn English when they are very young. When these returned students come back to their motherland, Taiwan, not surprisingly they usually use English as their communication medium. However, the elder (mostly their grandparents) will always complain that those who "have drunk foreign ink" (a Chinese idiom, indicating those who finished their education in Western countries) forget their identities and are not patriotic any more. As to the children's parents, they know that learning English is essential and important for their children; however, they are supposed to be obedient to their parents (children's grandparents) as well. Thus they would not stress the importance of English too evidently in front of the grandparents in fearing that it would be a threat to their Chinese identities; however, privately they do support and encourage their children to learn English as early as possible. As a result, a generation gap would exist among three generations in a family, which is still very common in traditional Taiwanese families.

The above worry exhibits the notion that engagement of learning a particular language, values, and cultures must also lead to identity formation (Pennycook, 2001). This stance simply regards language learner's identity fixed and homogenous. However, some also argue that identity should not be viewed as single category but it is likely for learners to possess multiple identities from multiple resources (Spack, 1997). This notion views identify transformation as an ongoing negation process between language, culture and society (Pennycook, 2001).

The Gourmet Culture

It is also noteworthy that English has changed the Chinese gourmet culture in Taiwan as well. Taiwanese people do not only learn English form America or Britain but also adopt the Western gourmet culture equivalently. According to the data form the Department of Agriculture in Taiwan, the demand of rice has been dramatically decreasing for the past few years; nevertheless, the requirement of flour is increasing every year. Hamburger culture, also termed as fast-food culture, has changed the demands between rice and flour gradually and this change even forces the government to re-consider the policy of agriculture. Moreover, as a tradition when two Taiwanese friends meet each other, their greeting always begins with the expression "Chi-bao-mei? 吃飽沒?" (Have you taken your meal yet?), but most young people merely would say "Hi!" or "Hello" now, which makes the aged consider the young generation lack the basic sense of caring others. This change is believed to be the by-product of importing English in Taiwan.

Values

Taiwanese people were always considered to be family-loyal and trustworthy in the past; however, we can find that nowadays this values has undergone a slightly change. Young people do not put too much emphasis on family-loyalty and trustworthiness any more, and most people believe this is the result of learning English and its culture excessively. Another noticeable cultural transformation is that since Taiwanese people stress the importance of learning English excessively, those who can speak fluent English especially native speakers would be adored. Any language can be a value-laden product of its particular context. In an English classroom, "No Taiwanese/Chinese! Speak English!" can always be heard by language learners. This teacher's warning will imply students, especially in kindergarten and primary school, that speaking their native languages is inferior to those who can speak English. Tang's study indicates that EFL learners believe native EFL teachers are superior to their non-native EFL teachers nearly in all aspects of language skills teaching (Tang, 1997). English including its values, cultures, and people is superior to Taiwanese/Chinese. For those whose English ability is lower, they are very likely to be isolated and discriminated by their peers. To sum up, Taiwanese people believe English is important and most things related to English might be good as well inclusive of its people, culture and traditions.

So far, we can see that English has brought many impacts on Chinese in Taiwan linguistically, socially and culturally indeed. Are these impacts all very positive and undisruptive? Should learning English indeed be an all-people-campaign in Taiwan? Or should we start to consider cautiously the issue that if these impacts of English have to be re-examined and then localised to fit Taiwanese context? Indeed, most too often imported educational change or instruction is not well culture-sensitive, and thus perhaps it subverts the values, morale, and characteristics of its local educational context furtively. Pursuing globalisation is unlikely if the concern of localisation is not catered properly. In the following section, I would like to take a critical view about the current situations of ELT and its practice in Taiwan.

CRITICAL ISSUES ON ENGLISH LANGUAGE TEACHING

As discussed in the previous sections, English learning has indeed become a 'blind' campaign, and English teaching also has become an enterprise in Taiwanese society. The impacts of English on Taiwan seem inevitable, and the learning of it embodies the spirit of 'fashion' and 'knowledge'. However, a number of potential and critical issues are worthy of addressing and reflecting behind such a prosperous situation i.e. since English learners have learnt it for many years why (1) students' English competency is still unsatisfactory in GEPT or TOFEL test, (2) students' English academic performance appears to be two-peaked statistically, and this huge gap had lead to a great difficulty in ELT among secondary and primary schools, (3) over half of university students are worried that they are unable to pass the threshold of English competency and believe English course in school is unreliable, and (4) also over half of the native speakers living in Taiwan are complained about the unfriendly environment of English using in Taiwan (黃以敬，民 93 a.；羅浩恩，民 93；黃旭昇，民 93；溫貴香，民 93)? Language educators and language policy-makers often apparently adopt uncritical assumptions about the influences of English and this does not reflect the reality of lives of English learners. Therefore, an appropriate means to re-address these issues should be taken through a critical look at the current trends in addressing ELT (Tollefson, 1995), and then we can critically examine its situations in Taiwan. This needs someone to play the devils' advocate, and this is what the following discussion aims for.

Critical English language planning and language rights

Learners' mother tongue is the base of studying all matter subjects, including English (蘇以文，民 93). However, due to the government's deliberate language policy planning, English status and the learning of it have become an all-people-campaign. Nevertheless, the fact is that learners cannot apply what they have learnt; instead they simply memorise many rules, vocabulary, and patterns. English is still not yet the mainstream communication tool in Taiwan and cannot be commonly used by most people either. This turns English language learning declarative knowledge rather than procedure knowledge. This problem indicates that our language policy is uncritically developed and implemented (Pennycook, 2001). "Language planning has tended to avoid directly addressing larger social and political matters within which language change, use and development, and indeed language planning itself are embedded" (Luke, McHoul & Mey, 1990: 27). Planning English langue policy superficially will reinforce the social inequality, unequal power distribution, and fixed social hierarchy. Pennycook (1995: 54) argues that English is "the language through which much of the unequal distribution of wealth, resources, and knowledge operates," and represents the role as the duplicate of global inequalities. Furthermore, as discussed in the preceding section, the demands of English uses and proficiency have marginalised professional skills and deprived the working chances of some certain classes in working places, English competence statistically appears a two-peaked distribution, and the huge English learning gap has existed between urban and rural areas in Taiwan (黃旭昇，民 93). These phenomena may result from the inappropriate English language education policy. It avoids examining the inequality existing in the Taiwanese society, including the social justice, the social classes, the races, the learning and teaching resources, and respective mother tongues. Under the unified English education policy, all English learners are assumed to be identical, ready to be programmed with unequal inputs. This is contradictory and ironical to what we have seen and what happened now in Taiwan's situation.

Pursuing globalisation is not to sacrifice the substance of localisation for the shadow but to embrace the differences and justice in-between. Global learning of English has seriously threatened the acquisition of other languages in the world (Pennycook, 1995). Contrarily, ones' native language should be the base of learning all subjects, including English learning. Appropriate learning of native language (Taiwanese or Mandarin) facilitates logical reasoning and organised thinking. Shattered base of mother tongue will deprive learners of their independent thinking and creativity. Form the perspective of globalisation, it is inspiring to see the prevalence and promotion of English learning in Taiwan (蘇以文，民 93). However, if the learning right of native languages is ignored and the English language policy is still implemented superficially, students will not acquire logical, independent, and critical thinking; neither can they learn English well. As Skutnabb-Kangas (1998) proposes, language learners should be empowered rights to indemnify, to maintain and fully develop their native languages. This is self-evident, fundamental individual linguistic human right, and essential localized step to advance to globalisation. As I proposed in the previous section, globalisation of English language is much unlikely if the local solid acquiring of a native language cannot be emphasised, fostered, and manifested.

Critical language teaching issues

This section will briefly discuss the current critical approaches to TESOL. We will examine this issue from three perspectives i.e. the domains of defining a critic approach to TESOL, the transformative pedagogy of TESOL to change things, and a self-reflexive stance on critical theory to TESOL. First of all, according to Pennycook (1999), the critical works in TESOL would include the issues about race, class, gender, sexual identity, violence, and power and inequality. For example, English language teaching has led Hong Kong learners to a reproduction or the transformation of class-based inequality, which has been discussed in the preceding section (Lin, 1999). Furthermore, a major theme about the power and inequality between native and non-native English teachers also has received great attention and discussion recently (Liu, 1999). Native English teachers have always been regarded superior to non-native teachers in terms of language proficiency; therefore, they would be accountable and highly valued comparatively. In

2004, the Taiwanese authorities' introducing native speakers to teach English can well exemplify the inequalities in the relation between the constructs of the native and non-native teachers in an EFL context. However, these above domains should be viewed interwoven rather than independent for they are all related to the particularities of a society, context or culture (Pennycook, 1999; 2001). If these concerns cannot be well catered, more resistance to English teaching and learning would be unavoidable in classroom, especially in an EFL context

Next, critical TESOL also seeks to make a change in pedagogy. It aims to conduct a critical need analysis before an ELT curriculum is designed and finalised. Too often, the need analysis of a language course is conducted neither in a 'top-down' nor a 'bottom-up' hierarchy but in a 'top-lateral' cross section. Those who are at the bottom are seldom entitled more power about what they are going to teach and learn about English. Canagarajah (1999) concludes in his research that undistributed and asymmetric need analysis of language curriculum places teachers and learners in the periphery resist in language classroom. Examining the situation of Taiwan, we find that English language curriculum has become a 'trick-or-treat'. Teachers and learners either have to accept what is apposed to them or to be regarded uncooperative by the superiors. They are supposed to teach and learn the needs of high authorities instead of their own. Pessimistically, language teachers are seemingly drifting with tides under the educational impacts of English. To cope with this problem, Pennycook

(1999) suggests a critical approach to pedagogy i.e. the stakeholders need to raise a political understanding of TESOL pedagogy and then develop a way of teaching aimed at transformation. This means that TESOL pedagogy needs to work at multi-levels, and teachers' voice, participation and power together with their own pedagogies about the issue should be suitably accommodated.

As the first half of this article discusses, English has brought in many influences to Taiwan linguistically, socially, and culturally. We may start to consider whether or not all these impacts will lead to positive development of English language education in Taiwan or they would cause a number of significant societal, cultural or language gaps damaging the values, language rights of native languages, self-identity, or power inequality of this society gradually. This requires teachers of a self-reflexive stance on critical theory to ELT. To put it differently, this process of self-reflection is a problematising practice, which can de defined as a rejection to English patriarchal rationality and power control over an EFL context (Pennycook, 1999). Problematising practice in EFL refers to that language teachers need to be more aware of the truth of their teaching conditions; not all of these conditions are taken-for-granted components of the reality of ELT in their peculiar contexts. It may be necessary to re-examine, skepticise, and reject common ELT assumptions continuously based on one's context. For example, ELT teachers of Taiwan are urged to be skeptical of the assumption that CLT can provide the most productive and effective method for teaching English, that the cultural content for ELT should be derived from the cultures of native speakers, or that only native speaker models can inform ELT curriculum and pedagogy (McKay, 2003). It is argued that culture-insensitive ELT theories, methods or materials should be critically examined before their applications. Perhaps it is the right time for Taiwanese ELT teachers to consider reflectively about these common assumptions and then make a transformative change rather than drift with fashions.

Critical ELT methods

Recently, most of the English teaching material writers claim they adopt CLT (communicative language teaching) method to compile the textbooks for students in Taiwan, and encourage language teachers to use CLT to maximise the effectiveness and efficiency of the books. However, there is, in fact, no best English teaching method in the world for the effective one relies much on individual particular context (Prabhu, 1990). On the one hand, some ELT teachers are very suspicious of the supposed good teaching methods to their own teaching context and show antipathy towards their imposition by experts from abroad (Pennycook, 1989). One the other hand, other teachers would enjoy applying foreign approaches or methods, but ignore a careful consideration of the context where teaching and learning occurs, including the cultural context, the political context, the local institutional context, and the context constituted by the teachers and learners in their classroom (Richards & Rodgers, 2001).

Many EFL educators are strongly criticising the blind application of 'methods.' For example, Richards and Rodgers (2001) regard 'method' exercising a 'top-down' power hierarchy over ELT teachers. They (p. 247) comment that,

> *Teachers have to accept on faith on the claims or theory underlying the method and apply them to their own practice. Teaching is regarded correct only by following its prescribed principles and techniques. Roles of teachers and students, as well as the type of activities and teaching techniques to be used in the classroom, are generally prescribed. Teacher's role is marginalised.*

In addition, Pennycook (1989) believes that 'ELT method' is embodied in the Western knowledge with a tailor-made configuration of its social, cultural, economic, political, and historical circumstances. This knowledge represents the interests of a certain group or culture, and is inevitably inscribed in relations of power. For him, 'ELT method' symbolises inequality in genders and international contexts. Method is a prescribed concept which conveys the notion of a positivist, progressivist, and patriarchal understanding of ELT. This concept leads to inequality between male academics and female teachers in a language classroom, "a hierarchically organised division between male conceptualises and female practitioners" (Pennycook, 1989: 611). Furthermore, as

Larsen-Freeman (2003) suggests, all ELT methods in history have one point in common i.e. they do not address the issues of English cultures; nor do they discuss how to teach cultures. This implies the notion that English culture is assumed to be a single but global culture, and it represents all.

Moreover, Pennycook (1989) also contends that promoting CLT methods in the world should be very careful for they may be very inappropriate for different contexts. This argument has been confirmed by many studies conducted in Asian countries, such as Burnaby and Sun (1989), Liao (廖曉青，民 90) in China, Li (1998) in Korea, Lai (1994) in Hong Kong, Kuo (1995) in Taiwan, Ellis (1994) in Vietnam, and Sano (1984) in Japan. All of these papers conclude that CLT confronts many unfavorable difficulties in its promotion in these countries due to their respective contextualised factors which cannot be altered very easily such as large class, test-oriented teaching, teachers' belief, non-native teacher's English proficiency, and anxiety. However, it appears that the Taiwanese authorities still promote CLT methods very deliberately, which makes most book publishers follow this policy to compile their teaching materials. This promotion also makes teachers mistakenly believe that only CLT methods are the best, correct, and plausible methods in teaching English.

Indeed, teachers should not focus one certain ELT method or implement one from a tailor-made context to their peculiar situations; otherwise, ELT teachers would be too culture-insensitive. Larsen-Freeman (2003) advises teachers that the adoption of teaching methods should involve 'relativism' and 'pluralism', acknowledging the advantages of each method, but adapting and integrating them with their teaching contexts and experiences. In other words, "teachers and teachers in training need to be able to use approaches and methods flexibly and creatively based on their own judgment and experience" (Richards & Rodgers, 2001: 250).

EFL teachers' critical awareness

In this section, I would like to discuss what a language teacher should do when s/he discovers English teaching, indeed, has led to great inequalities in classroom. There are two positions regarding to this issue. First, Pennycook (1995) proposes that language teachers be rebellions of subjugated knowledge of English, and be political agents to use English to reject the dominant discourse of Anglo-Saxon world and then help the articulation of counter discourse in English, the connections between English and the discourses of development, democracy, capitalism, and modernisation (Tollefson, 1995). However, this proposal seems very aggressive to the power authority and may be unlikely realised in Taiwanese context for teacher cultures of Taiwan are still very conservative and they tend to be lukewarm to politics. Compared with Pennycook's radical advice to EFL teachers, Rajagopalan (1999) contrarily addresses a more passive perspective. He maintains that if English is already what it is today such as leading to inequality or unequal empowerment, it is demonstrably owing to many historical reasons. "If the

English is threatening the survival of many regional languages all over the world, it has nothing to do with the brutal colonial contexts which originally made it possible for the language to the four corners of the world" (Rajagopalan, 1999: 202). By this, he means that it is unwise to blame English for its imperialism leading to the exercise of its power, violence, or dominance for these conditions are already there. Then, he advises that ELT teachers need not feel guilty of these imperial conditions occurred for authority and power is absolute, abstract, and unalleviated, and any negotiation will lead to the dominance of another language. Thus, teachers can do very little about this.

Canagarajah (1999: 210) disapproves this viewpoint strongly; he asserts EFL teachers will simply "concern themselves with the immediate tasks at hand within the narrow walls of the classroom or the pages of the textbook." Contrarily, he suggests that language teachers should be negotiators with divergent discourses to consider how they can expand a richer awareness of language and social contexts, finally enabling English teaching rewardingly in the classroom. Canagarajah (1999) also provides some examples illustrating what he advocates. For example, EFL teachers can allow learners to use their native languages to do pair-work or group-discussion in English class for they need to feel relaxed about the inhabitation against learning English. Learners can realise that their native languages are also valued, not inferior to English. Using native languages to discuss and interpret English literary tests can motivate pupils from the stand point of their native cultures. Furthermore, teachers can encourage pupils to bring into their

English writing, the discourse conventions and communicative strategies from their own local contexts (Belcher, 1997; Zamel, 1996).

All the above examples demonstrate that EFL teachers can be negotiators between a global imperialism and local context. They pluralise the form and content of learning English, and show equal respects to English and vernacular values and cultures. Indeed, this new role, language teachers as negotiators, embeds teachers with new identities to bridge the English learning gap between globalised learning and localised concerns. It is hoped that English teachers in Taiwan can also acknowledge this appeal.

SUGGESTIONS & CONCLUSION

The first half part of this chapter examines the influences of English on Taiwan in terms of linguistics, society, and culture. The second half part proposes critical approaches to ELT. It seems that these two sections are slightly contradictory and irrelevant at the first glance. However, it is, in fact, not. As an English teacher and educator, it is very joyful to perceive that English has gained its wide popularities and prospective official status in Taiwan. Learning English has become an all-people-campaign from the top authorities to bottom learners. Under the shed of pursuing globalisation within an international community, the learning of English has been regarded as a shortcut to this. It would be very unwise and radical if someone urges the authorities to reconsider the current intentional promotion of English in Taiwan for teachers who are at the basic level are still not empowered fully to voice about these issues and seldom are they interested in being involved with the political circle to make a change.

However, this cannot be treated as an excuse to ignore the critical issues to ELT. This article argues that though the prevalence of Englishlisation in Taiwan seems irresistible and inevitable presently, it is urgently indispensable to re-examine some critical issues and common assumptions about ELT from now on such as English education policies, language rights of mother tongues, power, learners' identities, and inequality. Hence, though this paper is not experiment-based, a number of suggestions still can be made. Owing to the increasingly abnormal phenomenon of two-peaked distribution in learners' English proficiency and learning resources（黃旭昇，民 93）, Taiwan indeed immediately deserves a reformed and consistent English education policy for a long-term. First of all, the authority should abandon the myth that the earlier learners learn English, the better performance they will promise, especially when there has been no agreed critical period for the best English learning so far, and huge differences about English teaching/learning resources between town and country exist.

Some educators in Taiwan advise that English learning should begin at the first grade in elementary school (戴維揚，民 92). While a recent study shows that studying English at a very early age does not necessarily promise any better proficiency in English for students (申慧媛，民 94). Besides, it is also claimed that the suitable age for English learning should depend on one's interest and intellectual development; otherwise, parents' being over-enthusiastic will likely do harm to their children's latter language learning (申慧媛與黃以敬，民 94). Indeed, the English education policy of Taiwan always seems contradictory by itself. For example, on the one hand the authority requires students and public servants to pass the GEPT, but on the other hand it also sets the limit of examinees' age under 12 due to the heat wave of it island-wide. However, this hasty policy leads to more tailor-made English proficiency tests for young learners to 'conquer', like Style/JET or YLE.

Similarly, on the one hand, the authority has decided that English education will start from the early age officially but on the other hand it also forbids the "All-English in Classroom" and English teaching in kindergartens. The MOE of Taiwan is advised to integrate the English curriculum and policies from the national scale to local scale, and from children English to Adult English. As 周中天（民 94）proposes, English learning hours should be very flexible and vary across levels in schools based on learners' intellectual and psychical development. Indeed, a centralised educational change without appropriate localised empowerment easily leads to failure (Yang, 2003). It is suggested that a national meeting about English education may be called to determine when to start teaching English, how to step up to a higher level, how to evaluate the learning, and then build some proficiency indicators of English for parents and students to follow (黃以敬，民 94 b.). A well sound and coherent English education policy can be defined as being prevalent to cater each learner's right, directive but empowered to allow alternatives, integrative to equally distribute resource, globalised to communicate with the world, and localised to accommodate vernacular characteristics.

Secondly, for English teachers, the effectiveness and appropriateness of native ELT methods, especially CLT, and materials also need to be re-considered cautiously for a large number of them are Anglo-Saxon-oriented and not culture-sensitive enough, and thus neglect to take localised factors into consideration. A language classroom is very dynamic and specific with many variables like age, proficiency, socioeconomic, political, or cultural factors, and it is very unrealistic if teachers hope one method i.e. CLT can fit all diversities. Thus, English teachers are advised to endeavor to gain their ownership for applying a local-fitted teaching method in their unique contexts. With regards to teaching materials, though those of the western content can 'correctly' inform learners the life, values, cultures, and experiences of native speakers but content of the source culture i.e. Taiwanese/Chinese cultures can not only encourage learners to obtain deeper understanding and insights of their own cultures to share with people from other cultures, but also ease local teachers' fear from trying to teach someone else's culture (McKay, 2002). Of course, this requires Taiwanese teachers' cooperative efforts to devote to designing localised teaching materials.

Thirdly, as McKay (2002) proposes, English teachers should teach their learners English as an international language instead of an American or British English. By this, she means that teachers need to teach learners the communication strategies to promote friendly relations rather than to achieve native-like competence. In addition, teachers also need to help language learners to develop a cultural awareness for these cultural factors do play a significant role in the success of learners' accessing to English information. That is the comprehension of an English text should be an interactive and active process through personal interpretation. In a word, English should not be taught in order to 'act' native-like but to 'use it' across cultures.

These above problematising practices do not intend to cause more anxiety to English teachers in Taiwan but aim to raising their awareness and reflection on rethinking the English status, impacts, cultures, teaching methods, and learners in their own peculiar teaching contexts. It is commonly believed that English will still openly and aboveboard exercise its linguistic, social, and cultural power over the Taiwanese society; however, the critical concerns of many localised issues urgently need to be addressed in order to achieve a productive and culture-sensitive English language teaching. After all, pursuing globalisation through English language learning is impractical and unilateral if the critical consideration of localisation is not taken. What should be pursued is 'to think globally but to act locally', for solid localisation is the accelerator of globalisation.

REFERENCES

中廣新聞網。**英研究指出英語的優勢至少還回維持五十年**（民 93 年 12 月 10 日）。 民 93 年 12 月 13 日，取自：http://tw.news.yahoo.com/041210/4/18suh.html

申慧媛（民 94 年 3 月 4 日）。教育部研究 早學英語 成績未必較好。**自由時報**，第 8 版。

申慧媛、黃以敬（民 94 年 3 月 4 日）。資質、興趣 影響學習效果。**自由時報**，第 8 版。

周中天（民 94）。中國大陸的英語教學（上）。師德會訊，28，4-6。

黃以敬（民 93 年 10 月 17 日 a.）。英檢畢業關、大學生心慌。**自由時報**。

黃以敬（民 94 年 3 月 4 日 b.）。英語政策 自相矛盾。**自由時報**，第 8 版。

黃旭昇（民 93 年 12 月 1 日）。平衡學習落差、台北縣國中小學將實施英檢。**中央社**。民 93 年 12 月 13 日，取自：http://tw.news.yahoo.com.tw/041201/43/17nae.html

溫貴香（民 93 年 12 月 1 日）。英語環境外籍人士滿意度提昇。**台灣日報**。民 93 年 12 月 13 日，取自：http://tw.news.yahoo.com/041201/46/17j0d.html

廖曉青 (民 90 年)。在中國實施交際教學法的不利因素。*New Zealand TESOL Journal*, 9, 57-70.

戴維揚（民 92b）。英語文課程革新的三大目標：文字、文學、文化。載於戴維揚、梁耀南（主編），**語言與文化**（23-38 頁）。台北市：文鶴出版社。

羅浩恩（民 93 年 11 月 30 日）。外國人看台灣英文環境、空有計畫不實用。**中廣新聞網**。民 93 年 12 月 13 日，取自：http://tw.news.yahoo.com/041130/4/17hmv.html

蘇以文（民 93 年 11 月 17 日）。母語是一切學習的基礎。**天下雜誌電子報**。民 93 年 12 月 13 日，取自：http://tw.news.yahoo.com/041117/22/161hy.html

Belcher, D. D. (1997). An argument for non-adversarial argumentation: On the relevance of the Feminist critique of academic discourse to L2 writing pedagogy. *Journal of Second Language Writing, 6* (1), 1-21.

Burnaby, B., & Sun, Y. (1989). Chinese teachers' view of Western language teaching: context informs paradigms. *TESOL Quarterly, 23* (2), 219-238.

Boyle, J. (1997). Changing Attitudes to English. *English Today, 51* (13/3), 3-6.

Canagarajah, A. S. (1999). On EFL teachers, awareness, and agency. *ELT Journal, 53* (3), 207-213.

Cheng, C. C. (1992). Chinese Varieties of English. The Other Tongue. In Kachru, B. B. (Ed.), *The Pragmatic of Non-native Varieties of English.* Urbana: University of Illinois Press.

Crystal, D. (1997). *English as a Global Language.* Cambridge: C.U.P.

Ellis, G. (1994). *The Appropriateness of the Communicative Approach in Vietnam: An Interview Study in Intercultural Communication.* Unpublished master's thesis. La Trobe University, Bundoora, Australia.

Kachru, B. B. (1981). *The Pragmatic of Non-native Varieties of English.* IL.: University of Illinois Press.

Kang, J. (1999). English Everywhere in China. *English Today, 51* (2), 46-48.

Kuo, H. (1995). The (in)appropriateness and (in)effectiveness of imposing communicative language teaching to Taiwan. *University of Hawaii's*

Working Papers in ESL, 13 (2), 21-47.

Lai, C. (1994). Communication failure in the language classroom: An exploration of causes. *RELC Journal, 25* (1), 99-129.

Larsen-Freeman, D. (2003). *Techniques and Principles in Language Teaching.* Oxford: OUP.

Li, D. (1998). It's always more difficult than you plan and imagine: Teachers' perceived difficulties in introducing the communicative approach in South Korea. *TESOL Quarterly, 32* (4), 677-703.

Lin, A. (1999). Doing-English-Lessons in the reproduction or transformation of social worlds? *TESOL Quarterly, 33* (3), 393-412.

Liu, J. (1999). Non-native-English-speaking professionals in TESOL. *TESOL Quarterly, 33* (1), 85-102.

Luke, A., McHoul, A., & Mey, J. L. (1990). On the limits of language planning: Class, state and power. In R. B. Balduaf, Jr., A. Luke (Eds.), *Language Planning and Education is Australia and the South Pacific* (pp.25-44). Clevedon, U.K.: Multilingual Matters.

McKay, S. L. (2002). *Teaching English as an international language.* Oxford: OUP.

McKay, S. L. (2003). Toward an appropriate EIL pedagogy: re-examining common ELT assumptions. *International Journal of Applied Linguistics, 13* (1), 1-22.

Ministry of Education (Taiwan). (1999). Retrieved from http://www.edu.tw/high-school/index-htm; http://www.edu.tw/bicer/chinese.htm

Pennycook, A. (1989). The concept of method, interested knowledge, and the politics of language teaching. *TESOL Quarterly, 23* (4), 589-618.

Pennycook, A. (1994). *The Culture Politics of English as an International*

Language. New York, NY.: Longman.

Pennycook, A. (1995). English teachers and the worldliness of English. In J. W. Tollefson (Ed.), *Power and Inequality in Language Education* (pp.34-58). Cambridge: CUP.

Pennycook, A. (1999). Introduction: critical approaches to TESOL. *TESOL Quarterly, 33* (3), 329-348.

Pennycook, A. (2001). *Critical Applied Linguistics: a critical introduction.* Mahwah, NJ.: LEA.

Prabhu, N. S. (1990). There is no best method- why? *TESOL Quarterly, 24* (2), 161-176.

Rajagopalan, K. (1999). Of EFL teachers, conscience, and cowardice. *ELT Journal, 53* (3), 200-206.

Richards, J. C., & Rodgers, T. (2001). *Approaches and Methods in Language Teaching.* Cambridge: CUP.

Sano, M., Takahashi, M., & Yoneyama, A. (1984). Communicative language teaching and local needs. *ELT Journal, 38* (3), 170-177.

Skutnabb-Kangas, T. (1998). Human rights and language wrongs- a future for diversity? *Language Sciences, 20*, 5-28.

Spack, R. (1997). The rhetorical construction of multilingual students. *TESOL Quarterly, 31* (4), 765-774.

Tang, C. (1997). The identity of the nonnative ESL teacher on the power and status of nonnative ESL teachers. *TESOL Quarterly, 31* (3), 577-580.

Tollefson, J. W. (1995). *Power and Inequality in Language Education.* New York, NY.: CUP.

Tsao, F. F.(1993). *Explorations in Applied Linguistics: Papers in Language Teaching & Sociolinguistics.* Taipei: Crane.

Wong, L. (1947). *Theory of Chinese Syntax.* Shangshai: Shung-wu

Publisher.

Wong, L. (1955). *Theory of Chinese Grammar.* Beijing: Shung-wu Publisher.

Yang, W. H. (2003). *An interpretative analysis of teachers' perceptions of educational change in Taiwan.* Unpublished doctoral dissertation. University of Exeter: Exeter, U.K.

Zamel, V. (1996). Transcending boundaries: Complicating the sense of teaching language. *College English, 6* (1), 1-11.

Zhang, A. (1997). China English and Chinese English. *English Today, 52* (13 /4), 39-40.

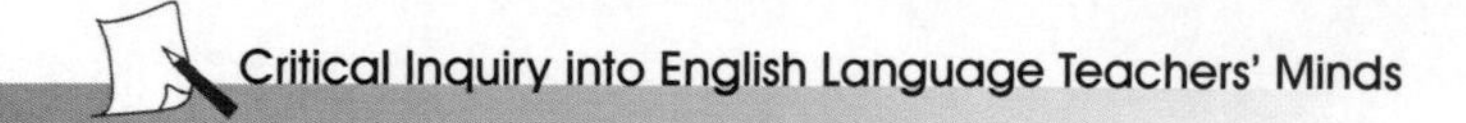

Chapter 3

English Teachers' & Learners' Attitudes Towards English Education in Taiwan

INTRODUCTION

Studies about English learners' perceptions and attitudes towards English language teaching as EFL have been abundant (Redfield, *et al.* 2003). Many of them investigated the situations in Japan and drew the conclusion that most of the students there expressed their strong dissatisfication with the traditional English teaching methodologies adopted among Japanese schools (Widdows & Voller, 1991). The students would prefer learning more about communicative skills of English to acquiring merely the forms of English, i.e. grammar rules or vocabulary. Some research also compared attitudes towards foreign language education across cultures (Durhm & Ryan, 1992; Ligget, 1988; Shawback & Redfield, 1996; Redfield, *et al.* 2003). For example, Ligget (1998) found that Japanese students and Egyptian students have very different attitudes towards English learning; furthermore, Durham and Ryan (1992) also concluded that Australian language learners and Japanese's regarded foreign language education very largely different, too.

In Redfield's *et al.* study (2003), they examined English learners' attitudes of similarities and differences towards English language learning between Chinese of PROC and Japanese college students. They found that the two groups have significantly different attitudes on nearly half of the measuring instrument items. Chinese learners are apparently more motivated to study English than their counterparts, Japanese learners. The contributions of these differences may owe to the changing society and boosting economical growth in China, and that Japanese learners' complaints of their teachers' unwilling to use English to teach communicative English skills in classroom (Redfield, *et al.* 2003). They claim that this study fractures English native speakers' illusion that most East Asian students (mainly referring to those countries, like China, Japan, Korea, and Taiwan) share a single culture entity and so should be their attitudes towards English language teaching. Their comparison motivated this study to investigate the situation of Taiwan.

METHODS

Research aims

As discussed in the preceding section, many studies have been conducted to investigate learners' perceptions about English language instruction in a single or cross-cultural scales, especially in the East Asian contexts. However, Taiwan appears to be the one left blank in this area. Thus, the first research aim is to examine if Taiwanese language learners basically belong to the stereotype group of all East Asian learners as well (Redfield, *et al.* 2004). Furthermore, "teaching is an activity which is embedded within a set of culturally bound assumptions about teachers, teaching, and learners" (Richards & Lockhart, 1996), and thus it would be useful if teachers' perceptions of English language instruction can be investigated and compared with learners' to gauge the potential gap about this issue in Taiwan. This is the second aim of this research.

Questionnaire

The Foreign Language Education Questionnaire (FLEQ) was chosen as the measuring instrument for this research. This questionnaire was designed by Allen (2002) in an effort to determine the efficiency of the Standards for Foreign Language Learning in the 21st century (National Standard, 1999), a document offering a vision for foreign language education in the US. The aim of this standard is to promote a standardised teaching in the US schools; the FLEQ was developed to scrutinise if the standard-based instruction cause any effect on pre- and in-service foreign language teachers' attitudes. In this study, FLEQ was adapted into a Chinese version (see Appendix) and some items have been revised or deleted in order to conform to Taiwanese context. For example, foreign language instruction was defined as English language education solely in this research. Before the Chinese FLEQ was conducted formally, its first version had been piloted by a number of learners and teachers, and thus revised accordingly.

Participants

The participants were categorised into four different groups. The first group (G1, N=77) is English-major students coming from 3 different universities (2 national; 1 private). The second group (G2, N=89) is all non English-majors from the same universities as G1. All participants in both groups have learnt English at least for six years formally and some of them have a longer period of study than others. The third group (G3, N=44) includes the pre-service English teachers, coming from a national teacher university and a teacher cultivation programme for secondary school English teachers of a private university. Similar to the previous groups in the time length of English learning, these participants are being trained to teach English and also continue learning English in universities. The last group (G4, N=14) is composed of all in-service English teachers in a municipal senior high school. Over half of these teachers have at least been teaching English for 10 years, and one –third of them even have accumulated 20-year experience. The participants were selected based on a purpose sampling for they could provide contributions to the questions probed in this research. The total number of the participants is 224.

Analysis

Excel was employed as the main statistical measure to compare the responses on the Chinese FLEQ of the language learner and teacher participants.

This is an integration-based research combing the quality of quantitative research and qualitative one. The number of the participants, data assessment, and measuring instrument reveal the characteristics of quantitative research while the interpretation and reflection of the data derive from the quality of qualitative research. Furthermore, my role i.e. as being an outside researcher and inside language teacher educator in this study also fosters the qualitative base for the research.

RESULTS & INTERPRETATION

In this section, the statistical data will be displayed with the interpretation. The results of most questions will be analysed and discussed comprehensively. The abbreviations used for this discussion are Q: Question number asked in the FLEQ, G1 (Group 1 EM): English Majors, G2 (group 2 NEM): Non-English Majors, G3 (Group 3 PET): Pre-service English Teachers, G4 (Group 4 IET): In-service English teachers, and ELE: English Language Education. (SA: strongly agree; A: agree; NI: not identified; D: disagree; SD: strongly disagree; #: number; %: percentage)

Q1.: The data shows that a very high percentage of all groups believes textbook plays a very significant role in ELT.

This indicates that both teachers and students rely on ELT textbooks very much, and may imply that teachers lack proficiency in designing self teaching materials. The reasons accounted for this can be (1) ELE is exam-oriented in Taiwan and textbooks are the sources of exam, and (2) teachers can avoid uncertainty provided a textbook on hand.

Table 1: Adopted materials and accompanying ancillaries

	1 (SA)	2 (A)	3 (NI)	4 (D)	5 (SD)
Group 1 #	25	45	3	3	1
EM (%)	32.5	58.4	3.9	3.9	1.3
Group 2 #	29	42	4	12	2
NEM (%)	32.6	47.2	4.5	13.5	2.2
Group 3 #	9	32	0	3	0
PET (%)	20.5	72.7	0	6.8	0
Group 4 #	6	7	1	0	0
IET (%)	42.9	50.0	7.1	0	0

Q2.: About half of the respondents in four groups agree ELE should begin from the lower grades in elementary school but nearly half of them also disagree with this statement. This response is slightly different from the current policy of the MOE for ELE will soon start from the 3rd grade in elementary school in the near future in Taiwan and some cities, in fact, have already implemented this policy like Taipei and Hsinchu. It can be assumed that these respondents do not believe the earlier one learns English, the better English proficiency can be enhanced. This also pinpoints the low average English competency among university students even after a long period of learning English.

Table 2: Ideal time of English learning in early elementary school

		1 (SA)	2 (A)	3 (NI)	4 (D)	5 (SD)
Group 1 EM	#	10	33	12	18	14
	(%)	13.0	42.9	15.6	23.4	5.2
Group 2 NEM	#	23	35	8	20	3
	(%)	25.8	39.3	9.0	22.5	3.4
Group 3 PET	#	6	19	6	12	1
	(%)	13.6	43.2	13.6	27.3	2.3
Group 4 IET	#	3	5	1	4	1
	(%)	21.4	35.7	7.1	28.6	7.1

Q4.: Compared with the other groups, the in-service English teachers' attitudes towards authentic materials are less positive. The reasons can be that firstly, the authentic materials may not be culture-sensitive i.e. unsuitable or inappropriate to Taiwanese context, secondly they are not evaluated beforehand, thirdly they demand more efforts for teachers and finally teachers may not know how to apply these authentic materials to their teaching.

Table 3: The incorporation of authentic materials

		1 (SA)	2 (A)	3 (NI)	4 (D)	5 (SD)
Group 1 EM	#	29	28	9	11	0
	(%)	37.7	36.4	11.7	14.3	0
Group 2 NEM	#	31	30	18	8	2
	(%)	34.8	33.7	20.2	9.0	2.2
Group 3 PET	#	11	19	2	11	1
	(%)	25.0	43.2	4.5	25.0	2.3
Group 4 IET	#	3	4	0	7	0
	(%)	21.4	28.6	0	50.0	0

Q5.: It is clearly shown that those who show neutral and disagreement take up more than 70% on average. Perhaps, this item may not be well applicable to Taiwan for English is taught as a first foreign language, not as a second language like the States. Seldom do Taiwanese learn another foreign language except English as their first foreign language; therefore, it is unlikely to determine if those who have learnt another foreign language, for example Japanese, can learn English better than others in Taiwan.

Table 4: Having learnt another language facilitates English learning

	1 (SA)	2 (A)	3 (NI)	4 (D)	5 (SD)
Group 1 #	4	15	28	26	4
EM (%)	5.2	19.5	36.4	33.8	5.2
Group 2 #	7	20	34	24	4
NEM (%)	7.9	22.5	38.2	27.0	4.5
Group 3 #	2	11	18	13	0
PET (%)	4.5	25.0	40.9	29.5	0
Group 4 #	1	5	7	1	0
IET (%)	7.1	35.7	50.0	7.1	0

Q6.: The four groups show 17.57% on average that they would prefer to use English solely in classroom, and it is very interesting to note that less than 5% of G3 agree to this statement. The reason accounting for this can be that the respondents are worried about their English competency is not proficient enough either in listening or speaking. This result identifies that using English completely is still demanding for non-native teachers but also implies that native-speaker teachers may confront some difficulties when using English only to teach in classroom (Medgyes, 2001). Besides, it is also very ironical to realise that in fact many English teachers, especially non-native ones for young learners still greatly emphasise 'Only English; no Taiwanese/Chinese' in classroom.

Table 5: English as dominant language in classroom

	1 (SA)	2 (A)	3 (NI)	4 (D)	5 (SD)
Group 1 #	7	13	7	45	5
EM (%)	9.1	16.9	9.1	58.4	6.5
Group 2 #	4	6	11	57	11
NEM (%)	4.5	6.7	12.4	64.0	12.4
Group 3 #	0	2	4	34	4
PET (%)	0	4.5	9.1	77.3	9.1
Group 4 #	0	4	2	8	0
IET (%)	0	28.6	14.3	57.1	0

Q7.: Except the G3 with 61%, 80% of all the other three groups believe English is useful for them. Learning English is very extrinsically motivated in Taiwan for it is equivalent to job promotion, guaranteed and higher pay. This can be proved by the large number of examinees (over 120,000) taking GEPT this year due to being secure of their official jobs (許敏溶，民 94; 羅浩恩，民 94). However, it is interesting that the percentages of G3 and G4 are slightly lower then those of G1 and G2. Perhaps, teachers hold a more realistic attitude towards ELE in that not everyone can indeed benefit from learning English.

Table 6: All students benefit from English learning

	1 (SA)	2 (A)	3 (NI)	4 (D)	5 (SD)
Group #	33	31	6	6	1
EM (%)	42.9	40.3	7.8	7.8	1.3

Group 2 #	39	36	8	8	0
NEM (%)	43.8	40.4	9.0	9.0	0
Group 3 #	5	22	8	8	1
PET (%)	11.4	50.0	18.2	18.2	2.3
Group 4 #	4	7	3	3	0
IET (%)	28.6	50.0	21.4	21.4	0

Q8.& Q9. : Nearly 80% of the groups on average believe English components are extremely important, and nearly 90% on average of them agree that communication skill is very important in learning English. The former response does not surprise us for traditionally Taiwanese students have been known for being good at learning rules and memorising them. The group of English teachers ranks the highest one in Q8 (85%), which may imply that most teachers still believe English is taught mostly for examination in Taiwan but in fact, learners may have their another need of learning it i.e. to communicate in English effectively.

Table 7: All class time devoted to learning language system

	1 (SA)	2 (A)	3 (NI)	4 (D)	5 (SD)
Group 1 #	34	27	7	9	0
EM (%)	44.2	35.1	9.1	11.7	0
Group 2 #	36	37	6	9	1
NEM (%)	40.4	41.6	6.7	10.1	1.1
Group 3 #	12	19	8	5	0
PET (%)	27.3	43.2	18.2	11.4	0
Group 4 #	2	10	1	1	0
IET (%)	14.3	71.4	7.1	7.1	0

Table 8: Teach specific communication strategies in English

	1 (SA)	2 (A)	3 (NI)	4 (D)	5 (SD)
Group 1 #	37	30	7	9	0
EM (%)	48.1	39.0	9.1	11.7	0
Group 2 #	46	32	9	9	1
NEM (%)	51.7	36.0	10.1	10.1	1.1
Group 3 #	26	18	0	5	0
PET (%)	59.1	40.9	0	11.4	0
Group 4 #	6	6	2	1	0
IET (%)	42.9	42.9	14.6	7.1	0

Q10.: On average 75% of the respondents believe English teaching should be integrated with technology. This implies that CALL has attracted teachers' and learners' attention recently in the net-time; however, very paradoxically, in my another paper investigating teachers' technology application of English teaching only 8.75% of the teachers have tried used technology on their English teaching while 81.25% of them never try it before (Yang, 2003). The most obvious reasons result from the inaccessible facilities and insufficient training. Therefore, the consequence of Q10 cannot suggest that these teachers will 'act' to use CALL but simply that they 'believe' it necessary and inevitable. Teachers' belief will not necessarily lead to action.

Table 9: Opportunities for accessing a variety technologies

	1 (SA)	2 (A)	3 (NI)	4 (D)	5 (SD)
Group 1 #	17	36	21	3	0
EM (%)	22.1	46.8	27.3	3.9	0
Group 2 #	24	38	21	4	2
NEM (%)	27.0	42.7	23.6	4.5	2.2
Group 3 #	11	22	10	1	0

PET (%)	25.0	55.0	22.7	2.3	0
Group 4 #	4	8	1	1	0
IET (%)	28.6	57.1	7.1	7.1	0

Q11.: Except the G4, all the other groups show a extreme support for adopting different materials for differentiated students with the average of 93.4%, while more than 20% of English teachers undecided their choice. The reason can be that though the claim of teaching students in accordance with their aptitude is commonly regarded as teaching dogma for teachers yet this appears to be very difficult when teachers face a large class with differentiated students in a real teaching context.

Table 10: Different topics for different students' interests

	1 (SA)	2 (A)	3 (NI)	4 (D)	5 (SD)
Group 1 #	35	38	4	0	0
EM (%)	45.5	49.4	5.2	0	0
Group 2 #	44	36	5	4	0
NEM (%)	49.4	40.4	5.6	4.5	0
Group 3 #	20	22	2	0	0
PET (%)	45.5	50.0	4.5	0	0
Group 4 #	4	7	3	0	0
IET (%)	28.6	50.0	21.4	0	0

Q12.: The responses of this question correspond to the consequences of Q8 and Q9. English learners and teachers believe both language components and skills for real communication are equally essential. However, these urgent demands for learning communication skills suggest that the current English teaching still cannot satisfy learners these needs but emphasises rules memorisation for tests.

Table 11: Using English for real communication in school and real life

		1 (SA)	2 (A)	3 (NI)	4 (D)	5 (SD)
Group 1	#	47	29	1	0	0
EM	(%)	61.0	37.7	1.3	0	0
Group 2	#	57	23	7	2	0
NEM	(%)	64.0	25.8	7.9	2.2	0
Group 3	#	28	16	0	0	0
PET	(%)	63.6	36.4	0	0	0
Group 4	#	7	6	1	0	0
IET	(%)	50.2	42.9	7.1	0	0

Q13.: With reference to Q6, responses of this item seem parallel with Q6. Neither do most respondents believe an effective English teacher should only speak English in classroom; nor do most of them consider an effective English programme should be instructed only by using English. Again, this is another example of a con for non-native teachers and learners in a real teaching context for they are worried about their English proficiency (Medgyes, 2001). However, about half of the G4 agrees to this statement and another half is undecided, which are significantly much higher than the other groups. The pre-service English teachers show a strong disagreement to this point (85%). Does this imply that these pre-service English teachers are more worried about their English proficiency and their proficiency indeed is descending, or are they just humble to say so? This phenomenon deserves further study.

Table 12: Only English used in instruction

	1 (SA)	2 (A)	3 (NI)	4 (D)	5 (SD)
Group 1 #	7	8	12	46	4
EM (%)	9.1	10.4	15.6	59.7	5.2
Group 2 #	5	10	18	43	13
NEM (%)	5.6	11.2	20.2	48.3	14.6
Group 3 #	0	2	5	32	5
PET (%)	0	4.5	11.4	72.7	11.4
Group 4 #	0	5	2	7	0
IET (%)	0	35.7	14.3	50.0	0

Q14.: Developing the critical and independent thinking skills has been highly emphasised and valued in recent years, especially for Asian students. Most of the respondents in four groups agree to this point but those who undecided still take up about 25 % on average. This can be assumed that those respondents do not have a clear idea of what critical thinking means.

Table 13: The promoting of learners' critical thinking

	1 (SA)	2 (A)	3 (NI)	4 (D)	5 (SD)
Group 1 #	23	35	16	3	0
EM (%)	29.9	45.5	20.8	3.9	0
Group 2 #	23	34	28	4	0
NEM (%)	25.8	38.2	31.5	4.5	0
Group 3 #	3	31	8	1	1
PET (%)	6.8	70.5	18.2	2.3	2.3
Group 4 #	5	6	3	0	0
IET (%)	35.7	42.9	21.4	0	0

Q15.: All four groups show a very positive attitude towards this statement.

Table 14: English learning related to learners' life

	1 (SA)	2 (A)	3 (NI)	4 (D)	5 (SD)
Group 1 #	28	36	11	2	0
EM (%)	36.4	46.8	14.3	2.6	0
Group 2 #	35	46	5	1	2
NEM (%)	39.3	51.7	5.6	1.1	2.2
Group 3 #	11	26	6	0	1
PET (%)	25.0	59.1	13.6	0	2.3
Group 4 #	6	7	1	0	0
IET (%)	42.9	50.0	7.1	0	0

Q16.: Both G1 and G4 show a higher degree of agreement to this point than G2 and G3. It is very likely that these non-English majors, and in-service teachers are those who need special strategy training immediately in learning English; however, a number of these pre-service teachers do not think so or are undecided. This may imply that they are not well-educated about how to teach their future students English learning strategies. Current language teacher educators need to notice this gap and then design courses for these pre-service teachers to cater this issue.

Table 15: Specific learning strategies for learning English

	1 (SA)	2 (A)	3 (NI)	4 (D)	5 (SD)
Group 1 #	24	39	10	4	0
EM (%)	31.2	50.6	13.0	5.2	0
Group 2 #	27	40	18	3	1
NEM (%)	30.3	44.9	20.2	3.4	1.1
Group 3 #	8	24	7	5	0
PET (%)	18.2	54.5	15.9	11.4	0
Group 4 #	7	6	0	1	0
IET (%)	50.0	42.9	0	7.1	0

Q17.: Compared with the results of Q2, the average percentage of the respondents agreeing to this statement is much less. A large number of them are either disagreed or undecided about the appropriate time of first English learning from junior high school. Half of them also do not support that learning English should begin from the lower grades in elementary school. This illustrates the argument of the critical period of English learning. Presumably, the most appropriate starting period of English learning may situate at the higher grades in elementary schools in Taiwan. This finding is worthy of attention while the educational authorities are amending English education policy.

Table 16: The best timing of English learning begins from junior high school

	1 (SA)	2 (A)	3 (NI)	4 (D)	5 (SD)
Group 1 #	5	17	21	27	7
EM (%)	6.5	22.1	27.3	35.1	9.1
Group 2 #	8	16	29	28	8
NEM (%)	9.0	18.0	32.6	31.5	9.0
Group 3 #	1	5	9	25	4
PET (%)	2.3	11.4	20.5	56.8	9.1
Group 4 #	1	1	3	8	1
IET (%)	7.1	7.1	21.4	57.1	7.1

Q18.: Both G1 and G2 show over 70% of agreement while pre- and in-service English teachers express a very strong agreement to this item with 93%. Taiwan, like many other Far Eastern countries, is very exam-oriented, and traditionally English is regarded as equivalence to paper-and-pencil test

(Redfield, Yang & Ueda, 2003). However, in this research, the participants express a very strong need for open-ended activities to assess some parts of their English grades. Teachers' tremendous agreement to this may imply that they are unsatisfied about the type of current English exams and its wash-back effects; contrarily, they need to be empowered to assess their students' English ability in open manners. It is likely that they do not believe traditional paper-and-pencil tests can properly evaluate learners' proficiency any more presently.

Table 17: Using open-ended activities to assess English learners

	1 (SA)	2 (A)	3 (NI)	4 (D)	5 (SD)
Group 1 #	15	40	14	7	1
EM (%)	19.5	51.9	18.2	9.1	1.3
Group 2 #	21	44	16	6	2
NEM (%)	23.6	49.4	18.0	6.7	2.2
Group 3 #	9	32	3	0	0
PET (%)	20.5	72.7	6.8	0	0
Group 4 #	4	9	0	1	0
IET (%)	28.6	64.3	0	7.1	0

Q19.: In this item, nearly 93% of the respondents agree to the notion that effective English language instruction should lead to an understanding of underlying values and beliefs of English societies. However, in fact the sources of understanding English values and cultures for Taiwanese people are multi-channels, and for critical applied linguists like Pennycook (2001) and Tollefson (1995) the responses of this item proves that English is quietly exercising its imperial linguistic power on many EFL contexts, which may lead to the hindrance to learners' identities, language rights, and language power and resources distribution. It can be presumed that either teachers or materials should function as the medium to convey these English values and cultures but in fact whether all non-native English teachers of Taiwan are well-qualified to do this job is highly doubtful. Moreover, most current EFL materials published by English-speaking nations would be very cautious when addressing the issues of cultures and values due to the consideration of global selling markets (Richards, 2001). This leads to firstly the superficial introduction of English cultures and values but not the true 'understanding' of them. Secondly, presumably it may be difficult in Taiwan if any writer tries to write localised English teaching materials or students are required to think about the local context by using English. In this way, English will be either learnt as an imported product without understanding its essences, or unlikely to be integrated with the local context.

Table 18: The understanding of underlying values and cultures of English

	1 (SA)	2 (A)	3 (NI)	4 (D)	5 (SD)
Group 1 #	35	36	5	1	0
EM (%)	45.5	46.8	6.5	1.3	0
Group 2 #	27	47	11	3	1
NEM (%)	30.3	52.8	12.4	3.4	1.1
Group 3 #	16	26	1	1	0
PET (%)	36.4	59.1	2.3	2.3	0
Group 4 #	8	6	0	0	0
IET (%)	57.1	42.9	0	0	0

Q20.: Compared with the item 8, though over 80% of the participants believe that an effective English teaching should focus on language components, nearly 60% on average of them do not think grammar and vocabulary should be the major focus. Again, teachers show a higher percentage than students by 25%. The reasons can be that students are most of time taught grammar and vocabulary in class and they believe these are exactly what most exams will assess them.

Table 19: English instruction focuses on grammar and vocabulary

	1 (SA)	2 (A)	3 (NI)	4 (D)	5 (SD)
Group 1 #	1	21	14	35	6
EM (%)	1.3	27.3	18.2	45.5	7.8
Group 2 #	6	18	19	36	10
NEM (%)	6.7	20,2	21.3	40.4	11.2
Group 3 #	0	3	3	33	5
PET (%)	0	6.8	6.8	75.0	11.4
Group 4 #	0	3	1	8	2
IET (%)	0	21.4	7.1	57.1	14.3

Q21.: Very interestingly, the responses of this item appear slightly contradictory to those of item 1. Though they believe good teaching textbooks play an important role in an effective teaching, over 50% of them do not consider effective teachers should only teach the contexts of textbooks. This implies that textbooks should not become the only source of obtaining English knowledge but contrarily teachers themselves play a significant role in transmitting knowledge i.e. they may be supposed to be learnt and accomplished in everything about English. One the one hand, teachers rely much on textbooks; on the other hand, they do not believe these books can convey appropriate or sufficient knowledge about learning English. This reaction apparently suggests that the respondents are not able to build a stable belief system about English instruction.

Table 20: Teacher's role is to help students learn what is in the text-book

	1 (SA)	2 (A)	3 (NI)	4 (D)	5 (SD)
Group 1 #	2	17	6	44	8
EM (%)	2.6	22.1	7.8	57.1	10,4
Group 2 #	11	19	10	36	13
NEM (%)	12.4	21.3	11.2	40,4	14.6
Group 3 #	1	8	2	27	6
PET (%)	2.3	18.2	4.5	61.4	13.6
Group 4 #	0	5	1	5	3
IET (%)	0	35.7	7.1	35.7	21.4

Q22.: The responses of this item are much divided. Nearly 50% of them on average do not believe tests accompanying the textbook can adequately assess students' English learning while another half of them do, especially for the in-service English teachers. This may account for the phenomenon that Taiwanese students are usually good at doing tests mechanically but may be incapable of using English communicatively. Teacher's equally divided responses of agreement and disagreement about this item may suggest that half of them are unsatisfied with current exam systems and doubt their effectiveness. Furthermore, students' responses almost equally distributed among agreement, unidentified, and disagreement also represent the worry that they are used to being assessed without clearly understanding the effectiveness and meaning of these tests. This would be very disappointed if English learners of

Taiwan need to take many tests but cannot ensure whether or not these texts are appropriate and effective to reflect their proficiency.

Table 21: The text-book provides adequate tests

	1 (SA)	2 (A)	3 (NI)	4 (D)	5 (SD)
Group 1 #	1	30	19	20	7
EM (%)	1.3	39.0	24.7	26.0	9.1
Group 2 #	4	26	19	29	11
NEM (%)	4.5	29.2	21.3	32.6	12.4
Group 3 #	1	12	7	20	4
PET (%)	2.3	27.3	15.9	45.5	9.1
Group 4 #	1	6	0	7	0
IET (%)	7.1	42.9	0	50.0	0

Q23. & Q29.: Over 80% of all groups on average believe that those who are incapable of learning other subjects well still can learn English. This proves that English has become an all-people-campaign in Taiwan, and that diligence is the means by which one makes up for his/her incapability, which is the traditional dogma in education asserted by Confucius and his followers.

Table 22: English is not suitable for students having difficulties with learning

	1 (SA)	2 (A)	3 (NI)	4 (D)	5 (SD)
Group 1 #	1	0	5	38	33
EM (%)	1.3	0	6.5	49.4	42.9
Group 2 #	0	4	11	41	33
NEM (%)	0	4.5	12.4	46.7	37.1
Group 3 #	0	0	0	23	21
PET (%)	0	0	0	52.3	47.7

Group 4 #	0	0	2	6	6
IET (%)	0	0	14.3	42.9	42.9

Table 23: All students can successfully learn English even with learning difficulties

	1 (SA)	2 (A)	3 (NI)	4 (D)	5 (SD)
Group 1 #	22	37	16	1	1
EM (%)	28.6	48.1	2.8	1.3	1.3
Group 2 #	26	47	11	4	1
NEM (%)	29.2	52.8	12.4	4.5	1.1
Group 3 #	13	29	2	0	0
PET (%)	29.5	65.9	4.5	0	0
Group 4 #	3	8	3	0	0
IET (%)	21.4	57.4	21.4	0	0

Q24.: This item may not be well applied to Taiwan context for English is learnt as a foreign language and most of Taiwanese learn it as their first foreign language. This is because Taiwan is not an officially multilingual country like the U.S.; therefore,this is a very America-centric item.

Table 24: Little or no benefit for students who have learnt another language other than English

	1 (SA)	2 (A)	3 (NI)	4 (D)	5 (SD)
Group 1 #	1	3	15	35	23
EM (%)	1.3	3.9	19.5	45.5	29.9
Group 2 #	3	2	20	45	19
NEM (%)	3.4	2.2	22.5	50.6	21.3
Group 3 #	0	1	6	25	12
PET (%)	0	2.3	13.6	56.8	27.3
Group 4 #	0	0	4	8	2
IET (%)	0	0	28.6	57.1	14.3

Q25. & Q30.: These two items show that nearly 85% of all respondents perceive that English tests should not be confined to the components of English language but instead should contain testing items about English cultures. However, there are still some slight differences between students' and teachers' responses. Only about half of students do not believe grammar and vocabulary tests are important while nearly 90% of the pre- and in-service teachers do not think so. The responses of these two items reflect that first traditional English tests, which only assess learners' linguistic competency, frustrate not only most students but teachers. Second, another half of students still believe traditional tests may still be necessary for they do not have adequate knowledge about English cultures and the assessment of understanding of English cultures will perhaps become value judgement. Furthermore, the understanding of a culture can be interpreted and assessed from many different perspectives, which makes the answer multiple. This is what Taiwanese students are not used to for most of them always expect a single-reality for an answer in tests.

Table 25: Assessing learners' English culture learning

	1 (SA)	2 (A)	3 (NI)	4 (D)	5 (SD)
Group 1 #	37	30	7	9	0
EM (%)	48.1	39.0	9.1	11.7	0
Group 2 #	46	32	9	9	1
NEM (%)	51.7	36.0	10.1	10.1	1.1
Group 3 #	26	18	0	5	0
PET (%)	59.1	40.9	0	11.4	0
Group 4 #	6	6	2	1	0
IET (%)	42.9	42.9	14.6	7.1	0

Table 26: Assessing vocabulary and grammar mainly

	1 (SA)	2 (A)	3 (NI)	4 (D)	5 (SD)
Group 1 #	2	13	17	35	10
EM (%)	2.6	16.9	22.1	45.5	13.0
Group 2 #	9	11	21	34	14
NEM (%)	10.1	12.4	23.6	38.2	15.7
Group 3 #	0	2	3	31	8
PET (%)	0	4.5	6.8	70.5	18.2
Group 4 #	0	0	2	11	1
IET (%)	0	0	14.3	78.6	7.1

Q26. & Q31.: The responses of these two items are very correspondent. Nearly 75% of them on average consider English beneficial for their future careers. This suggests that most of Taiwanese people learn English for an extrinsic and instrumental purpose. That is, they learn English because of some external incentives such as job promotion, higher salaries, certificates or thresholds. In addition, this also implies that the Taiwanese government's deliberate promotion for learning English is successful to some extent for it has led its people to regard learning English as being important and necessary.

Table 27: English learning only enhances certain professions

	1 (SA)	2 (A)	3 (NI)	4 (D)	5 (SD)
Group 1 #	0	4	4	39	30
EM (%)	0	5.2	5.2	50.6	39.0
Group 2 #	3	8	12	45	21
NEM (%)	3.4	9.0	13.5	50.6	23.6
Group 3 #	0	5	5	25	9
PET (%)	0	11.4	11.4	56.8	20.5
Group 4 #	0	0	1	11	2
IET (%)	0	0	7.1	78.6	14.3

Table 28: English learning benefits to every future occupation

	1 (SA)	2 (A)	3 (NI)	4 (D)	5 (SD)
Group 1 #	37	31	5	4	0
EM (%)	48.1	40.3	6.5	5.2	0
Group 2 #	34	28	19	8	0
NEM (%)	38.2	31.5	21.3	9.0	0
Group 3 #	7	22	11	4	0
PET (%)	15.9	50.0	25.0	9.1	0
Group 4 #	4	6	2	2	0
IET (%)	28.6	42.9	14.3	14.3	0

Q28.: The responses of this item are dividedly distributed. About half of the teacher groups do not perceive English culture learning should be secondary to vocabulary and grammar while only one-third of student groups do not think so. There is seemingly a gap between students' and teachers' perceptions of culture learning. It appears that teachers are more positive about culture learning while most students are either undecided or disagreed. The reasons can be that first students do not know much about English culture learning, second they have been long used to traditional grammar teaching already, and third they may be worried about that there will be an extra assessment of their competency about English culture if it is taught.

Table 29: English culture learning subordinate to grammar and vocabulary

	1 (SA)	2 (A)	3 (NI)	4 (D)	5 (SD)
Group 1 #	5	14	26	24	8
EM (%)	6.5	18.2	33.8	31.2	10.4
Group 2 #	6	21	29	26	7
NEM (%)	6.7	23.6	32.6	29.2	7.9
Group 3 #	0	12	6	22	4

PET (%)	0	27.3	13.6	50.0	9.1
Group 4 #	0	3	4	6	1
IET (%)	0	21.4	28.6	42.9	7.1

IMPLICATION & SUGGESTIONS

From the above discussion, the following implication can be drawn. Firstly, English culture learning is still insufficiently accommodated in Taiwan. Learning a language is also learning its cultures; language is the core component in culture while culture influences the use of its language (Brown, 2002; 游毓玲，民 92). This means learning English language is not definitely equal to understanding English and its underlying cultures or values (黃以敬，民 94 b.). According to a survey (陳英暉，民 92), most English departments in Taiwan only value 'language teaching' but neglect 'culture teaching.' Thus, English teachers are imposed a tough task to teach English culture even if they were not provided enough courses to learn English cultures while in university. A holistic language education should aim at facilitating learners' linguistic competence and cultural literacy (戴維揚，民 92 a. b.). Only teaching students the 'outer forms' of English is simply like letting them examine the skeleton of a human body in anatomy, which is not complete at all. 'Inner culture' is truly the fresh and blood for a language. Furthermore, cultural awareness helps students to critically reflect on their native cultures and then can become global villagers. Hence, it is advised that the professional development for pre-service and in-service English teachers be focused on providing more courses about English cultures.

Secondly, present English tests in classroom cannot appropriately evaluate learners' communicative proficiency and lack of flexibility in forms. The best English language testing is teacher-designed materials (Heaton, 1988); however, currently what English learners are tested relies much on the ready-made tests, which usually lack of flexibility and communicative functions. The wash-back effects of entrance examinations may account for this phenomenon for they mainly test learners' knowledge about language forms and students only learn what will be tested (陳楷, 民 94 b.). As Brown (2001) suggests, the present trend for language testing is centred on catering different intelligences of all learners, and designing performance-based, interactive and alternative tests like a task-based or a project test. These alternatives may satisfy the participants' urges of this research; however, these flexible tests may be criticised as time-, energy-, and money-consuming, and subjective, compared with the traditionally adopted ready-made tests.

Thirdly. there is a perception gap existing between teachers and learners about the issue that if the current English teaching should be traditionally form-focused or communicatively learner-centred. Compared with other groups, English teachers emphasise more on learning the components of English, i.e. grammar rules, or vocabulary; however, learners would eager to learn more about communication skills. This perception gap involves the beliefs about English language, and language teachers' role. In Richards & Lockhart's (1996) book, they argue that English teachers in Taiwan and Hong Kong perceive that English is a rule-bound but illogical language, and they believe their roles as English teachers are mainly to provide a correct model of language use and correct learners' errors. Perhaps this can partially account for the reason of why teachers in this study emphasise the teaching of English rules. Therefore, it is advised that in order to meet both sides' beliefs and expectations teachers can negotiate with learners about what they will teach and learn, and set the proportions of different focuses in advance.

Next, the critical period for English language education is still uncertain (Brown, 2000). Indeed, as the data reveal, the participants cannot reach an agreement about when is the right starting age for Taiwanese students to learn English officially in school. Though it is presumably believed that the critical period for a successful second language learner is before the adolescence, yet it is still disputed about how to define "successful", especially when authentic accent is highly emphasised, not to mention considering the neurological, phonological, cognitive, affective, and linguistic factors (Brown, 2000). However, one of the distinguished TESOL educators, Prof. 戴維揚(民 92 b.)of Taiwan advises that English learning should begin at the first grade in elementary school. While a recent study shows that studying English at a very early age does not necessarily promise any better proficiency in English for students (申慧媛，民 94). Some experts also claim that the suitable age for English learning should depend on one's interest and intellectual development; otherwise, being over-enthusiastic will likely do harm to students' latter language learning (申慧媛與黃以敬，民 94). Indeed, the

English education policy of Taiwan always seems contradictory by itself. For example, the authority's requirement of passing GEPT among students and public servants lead to the limit of examinees' age due to the heat wave of it island-wide. Furthermore, on the one hand, the authority has decided that English education will start from the early age officially but on the other hand it also forbids the "All-English in Classroom" and English teaching in kindergartens. The MOE of Taiwan is advised to integrate the English curriculum and policies from the national scale to local scale, and from children English to adult English. In addition, a national meeting about English education may need to be called to determine when to start teaching English, how to step up to a higher level, how to evaluate the learning, and then build some proficiency indicators of English for parents and students to follow. In a word, English education policy should be consistent for a long-term (黃以敬，民 94 e.).

Finally, English is mostly learnt out of instrumental orientation in Taiwan. The data of this research and other reports indicate that English instruction in classroom is not welcomed by Taiwanese learners and teachers, though they still perceive English learning is beneficial for 'everyone.' A certificate of any English proficiency test is the proof guaranteeing learners the benefits of English learning in the careers (朱正庭，民 94 a. b.). Thus, it is not surprising that GEPT (General English Proficiency Test) has become an all-people-campaign in Taiwan (劉俊言等，民 94；許敏溶，民 94), which, however, also leads to some debates and educators' serious concerns about this heat-wave of English proficiency test. For example, the authority is considering setting a limit on the examinees' age (陳楷， 民 94 a. ;黃以敬, 民 94d). Whereas, English instruction, ironically, in classroom cannot have learners' approval (黃以敬，民 94 a.). This contradictory phenomenon pinpoints the instrumental orientation of English learning in Taiwan. For a country, indeed, like Taiwan where English is learnt as a foreign language, English used as a communicative or instructive purpose is apparently considerable if the status of English needs to be positioned as a second or international language (黃以敬，民 94 c.). Appealing for motivating English learners intrinsically, thus, becomes an urgent task for teachers. Language teachers are encouraged to integrate content-based instruction and learner-centred cooperative learning, and to help students set their intrinsic goals of English learning (Brown, 2001).

CONCLUSION

This article investigates the attitudes toward ELT of four different groups by using FLEQ. The results reveal that most of the participants have a very positive attitude towards English language learning in Taiwan; however, the four groups also express different degrees of beliefs and concerns in a number of areas of current English teaching in Taiwan. The findings may reveal that firstly the deliberate promotion of English status from the Taiwanese government has greatly increased the value and importance of English for language learners. The degree of these positive attitudes greatly outnumbers that of Redfield's *et al.* (2003). Yet secondly, the in-service teacher group comparatively hold a more realistic and cautious attitude towards English learning. This chapter, in the end, concludes that learners' perceptions of English language learning may not share a single entity with English teachers in Taiwan, and this perception gap should be came into notice by those prospective, non-native in-service, and newly-introduced native English teachers.

REFERENCES

申慧媛（民 94 年 3 月 4 日）。教育部研究 早學英語 成績未必較好。**自由時報**，第 8 版。

申慧媛、黃以敬（民 94 年 3 月 4 日）。資質、興趣 影響學習效果。**自由時報**，第 8 版。

朱正庭（民 94 年 1 月 9 日 a.）。全民英檢 各大學認同 紛列畢業門檻。**聯合新聞網**。民 94 年 1 月 10 日，取自 http://tw.news.yahoo.com/050109/15/1cyty.html

朱正庭（民 94 年 1 月 9 日 b.）。英語檢定來加持 證明能力有依據。**聯合新聞網**。民 94 年 1 月 10 日，取自 http://tw.news.yahoo.com/050109/15/1cytx.html

陳英暉（民 92）。重語輕文的英語教育－從技職體系「應外系」的文化文學課程談起。載於戴維揚、梁耀南（主編），**語言與文化**（39-80 頁）。台北市：文鶴出版社。

陳楷（民 94 年 1 月 9 日 a.）。全民英檢 早考不一定早好。**中廣新聞網**。民 94 年 1 月 10 日，取自 http://tw.news.yahoo.com/050109/4/1cypw.html.

陳楷（民 94 年 1 月 9 日 b.）。有考才會唸 應檢考試大熱門。**中廣新聞網**。民 94 年 1 月 10 日，取自 http://tw.news.yahoo.com/050109/4/1cypx.html.

許敏溶（民 94 年 1 月 9 日）。全民英檢初級初試 十二萬人應考。**自由時報**。第 6 版。

游毓玲 （民 92）。文化、脈絡與語言學習。載於戴維揚、梁耀南（主編），**語言與文化**（1-21 頁）。台北市：文鶴出版社。

黃以敬（民 94 年 1 月 17 日 a.）。英語授課流行 不少學生鴨聽雷。**自由時報**，第 10 版。

黃以敬（民 94 年 1 月 17 日 b.）。英語與學識 不能劃等號。**自由時報**，第 10 版。

黃以敬（民 94 年 1 月 17 日 c.）。追求國際化 1300 門課改說英語。**自由時報**，第 10 版。

黃以敬（民 94 年 1 月 17 日 d.）。學童考英檢 年齡將限制。**自由時報**，第 10 版。

黃以敬（民 94 年 3 月 4 日 e. ）。英語政策 自相矛盾。**自由時報**，第 8 版。

劉俊言、洪敬浤與梁靜于（民 94 年 1 月 8 日）。全民英檢 全民運動 12 萬人應試。**聯合新聞網**。民 94 年 1 月 10 日，取自 http://tw.news.yahoo.com.tw/050108/15/1cxwr.html

戴維揚（民 92a）。九年一貫新課程文化學習與英語文教學。載於戴維揚、梁耀南（主編），**語言與文化**（1-21 頁）。台北市：文鶴出版社。

戴維揚（民 92b）。英語文課程革新的三大目標：文字、文學、文化。載於戴維揚、梁耀南（主編），**語言與文化**（23-38 頁）。台北市：文鶴出版社。

戴維揚、梁耀南（主編）（民 92）。**語言與文化**。台北市：文鶴出版社。

羅浩恩（民 94 年 1 月 7 日）。英檢初試明登場 考生爆增 上班族增加。**中廣新聞網**。民 94 年 1 月 10 日，取自 http://tw.news.yahoo.com/050107/4/1ctvm.html

Allen, L. Q. (2002). Teachers' pedagogical beliefs and standards for foreign language teaching. *Foreign Language Annals, 35* (5), 34-48.

Brown , H. D. (2000). *Principles of language learning and teaching*. NY.: Pearson Education.

Brown, H. D. (2001). *Teaching by principles: An interactive approach* to *language pedagogy*. NY.: Pearson Education.

Brown, H. D. (2002). *Strategies for Success*. NY: Pearson Education

Celce-Murcia, M. (Ed). (2001). *Teaching English as a second or foreign language*. Boston, MA.: Heinle & Heinle.

Heaton, J. B. (1988). Writing English language tests. NY.: Longman.

Medgyes, P. (2001). When the teacher is a non-native speaker. In M. Celce-Murcia (Ed.), *Teaching English as a second or foreign language* (pp. 429-442). Boston, MA.: Heinle & Heinle.

National Standards in Foreign Language Education Project. (1999). *Standards for foreign language learning in the 21st century.* Yonkers, NY.: National Standards in Foreign Language Education Project.

Pennycook, A. (2001). *Critical Applied Linguistics: a critical introduction.* Mahwah, NJ.: LEA.

Redfield, M., Yang, Y., & Ueda, T. (2003, October). *Comparing Chinese and Japanese learners' attitudes to EFL teaching.* Paper presented at The 12th Korea TESOL International Conference, Seoul, Korea.

Richards, J. C. (2001). *Curriculum development in language teaching.* Cambridge: CUP.

Richards, J. C., & Lockhart, C. (1996). *Reflective Teaching in Second Language Classrooms.* Cambridge: CUP.

Tollefson, J. W. (1995). *Power and Inequality in Language Education.* New York, NY.: CUP.

Widdows, S., & Voller, P. (1991). PANSI: A survey of the ELT needs of Japanese University Students. *Cross Currents, XVIII* (2), 127-138.

Yang, W. H. (2004, October). *CALL: Assistance or Anxiety for Language Teachers.* Paper presented at The 12th Korea TESOL International Conference, Seoul, Korea.

APPENDIX

English Language Education Questionnaire (ELEQ)

英語教學問卷調查

請指出你對於下列各有關英語教學之敘述的同意程度為何，勾選時請根據你心中所相信的認知來作答，而非根據你實際遇到的現況作答。謝謝您的協助。

【1、非常同意。2、同意。3、不清楚。4、不同意。5、非常不同意。】

□1. 好的英語教學有賴於所選用的教科書及其補充教材。

□2. 學習英語的最佳起步階段是由小學的低年級開始。

□3. 好的英文老師應該能將英語教學與其他學科的學習做一統整。

□4. 有效的英語教學應使用真實的原文材料當作教材（如：英美國家當地的英文報紙、雜誌、 電視節目或廣播等。）。

□5. 已經學過另外一種外語的學生學習起英語會更有效。

□6. 好的英文老師應該上課時只使用英語來教學。

□7. 學習英語對每一位台灣學生的將來都是有助益的。

□8. 好的英語課程應該著重於教導學生學習英語的各個語言成份（如：發音、單字、文法、拼字和語法等。）。

□9. 好的英語教學有時也必須教導學生如何使用特殊的語言溝通技巧（如：婉轉拒絕、融入圈子或肢體手勢等。）。

□10.好的英語學習課程應該融入科技的運用。

□11.好的英文老師能夠針對不同的學生提供其感興趣的英語學習內容。

□12.好的英語課程應該教導各種程度的學生不論在課堂上或現實生活中能使用英語做真實的溝通。

□13.好的英語課程在課堂上應只使用英文教學。

□14.好的英語教學應該要能提升學生批判性思考的能力。

□15.好的英語課程教學應該和學生的學校、社區、家庭或同儕生活息息相關。

□16.好的英語老師應該教導學生特定的學習策略（如：預習、略讀、會意等技巧。）。

□17.最佳學習英語的階段是在國中開始學。

□18.好的英語教學應該使用開放性的活動來評量學生的部分成績（如：學生的學習檔案、表演示範、發表或提案計畫等。）。

□19.好的文化教學應該能使學生對英語國家的文化價值觀有更深一層的了解。

□20.好的英語課程應該著重於單字和文法教學兩方面。

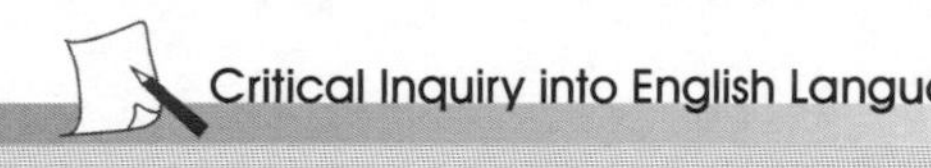

□21.英文老師的角色主要是在幫助學生學習課本上的知識。

□22.英語課本中所附的測驗題應能評量出學生的學習情形。

□23.對於學習其他科目上有障礙的學生不適合再學英語。

□24.對已經學過另一種外語的人、學習英文對他們來說並沒有學習上的幫助。

□25.好的英語課程不應只是設定和評量學生的文法、字彙學習目標，更應該設定和評量學生對英語文化的了解程度。

□26.學習英語只是對某些特定的職業有幫助而已。

□27.好的英語老師應該能將所要　的英語和學生已知的東西做相關的連結。

□28.英語文化教學的重要性應該次於單字和文法教學。

□29.即使是在其他科目上有學習障礙的學生也能夠成功的學習英語。

□30.好的英語學習評量應著重於測驗學生的英文單字和文法能力。

□31.不管學生以後要從事什麼行業、學習英語對他們來說一定是有幫助的。

問卷至此結束。謝謝您的協助和寶貴的意見！

實踐大學 高雄校區 應用外語系
楊文賢

Chapter 4

Non-Native English Speaking Teachers (NNEST) vs. Native English Speaking Teachers (NEST)- Who are better?*

LITERATURE REVIEW

Introduction

Among the trends which have recently emerged in the field of English Language Teaching, one of them is to get rid of the native speaker teacher versus non-native speaker teacher division. Although native speaker teachers have the advantages of teaching English in many aspects, it is arguable, according to Phillipson (1992), that non-native teachers may actually be better qualified than native speakers, if they have gone through the complex process of acquiring English as a second/foreign language, have insight into the linguistic and cultural needs of their learners, and own a detailed awareness of how mother tongue and target language differ and what is difficult for learners. The following article will discuss and evaluate critically the generally believed extra value that native speaker teachers can provide while teaching English from three different perspectives: the expertise in language use, the superiority of cultural knowledge, and the value of creating a more effective teaching and learning environment.

The expertise in language use

It is generally agreed that the native-English speaking teachers are intrinsically better qualified than the non-native because of their greater facility in demonstrating fluent, and idiomatically appropriate language. Theoretically speaking, these innate advantages of NESTs would have attracted Taiwanese English learners; however, according to MCU's survey (2005), it is found that a vast majority of English learners have no specific preference to NEST or NNESTs. This implies that language expertise should not be regarded as the major and only criterion for students to evaluate their English teachers. Indeed, based on Rampton's (1990) notion, language expertise contains at least three metaphorical meanings:

(1) Expertise is learned, not fixed or innate.

(2) Expertise is partial. People can be expert in several fields, but they are never omniscient.

(3) To achieve expertise, one goes through processes of certification, in which one is judged by other people. Their standards of assessment can be reviewed and disputed.

This notion apparently has shifted the focus from "who you are" to "what you know;" that is to say, native speakers are not necessarily more proficient than non-native in terms of language use, depending on how much they know about the language. In addition, Phillipson (1992) indicates that the untrained or unqualified native speaker would become potentially a menace for the ignorance of the structure of the language itself and there would be indeed strong grounds for concern about the deficient metalinguistic awareness of any under-trained native speakers. This implies the importance of training English language teachers and the potentially negative effect on learners owing to the discrepant qualities of untrained native teachers. Furthermore, Medgyes (1999) argues that while native speakers might have the advantage of vocabulary, oral fluency, and pronunciation in using English, the non-native might have good control over grammar, reading and writing abilities. In addition, as Saminy (1997) claims, can a competent English speaker necessarily be a good English teacher, and is English linguistic competency the only criterion to determine if an English teacher is good or not? This issue is, indeed, still arguable. Therefore, we conceive that though nationality plays a crucial role in deciding the expertise of English language use, as far as the teaching of English is concerned, the non-native speaker teachers can attain their expertise through appropriate training and development.

The superiority of cultural knowledge

In terms of the superiority of cultural knowledge, it is commonly believed that the native speakers are better off in the cultural knowledge of the target language and thus can offer more extra value than the non-native speaker teachers. Nevertheless, Christophersen (1992) suggests that with all the aids and facilities that are available, including easier travel and closer international contacts, the traditional view that "native-like" command of a second language is an unattainable goal is becoming difficult to sustain. This implies that the non-native can gain more access to the English culture by means of modern technology and therefore cultural knowledge is no longer the privilege of native speakers. Meanwhile, according to Medgyes (1999), although the native speaker teachers are genuine specimens of their culture, they often have stunningly little factual knowledge about it. With the spread of various channels of mass media and travel, devoted non-native speaker teachers can become just as informed as their average native counterparts. Moreover, some native speakers are restricted to the view of so-called "standard English" and fail to introduce globally the varieties of English culture. While on the other hand, their non-native colleagues, thanks to the non-native nature, are more willing and tolerant of other English cultures and can thus possibly become more well-informed of the varieties of English culture than the native speaker teachers. In a nutshell, the more the English language spreads and diversifies in the world, the less it will remain the cultural privilege of the native speakers.

The value of creating a more effective teaching and learning environment

Intriguing motivation

It has been assumed that native speaker teachers seem more capable of creating motivation and an "English" environment in the beginning of teaching English because of the learners' curiosity toward them. However, with regard to long-term motivation, the non-native teachers are better off for they can serve as imitable models of the successful learners of English, which encourages the learners more than curiosity in the process of learning English (Medgyes, 1992). Depending on the extent to which they are proficient as users of English, they are more or less trustworthy models. In addition, as a language model, they are deficient learners of English just like their students, albeit at a high level. The closer they are to native-speaker proficiency, the greater language models they are (Medgyes, 1999). Lee (2000) concurs with the point, arguing that the presence of non-native speaker teachers brings the message that mastering English as a second/foreign language is an achievable goal and their presence can help dismantle the false dichotomy between native speakers and non-native speakers.

The interaction with learners

Based on Lee's (2000) research, students' perceptions of a good English teacher are often affected by two factors: the quality of helping students to get from the teacher and their relationship with the teacher. Although native speakers are generally casual and easy-going and are believed to be able to develop a better interaction with learners, it is important not to overgeneralise this notion. In fact, due to the cultural gap or some misled preoccupations, there are still many native speaker teachers who fail to develop close rapport or friendship with their students and thus remain "foreign friends" to them. As Richards (1996: 55) asserts, "learners from different cultures may have different beliefs about what constitutes good teaching." With the aid of cultural and language affiliation, the non-native teachers can comparatively have better understanding of learners' backgrounds and meet their expectations, initiating more interaction with the learners (ELT Calendar, 2004).

Pedagogic strategies

While the native speakers can introduce more flexible and innovative approaches of teaching English, the non-native teachers, from Medgyes' (1992) point of view, can teach learning strategies more effectively because they have adopted language learning strategies during their own learning process. Therefore, in theory they all know more about the employment of these strategies than their native colleagues who have simply acquired the English language. In spite that some native teachers, in reality, can speak and even use non-native learners' mother tongue, Medgyes (1992) further pinpoints that only non-native speaker teachers could benefit from sharing the learners' mother tongue, which is an effective vehicle of communication in the language classroom and is often used to provoke discussion and speculation, to develop clarity and flexibility of thinking, and to increase students' awareness of the inevitable interaction between the mother tongue and the target language that occurs during any type of language acquisition (Harbord, 1992). Another advantage of the non-native teachers elicited in Reves and Medgyes's (1994) study is that they prepare their lessons more thoroughly and, as a rule, have fewer discipline problems. In addition, NNESTs also set good examples of how to be successful language learners for their students, which positively facilitate learners' motivation and beliefs about English learning (ELT Calendar, 2004).

Tackling learners' difficulties

It is argued that the native teachers attend to learners' perceived needs while the non-native teachers cater to learners' real needs. This is because the non-native teachers, in a linguistic and cultural sense, are intrinsically more sensitive to learners' needs and difficulties than the native speakers. Medgyes (1992) stresses that the non-native teachers were better than their native counterparts in two aspects when tackling their students' difficulties. Firstly, the non-native speaker teachers are more able to anticipate language difficulties. This anticipatory skill, which becomes more and more sophisticated with experience, enables them to help learners overcome language difficulties and avoid pitfalls. Secondly, the non-native teachers can be more empathetic to the needs and problems of their learners because they have encountered difficulties similar to those of their students, albeit at an apparently higher level. As a rule, this constant struggle makes the non-natives more sensitive and understanding. In favor of this viewpoint, Reves and Medgyes (1994) elucidate that the non-native speaker teachers had a better control over estimating the learners' potential, reading their minds, and predicting their learning difficulties.

SUMMARY

As discussed above, the preoccupation that the native speaker teachers provide the best model of English language teaching has been challenged and questioned from several different perspectives. Nonetheless, our intention is not to marginalise the importance of the native teachers or have a bias toward the non-natives. Rather, we would like to highlight Medgyes' (1992) statement that both groups of teachers serve equally useful purposes in their own terms. In an ideal school, there should be a good balance of the native speaker teachers and the non-native speaker teachers, who complement each other in their strengths as well as weakness (Medgyes, 2001).

Furthermore, given a favourable mix, various forms of collaboration between these two groups are possible both inside and outside the classroom—using each other as language consultants or teaching in tandem. Above all, we should sensitise teachers both to their limitations and potentials, and suggest ways they could make progress within their own constraints. We are firmly convinced that good English teachers have nothing to do with their nationalities or accents and that by means of proper forms of collaboration, both the native and non-native teachers can be of great benefit to their students in the process of learning English.

A FURHTER DISCUSSION BASED ON REFLECTIVE TEACHING

As for this part, we would like to continue discussing whether the native speaker teachers provide the best model and extra values of English language teaching based on the real situation at the senior high school level in Taiwan. Again we will follow the framework discussed in the previous part by discussing the notion from three different perspectives: the expertise in language use, the superiority of cultural knowledge, and the value of creating a more effective teaching and learning environment.

To begin with, almost all English teachers in senior high schools in Taiwan are well-qualified and experienced in language teaching and they especially have their expertise in reading and writing skills. However, when it comes to listening and speaking ability, many of them, frankly speaking, are not as proficient as the native speaker teachers. This concern of linguistic handicap has been, indeed, confirmed in a number of studies (Medgyes, 2001). In view of this deficiency, some schools adopt measures to compensate the weakness of the non-native teachers in listening and speaking skills. Take our school for example; our colleagues and we invited several native speaker teachers who came from the United Kingdom to design a program which included courses like speeches, listening comprehension practice, and interactive teaching techniques in order to reinforce our productive as well as receptive abilities. Meanwhile, the native teachers gave some demonstrations to put those techniques into practice and then held a seminar to evaluate the teaching process and the responses of students. After several weeks of training, we all felt more confident in using English for communication, both in the office and in the classroom and we started to be convinced that the non-native teachers could gain their expertise in language use through appropriate training programs. Edge (1988 : 156) makes a supportive point as follows:

> *As far as the teaching of English is concerned, it seems more and more important that …training and development should help us escape from the essentially nationalistic view of native speaker/non-native speaker and get us involved in furthering an interna-*

> *tionalist perspective in which users of English are simply more or less accomplished communicators.*

Moreover, the collaboration between the native and non-native speaker teachers in our case sets a successful example of Medgyes' (1992) assertion that both groups of teachers have their own assets and can benefit their students most through proper forms of collaboration.

With regard to the superiority of cultural knowledge, the native speaker teachers undoubtedly have the advantage of introducing their native culture to their students. However, we agree to Medgyes' (1999) implication that with the spread of various channels of mass media and travel, dedicated non-native speaker teachers can become just as informed as their average native counterparts. In our opinion, what counts in teaching cultural knowledge is that an ideal teacher should be able to serve as a cultural bridge to connect the target culture with the local one so that learners will not only feel motivated but also make themselves familiar with the contents of the courses. We have an example for this point. Years ago we invited a native speaker teacher, Paul, to teach English conversation to a group of students in our school as a kind of extracurricular activity. The students who registered in the conversation course were all voluntary; that is, they were all highly motivated and expected to gain more exposure to English, linguistically, and culturally. In the beginning, the students welcomed this new native speaker teacher with enthusiasm and felt curious about Paul. They asked him a lot of questions about his country and culture, and Paul gave them absolutely satisfying answers. Obviously they all enjoyed the class periods in the beginning. A few weeks later, Paul adjusted his teaching approach and introduced some specific topics like popular music, social manners, and school education, trying to raise students' active discussion on these topics according to their own experience and cultural background. Nevertheless, some problems occurred because Paul was deficient in the knowledge of the local culture as well as the students' sub-culture and often failed to understand what students tried to express. Thus the students started to feel demotivated and gradually lost their interest in this conversation course. In the end, both Paul and the students came to us with discouragement and they decided to halt the conversation course. In view of this case, we tend to imply that the non-native speaker teachers may have a better grasp of introducing the target culture into the local one than their native colleagues because they share the same language and cultural values with their learners, which corresponds to Medgyes' (1999) concept that the non-native teachers are better qualified for their comprehensive familiarity with the students' linguistic, cultural, and personal backgrounds. Therefore, we believe that the non-natives are more capable of taking the role as cultural bridge to compensate the cultural gaps.

Finally, we would like to discuss the value of creating a more effective teaching and learning environment. In Taiwan, it is the current trend that more and more schools start to invite the native teachers to teach English conversation courses because many parents and students are convinced that the native teachers can provide the standard models of English and bring more innovative pedagogical techniques, especially in speaking and pronunciation. However, the conversation courses only occupy a small proportion of the whole class periods. The training of reading and writing ability, which is taught by the non-native speaker teachers, still takes the majority of the class hours because students at senior high school are under heavy pressure from the college entrance examination which approximately consists of questions involving reading and writing skills. Most parents and students have more confidence in the non-native teachers for their pedagogical strategies, albeit traditional and vapid, are more effective in enhancing students' reading and writing ability desperately essential for grasping excellent marks in the entrance examination. In addition, parents and students expect the non-native teachers to provide effective and efficient learning strategies of mastering English, to diagnose students' learning difficulties and to help them overcome the problems they encounter in the process of learning English. By contrast, parents and students' expectations toward the native speaker teachers are merely to create more chances for oral practice and fulfill their curiosity together with a sense of novelty. As for the interaction with students, it is generally presumed that the native teachers are friendly and gentle, and thus they should be able to develop a better interaction with learners. Nonetheless, most of the students in our school actually do not feel at ease approaching the native teachers. Though the students are encouraged to speak to the native speaker teachers about their feelings, they fail to develop intimate relationship with the native teachers on account of the cultural gap and their deficiency of linguistic competence. Therefore, based on our close observation, the students always turn to the non-native teachers for help when encountering problems during the learning process. In relation to these cases, we would like to quote a bolstering viewpoint from Medgyes (1999) that the non-native speaker teachers are more able to provide their learners with a good learner model for imitation, to teach them effective language learning strategies, to supply them with information about the English language, to anticipate and prevent their language difficulties, to show empathy, and finally to benefit from the shared mother tongue. We believe that the non-native teachers have contributed more than their native counterparts in creating an effective and interactive environment for teaching and learning English in Taiwan.

In summary, it is true that the native speaker teachers are a valuable boon to learners in Taiwan and they help learners develop interest in the people and culture represented by them. However, it is tremendously important for both teachers and learners to keep in mind that nationality and ethnicity are not necessarily equal to qualifications or criteria of an ideal language teacher. Rather, an ideal language teacher, according to Medgyes (1992), should be a native speaker teacher who has achieved a high degree of proficiency in the learners' mother tongue or a non-native speaker teacher who has attained near-native proficiency in English. In fact, Medgyes (1992) contends that both groups of teachers arrived from different directions but eventually stood close to each other. Therefore they will never become indistinguishable. As discussed in the preceding part, a truly liberal attitude towards the issue of the native and the non-native teachers is that both groups of teachers should work together for the purpose of utilising their expertise as well as complementing their limitations and thus enlighten their learners in the most effective and efficient way. "NESTs and NNESTs are potentially equally effective teachers, because in the final analysis their respective strength and weakness balance each other out. Difference does not imply better or worse!" (Medgyes, 1999: 76). NESTs and NNESTs are, therefore, supposed to cooperate with each other rather than to compete. What learners are concerned about is not whether their English teachers are natives or non-natives but whether they possess the qualities and competencies of being good English teachers, which usually are very culture-oriented, contextualised, and differentiated from context to context (Yang, 2005). Ultimately, we hope that our students can benefit from an appropriate form of collaboration between the native teachers and their non-native colleagues, and can enjoy the pleasure of learning English.

REFERENCES

Celce-Murcia, M. (2001). (Ed.). *Teaching English as a Second or Foreign Language.* Boston, MA.: Heinle & Heinle.

Christophersen, P. (1992). Native' models and foreign learners. *English Today,* 31: 16-20.

Edge, J. (1988). Natives, Speakers, and Models. *JALT Journal,* 9 (2), 153-157.

ELT Calendar. (2004). *The Non-Native English Speaking Teacher in the Oral Class.* Retrieved 30 August, 2005, from http://www.eltcalendar.com/events/details/2063

Harbord, J. (1992). The use of the mother tongue in the classroom. *ELT Journal, 46* (4), 350-355.

Lee, I. (2000). Can a Nonnative English Speaker Be a Good English Teacher? *TESOL Matters 10,* (1), 1-2.

MCU (Ming-chuan University). (2005). *No Title.* Retrieved 30 August, 2005, from http://www.mcu.edu.tw/department/app-Lang/elcenter/english/elc/Info/ProfDevelop/Scott/3_mcu.htm

Medgyes, P. (1992). Native and non-native: who's worth more? *ELT Journal, 46* (4), 340-49.

Medgyes, P. (1999). *The Nonnative Teacher.* Ismaning, Germany: Hurber Verlag.

Medgyes, P. (2001). When the Teacher Is a Non-native Speaker. In M. Celce-Murcia (Ed.), *Teaching English as a Second or Foreign Language* (pp. 429-442). Boston, MA.: Heinle & Heinle.

Phillipson, R. (1992). ELT: the native speaker's burden? *ELT Journal, 46* (1), 12-17.

Rampton, M. B. H. (1990). Displacing the native speaker: expertise, affiliation, and inheritance. *ELT Journal 44,* (2), 97-101.

Reves, T., & Medgyes, P. (1994). The Non-native English Speaking EFL/ESL Teacher's Self-image: An International Survey. *System,*

22 (3), 353-367.

Richards, J. C. (1996). *Reflective Teaching in Second Language Classroom.* Cambridge: CUP.

Samimy, K. K. (1997). A review on the non-native teacher. TESOL *Quarterly, 31* (4), 815-817.

Yang, W. H. (2005). *What makes a good English teacher- based on learners' perceptions.* The 14th International Symposium and Book Fair on English Teaching. Chien-tan: Taipei.

*This chapter is co-authored with Mr.Tsai, Feng-jou.

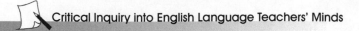

Chapter 5

What Makes A Good English Teacher in Taiwan?

INTRODUCTION

Learning English has become an all-people-campaign recently in Taiwan. English language education also has expanded its span from elementary school level to university level island-wide; consequently, being and recruiting English teachers seemingly become a roaring job market. Taiwanese government even 'imported' some native-speaking English teachers from the inner cycle of English countries such as the US, Canada, the UK, or Australia (Yang, 2005 a.). The effectiveness of this policy is still unknown so far. However, one group of stakeholders' views of English teaching is largely ignored, i.e. English learners. Learners as well as teachers are, indeed, the core component in English language education. Yet, learners' perceptions and attitudes towards what qualities and competencies they expect from a good English teacher are not widely researched. Besides, many private language schools in Taiwan recruit their English teachers without taking teachers' qualities and competencies into well consideration provided that they are "native speakers." Learner's perceptions of this concern cannot represent a holistic image of what constitutes good English teachers but instead this chapter can provide another perspective to examine the question and hopefully the implications generated from the results can be useful in the concern of determining good English teachers.

LITERATURE REVIEW

In this section, we would like to construct a theoretical framework for this study concisely. This part will review the three different issues related to this research, i.e. the profession of language teachers, the differences between native English speaking teachers (NESTs) and non-native English speaking teachers (NNESTs), and the results of a number of relevant studies.

To begin with, it seems manifest to discuss the issue about the profession of being teachers and its training education if we intend to investigate what the good qualities and competencies an English language teacher is supposed to possess. Language teacher education certainly influences, filters, and determines the qualities and competencies of teachers. However, the premise of discussing good English teachers' qualities and competencies is that we need to recognise English teaching is a 'profession' which requires specific characteristics such as homogeneous consensual knowledge, high social status, self-regulations, restricted entry and the legal right to govern daily work affairs (Lortie, 1975). In fact, the argument that whether teaching as a profession is still very of great debate (Pennigton, 1991). Richards (1996) and Lortie (1975) claim that English teaching is not globally viewed as a profession for this 'work' lacks for unique characteristics, specialised skills and training, a valued career choice, and a high degree of job satisfaction. However, in recent years "language teaching has done much to conceptualise and define its knowledge base, to regulate entry to profession, and to monitor the practices of teaching institutions" (Richards, 2001: 209). Teacher's knowledge about teaching content, contexts, pedagogy, teacher training for qualification, and their realisation between classroom practices and social ideas have been greatly emphasised in training courses, and they surely are the keys to converting teaching into a 'profession' (Barlette, 1987; Roberts, 1988; Richards, 1996). Hence, English language teaching has been recognised as a profession by UNESCO (Yang, 2005 c.). Unless the status of teaching English as a profession has reached consensus, the discussion about characteristic qualities and specific competencies of good English teachers cannot be continued.

Second, research shows that there are some distinguished innate and acquired differences existing between NESTs and NNESTs such as teacher's perceived roles, teaching skills, priority of teaching tasks, or linguistic proficiency in English, which will definitely also influence their learners' views about what constitutes a good English teacher in different contexts (Roberts, 1988; Medgyes, 2001; Tsai & Yang, 2005). According to Medgyes (2001: 436), compared with NESTs, the bright sides of being a NNEST are they are assumed to be able to "provide a better learner model, teach language-learning strategies more effectively, supply more information about the English language, better anticipate and prevent language difficulties, be more sensitive to their students, benefit from their ability to use the students' mother tongue." In addition, based on much literature, it has been confirmed that a good command of English proficiency is a must for being a NEST and NNEST, and thus the most important obligation for NNESTs seems to improve their English linguistic competencies in order to compete with their counterparts, i.e. NESTs (Britten, 1985; Lange, 1990; Murdoch, 1994; Liu, 1999; Medgyes, 2001). However, as Samimy (1997) argues, can a competent English speaker be a good English teacher, and is English linguistic competency the only criterion to determine if an English teacher is good or not? Are there other qualities and competencies that needed to be addressed with regarding to this issue? This concern is exactly what this study aims to cater for.

Furthermore, learners from diverse contexts would have different expectation of their English teachers. Thus, it can be argued that learner's perceptions of good quality and competencies of a good English teacher would be influenced by their beliefs about the nature of English, speakers of English, the four language skills, teaching, language learning, appropriate classroom behaviour, self and goal of learning English (Richards & Lockhart, 1996). These beliefs are largely diverse in different English learning contexts and English learners from different cultures possibly have different beliefs about what composes good teaching. For example, Chinese teachers of English are supposed to correct learners' errors and provide a good model for language using (Richards & Lockhart, 1996).

Third, we would like to review a number of relevant studies conducted in Taiwan. However, not much research investigated learners' perceptions of their teachers, not to mention those of English teachers. Nearly all related studies reviewed investigated the question about how teachers view themselves as professionals, i.e. their perceived qualities and competencies of good English teachers. Though these studies used teachers as their participants, yet we believe a comparison about this issue can be made to gauge if there is any gap. Except for Hsiao's (2004) and Hsieh's (2001) quantitative research methods, all the other studies used qualitative methods like interviews, questionnaire, observation or literature review to investigate this issue (Lin, 2000; Tsai, 2001; Liu, 2001; Lai, 2002; Fang, 2003; Li, 2003). However, all of them conclude that certain qualities and competencies do mold good English teachers. For example, Lai (2002) argues that a good English teacher should teach effectively, contextually, and reflectively. Furthermore, good English teachers should possess core ability (e.g. good command of English proficiency), subordinate ability (e.g. selection and teaching of materials), peripheral ability (e.g. skills of counselling, using multimedia, or culture teaching) together with profound content, teaching, and professional knowledge while teaching English (Lin 2000; Liu, 2001). Nevertheless, some of them also pinpoint the difficulties Taiwanese teachers perceived in their teaching; for instance, insufficient English culture knowledge hinders the instruction of it in classroom or teachers are less willingly to teach English learning strategies, adopt innovative teaching methods like CLT or cooperative English learning, and apply technology to English teaching (Tsai, 2001; Li, 2003). Interestingly, these findings are slightly different from what Medgyes (2001) proposes about the assumptions of NNESTs'. A foreign study reviewed was Richards' *et al.* (1991), which found that English teachers in Hong Kong believe their primary role in classroom is to provide useful learning experiences, a correct model of English usage, correct answers to questions, and to correct errors. We assume that this argument can be applied to Taiwanese context more or less for the two contexts may share similar cultural backgrounds.

RESEARCH METHOD

Research Question

Teachers have always enjoyed a high status and been embedded with the image of unchallenged authority in a traditional Confucian society like Taiwan (Yang, 2005 c.). However, due to the demands of accountability in teaching recently, teacher appraisal and professionalism has drawn the publics', the authorities' concerned, institutions', and teachers' attention (Lewis, 1989); nevertheless, Taiwan is just beginning its first step towards teacher appraisal, *ad hoc* for teachers who teach under the high school level. Therefore, it would be very demanding and radical if a complete appraisal system like the ones in the U.K. or the US is considered to be implemented, which, indeed, have evolved for more than 20 years (Yang, 2003). Currently, student appraisal about teachers is seldom conducted or even not emphasised. This means that learners' views of what qualities and competencies constitute of a good teacher are rarely proved; hence this paper would like to investigate English learners' perceptions of this question towards their English teachers.

Instrument

In order to elicit learner's opinions, a questionnaire was conducted for this purpose. This questionnaire was designed by Murdoch (1997) and was organised based on there sections-ELT Competencies, General Teaching Competences, and Knowledge and Attitudes (see Appendix). There are, indeed, still numerous other checklists and guidelines provided for appraising qualities or competencies of a/n (English) teacher such as UCLES (1998), Brown (1994), Britten and O'Dwyer (1995), which have different focuses; however, to answer the research question of this study Murdoch's (1997) is adopted for it is centred on English learners' views.

Participants

The participants joining this research came from my teaching university in southern Taiwan and all enrolled in the course "ELT Course Design", which is a tailor-made course for those English-majored students taking ELT module as their specialist. They are in the final year and the number of them accounts to forty-nine in total.

Analysis

SPSS 10 for Windows (Chinese edition) was used to calculate the frequencies of the responses in each question. The results will be displayed in the next section together with discussion. However, due to the limit of space, not all of the results will be presented; only a number of them will be selected for discussion.

Limitations

The limitations of this research are first, the number of the participants is not large enough and thus the results of it may not be representative and applicable to other English learners in Taiwan. Second, the participants have very similar education background i.e. English majors taking the English Language Teaching Module, and thus may be highly motivated to learn English and have a more positive attitude towards English and teachers than other non English-majors. Hence, their views may be different from other English learners. Third, since the participants are all senior students they would respond to the questions based on their English learning experience at different stages such as high school or university; therefore, their views of good English teachers cannot be clearly classified whether they are pertinent to high school English teachers or university ones.

DATA ANLYSIS & DISCUSSION

The percentages of the responses are displayed in the following tables. Presumably the participants would rank all the choices above 3 i.e. 'important, very important or absolutely essential'. Therefore, we will be focused on the items with comparatively high or low percentages in our discussion.

ELT Competencies

Table 1: ELT COMPETENCIES (%)

	A1	**A2**	**A3**	**A4**	**A5**	**A6**	**A7**	**A8**	**A9**	**A10**	**A11**	**A12**	**A13**	**A14**	**A15**
1.	0	0	6.1	2.0	12.2	0	0	2.0	2.0	6.1	0	4.1	2.0	2.0	8.2
2.	10.2	20.4	2.0	16.3	40.8	6.1	10.2	18.4	8.2	20.4	16.3	16.3	6.1	6.1	51.0
3.	18.4	49.0	30.6	44.6	40.8	18.4	34.7	4.08	28.6	44.9	44.9	36.7	24.5	24.5	26.5
4.	34.7	22.4	46.9	32.7	4.1	40.8	34.7	26.5	32.7	26.5	26.5	26.5	32.7	30.6	10.2
5.	36.7	8.2	14.3	4.1	2.0	34.7	20.4	12.2	28.6	2.0	12.2	8.2	34.7	32.7	4.1
NS	0	0	0	0	0	0	0	0	0	0	0	8.2	0	4.1	0

	A16	**A17**	**A18**	**A19**	**A20**	**A21**	**A22**	**A23**	**A24**
1.	4.1	2.0	6.1	2.0	4.1	16.3	14.3	2.0	2.0
2.	22.4	8.2	16.3	6.1	10.2	32.7	30.6	22.4	8.2
3.	42.9	30.6	38.3	34.7	40.8	26.5	38.8	24.5	38.8
4.	28.6	40.8	24.5	42.9	30.6	16.3	6.1	40.8	28.6
5.	2.0	14.3	8.2	14.3	12.2	8.2	10.2	4.1	22.4
NS	0	4.1	6.1	0	2.0	0	0	6.1	0

These 24 questions can be mainly categorised into several groups, i.e. teaching techniques (A2, 4, 5, 6, 8, 9, 10), presentation (A1, 14, 22), error treatment (A15, 16, 17, 18), learning strategies (A19, 24), motivation (A3, 10, 11, 20), use of mother tongue (A12), accuracy model (A13), and empowerment (A21). First of all, it can be found that over half the students do not view setting up pair/group activities is an essential competencies for a good English teacher (in A5). This result is identical to Nunan's (1988) research suggesting that learners rank pair/group activities very low in classroom activities while instead teachers view it as a priority. This tendency may reveal a strong contextual influence in Confucian countries. Learners in the Confucian circle are inclined to study alone (not equal to be independent or autonomous learning) or work together towards a common goal under an unthreatening and harmonious environment (Littlewood, 1996), which mitigates the necessity of accountability and competitiveness among pairs/groups.

In the items of error treatment, self-correction or peer-correction seems new or even unsure for them. The students do not believe that using correct English is fundamental any more but contrarily error tolerance is required for teachers. Perhaps the claim that Asian learners are very concerned to perform correctly in classroom should be re-addressed (Littlewood, 1996). In addition, comparatively high percentages in the "motivation" items may imply that NNESTs are "bookish" and do not often adopt appropriate means to motivate English learners (Medyges, 2001).

Furthermore, teachers do not or are reluctant to teach students strategies for English learning, which is a common phenomenon across different subjects in Taiwan (Li, 2003). Yet, if the concerns of motivation and learning strategies cannot be accommodated appropriately, the learner-centred English learning seems unlikely. Besides, in the item A21 the students do not regard empowerment important for them. It appears that our learners do not need the power to make decisions and thus take responsibility for their learning. They still suppose that teacher is an authoritarian and responsible for English learning (Littlewood, 1996), which unfortunately impede the pursuit of learner autonomy (Gardner & Miller, 1999).

General Teaching Competencies

Table 2: GENERAL TEACHING COMPETENCIES (%)

	B1	B2	B3	B4	B5	B6	B7	B8	B9	B10	B11	B12	B13	B14	B15
1	2.0	2.0	0	4.1	0	0	0	2.0	0	4.1	0	0	0	0	0
2	8.2	0	12.2	20.4	0	8.2	4.1	12.2	4.1	6.1	2.0	0	6.1	6.1	4.1
3	24.5	22.4	32.7	34.7	30.6	24.5	40.8	16.3	38.8	26.5	20.4	24.5	40.8	20.4	34.7
4	38.8	38.8	26.5	32.7	40.8	49.0	30.6	32.7	32.7	34.7	34.7	46.9	22.4	34.7	36.7
5	26.5	36.7	28.6	8.2	28.6	18.4	24.5	20.4	20.4	22.4	40.8	24.5	26.5	38.8	22.4
NS	0	0	0	0	0	0	0	16.3	16.3	6.1	2.0	4.1	4.1	0	2.0

	B16	B17	B18	B19	B20
1	2.0	0	8.2	0	0
2	4.1	6.1	28.6	22.4	4.1
3	32.7	40.8	26.5	26.5	34.7
4	30.6	30.6	26.5	36.7	40.8
5	30.6	20.4	10.2	14.3	20.4
NS	0	2.0	0	0	0

In this section, we would like to discuss the items about relationship (B6, 8), teaching aids application (B18, 19), and need analysis (B12, 20). First, in terms of relationship (*guanxi*), Confucian learners (subordinates) and teachers (superiors) are always deemed to keep a harmonious relationship without threats to each other (Yang, 2005 c.). Harmonious *guanxi* is an essential unseen rule governing the interaction between people in Confucian societies, certainly including classroom; therefore, obvious competitiveness will be oppressed. Next, the respondents ostensibly do not view the application of visuals and other media vital for evaluating English teachers. This result is the same to Nunan's (1998) argument suggesting that learners rank the application of multimedia in English learning in a very low need. Indeed, technology is still not yet widespread in English teaching so far in Taiwan; English teachers would view technology as anxiety rather than assistance to their teaching (Yang, 2004). Thus, they are less likely to use multimedia (Li, 2003).

The responses in B12 are significant due to the higher percentages in the choice 1 and 2, especially when need analysis has become a major issue in language programme planning. Taiwan is a country where the educational policy-making is in a top-down hierarchy; English curriculum is thus implemented based on the authorities' perceived needs instead of learners' and teachers' perceived needs (Richards, 2001). However, in fact, at a macro-level a critical need analysis of stakeholders in a language programme such as institutions, teachers, learners, or parents should be conducted before the implementation of it. At a micro-level, learners' needs are various and they have different expectations to English learning; hence, teachers are supposed to adapt their teaching methods and materials to fit learner's needs as a reflective circle. Yet, the students' views to this issue outwardly illustrate the lack of critical need analysis in our English language programme.

Knowledge and Attitudes

In this section, we are focused on English teachers' general attitudes towards their profession. Compared with Part A and B, the respondents chose the option "NOT SURE" more frequently in Part C for they may not know very much about the profession of teaching and teachers' belief.

Table 3: KNOWLEDGE AND ATTITUDES (%)

	C1	C2	C3	C4	C5	C6	C7	C8	C9	C10
1	6.1	0	0	0	2.0	0	2.0	0	0	0
2	10.2	12.2	16.3	6.1	8.2	4.1	6.1	4.1	2.0	12.2
3	40.8	30.6	36.7	34.7	26.5	34.7	32.7	24.5	26.5	22.4
4	20.4	30.6	28.6	40.8	38.8	36.7	40.8	38.8	49.0	32.7
5	18.4	24.5	12.2	16.3	24.5	18.4	14.3	30.6	20.4	26.5
NS	4.1	2.0	6.1	2.0	0	6.1	4.1	2.0	2.0	6.1

However, in fact "learners often have specific expectations as to how teachers teach and what their roles and responsibilities are" (Richards & Lockhart, 1996: 54). The gap may lie in that participants interpret the questions in different ways and they are used to expressing their views in their specific terms which are very different from a formal questionnaire. Yet, there are still a number of interesting findings here. First, the positive responses in C9 reveal that not only teachers but learners would regard English teaching as a profession nowadays, which requires specific qualities, competencies, professional development and growth. Second, the positive responses in C4 and C7 confirm the literature that a good command of English proficiency is still a major concern for NNESTs and their learners (Roberts, 1997; Medgyes, 2001). This worry may bring English teachers of Taiwan extra burden psychologically for on the one hand they are worried about their English proficiency, and on the other hand they still need to model as correct English users for their learners simultaneously (Richards, *et al.* 1991).

Contrarily, from the responses of C1 and C3 it can be assumed that a number of learners do not believe English learning is vital in determining the success of future, and therefore they instinctively would not rank this criterion as a high requisite for a good English teacher. Another interesting finding is the responses in C6. Though they express the stronger desire of being empowered here yet they reveal less enthusiastic attitudes toward the similar topic in A21 (see Table 1). The responses between A21 and C6 are, indeed, slightly contradictory. Learners apparently follow the doctrine of the mean. On the one hand they would like to be empowered to share some responsibility in their English learning, and on the other hand they also hope teachers can dominate the procedure and activities in the classroom. This contradictory balance exhibits the influences of Confucianism (the doctrine of mean), the changes of traditionally embedded roles of learners and teachers, and the transformation of education hierarchy.

IMPLICATIONS & CONCLUSION

Implications for Further Research

As discussed in the research method section, there are a number of limitations of this research due to the concerns of sampling, contexts, model boundary, and evidence; therefore, some suggestions will be made for future research. To begin with, the sample in this study is not large and representative enough; therefore, it is advised that the prospective participants could come from different education levels island-wide to make the study more reliable and representative. Second, a comparative study can be conducted to investigate teachers' and learners' respective opinions to gauge if there is any perceptional gap about this issue, which has been less explored so far in Taiwan. Third, in terms of result analysis, the means of factor and relative analysis is recommended for future studies in order to calculate the factor loading, Eigen-values, and degree of each item to total to see if any factor will significantly or non-significantly influence the whole. Finally, a cross-cultural study would be advised to survey if the qualities and competencies will vary in different contexts. This research can be practical *ad hoc* when English teaching has become an international profession and English teachers can circulate from country to country very frequently nowadays.

Implications for Practice

This section will provide implications for Taiwanese English teachers, teacher education institutions, and the authorities concerned. Firstly, for the educational authorities, it is urgent to define English teaching as a profession requiring specific qualities and competencies. Hence, the pathways to becoming English teachers should be limited and sieved. At present, the sources of our English teachers vary a lot and thus it is difficult to ensure the quality of them. Indeed, current policies of recruiting, developing, and appraising teachers should be modified or established. National standards should be settled to select, train and evaluate our English teachers for the present policy of multiple-sources of recruiting teachers has led to many problems and public criticism so far such as the outnumbering teachers and descending qualities. Most important of all, the appraisal system should be founded practically and implemented easily to ensure continuous professional growth for teachers, which would convert teaching as a life-long-valued profession.

Secondly, for the teacher training institutions, they are advised to train the perspective English teachers to be not only proficient users of English which is a major concern for most NNESTs and learners but also profound knower about English cultures. Aside from that, they also need to emphasise the practices of motivating learners and the instruction of English learning strategies which are fairly important but perhaps less centred and transmitted to pre-service English teachers by institutions. In addition, conducting classroom action research is vital for English teachers to discover their contextualised teaching problems for they can find solutions to improving teaching. However, according to Yang's (2005 c.) research, many teachers complain that they were not taught how to conduct classroom action research in the institutions. Therefore, courses about training teachers' research skills in different contexts should be necessarily introduced beforehand in training institutions.

Finally, for the in-service English teachers, the advice goes to the adaptation of teaching goals, beliefs, and values. Teachers' believe system deriving from their learning experiences, classroom practice, personal qualities or training education make them believe what constitutes effective English teaching. However, not only teachers but learners bring their experience to the classroom which affects their perceptions in subtle ways (Richards & Lockhart, 1996). Teachers' views towards English, learning and teaching can be very different from learners', and it is not appropriate to force learners to accept teachers' views. Yet teaching and learning cannot be formed if each party simply insists his/her respective beliefs and expectation. Thus, the adaptation is required. The modification of beliefs will definitely lead to its corresponding action and practice in classroom. For example, teacher's empowerment for students is traditionally lacked in a Confucian context; however, teachers can empower their learners to make decisions too about their learning in a gradual way if they perceive that teacher-fronted teaching should be changed. Students are then given chances to select part of their learning materials, decide their learning pace, set their goals, design learning activities, and even choose the evaluation type. Yet, teachers still play the role of director, instructor, and facilitator. This may be an acceptable, practicable and balanced way between extreme learner-centred learning and extreme teacher-fronted teaching in Taiwanese context.

Conclusion

We do not intend to identify what constitutes a "perfect English teacher" in this chapter and thus naively have our teachers develop all the required qualities and competencies perceived by the learners; instead we would like our English teachers to become welcome, professional, humanistic, and profession-loving people after listening to our learners' voices about what can make English teaching more effective and better. There is, in fact, no golden rule for teachers to follow in order to become good English teachers; instead, teaching is a much individualised activity and a contextualised product. "Individual teachers bring to teaching very different beliefs and assumptions about what constitutes effective teaching" (Richards & Lockhart, 1996: 36), and so do our learners. It is difficult to cater for all diverse expectations and to insist beliefs all the time. However, at least what teachers can do is continue reflecting on their teaching to adapt, to change, to transform, and to listen. Our learners are serving the role of a mirror clearly reflecting what constitutes a good English teacher.

REFERENCES

Bartlett, L. (1987). History with hindsight: curriculum issues and directions in the AMEP. In T. Burton (Ed.), *Implementing the Learner-centred Curriculum* (pp.141-155). Adelaide, Australia: National Curriculum Resource Centre.

Britten, D. (1985). Teacher training in ELT. *Language Teaching,18* (2), 112-118; *18* (3), 220-238.

Britten, D., & O'Dwyer, J. (1995). Self-evaluation in in-service teacher training. In P. Rea-Dickins & A. Lwaitama (Eds.), *Evaluation for development in English language teaching* (pp.87-106). London: Macmillian.

Brown, H. D. (1994). *Teaching by Principles.* Englewood Cliffs, NJ.: Prentice Hall.

Fang, C-Y. (2003). *A Study of English Teacher's Teaching Belief in Elementary School.* Unpublished MA Thesis. Chia-yi: CCU.

Gardner, D., & Miller, L. (1999). *Establishing Self-Access.* Cambridge: CUP.

Hsiao, Y-C. (2004). *A Study of the Relationship between Educational Profession Belief and Teaching Willingness of Elementary School English Teachers -- A Case in Taichung City.* Unpublished MA Thesis. Taipei: NTTC.

Heieh, H-J. (2001). *Teachers' Beliefs about EFL Learning: A Study of Elementary School English Teachers in Taipei County.* Unpublished MA Thesis. Taipei: NTTC.

Lai, H-F. (2002). *The Practical Knowledge of an Expert English Teacher in Junior High School.* Unpublished MA Thesis. Chia-yi: CCU

Lange, D. L. (1990). A blueprint for a teacher development program. In J. C. Richards & D. Nunan (Eds.), *Second language teacher education* (pp.245-268). Cambridge: CUP.

Lewis, L. (1989). Monitoring: prerequisite for evaluation. *Prospect,4* (3), 63-79.

Li, F-H. (2003). *An Investigation of Middle School EFL Teachers' Beliefs in and Attitudes toward English Teaching in Southern Taiwan.* Unpublished MA Thesis. Tainan: STUT.

Lin, M-L. (2000). *The Study on Professional Knowledge and Skills for Elementary English Teachers.* Unpublished MA Thesis. Hualien: NHLTC.

Littlewood, W. (1996). Autonomy in communication and learning in Asian context. In *Proceeding of Autonomy 2000: the Development of Learner Independence in Language Learning* (pp. 124-140). King Mongkut's Institute of Technology Thonburi: Bangkok.

Liu, D. (1999). Training non-native TESOL students: Challenges for TESOL teachers education in the West. In G. Braine (Ed.), *Nan-native educators in English language teaching.* Mahwah, NJ.: Lawrence Erlbaum.

Liu, F-L. (2001). *The Study of Professionalism in Educational knowledge and English subjects.* Unpublished MA Thesis. Pingtong: NPTTC.

Lortie, D. (1975). *Schoolteacher: a sociological study.* Chicago: University of Chicago.

Medgyes, P. (2001). When the Teacher Is a Non-native Speaker. In M. Celce-Murcia (Ed.), *Teaching English as a Second or Foreign Language* (pp. 429-442). Boston, MA.: Heinle & Heinle.

Murdoch, G. (1994). Language development is teacher training curricula. *ELT Journal,48* (3), 253-259.

Murdoch, G. (1997). What makes a good English language teacher? In *TESOL Arabia 1997 Third International Conference* (pp.96-108). vol. 11, Conference Proceedings Selected Papers, March.

Nunan, D. (1998). *The Learner-centred Curriculum.* Cambridge: CUP.

Pennington, M. (1991). *Work satisfaction in teaching English as a second language.* Department of English Research Report No. 5. City Polytechnic of Hong Kong.

Richards, J. C. (2001). *Curriculum Development in Language Teacher.* Cambridge:CUP.

Richards, J. C., & Lockhart, C. (1996). *Reflective Teaching in Second Language Classrooms.* Cambridge: CUP.

Richards, J. C., Ting, P., & Ng, P. (1991). *The culture of the English language teacher: a Hong Kong example.* Department of English Research Report No. 6. City Polytechnic Hong Kong.

Robert, J. (1998). *Language Teacher Education.* London: Arnold.

Samimy, K. K. (1997). A review on the non-native teacher. *TESOL Quarterly, 31* (4), 815-817.

Tsai, Y-J. (2001). *Culture and English Teaching: How Do Secondary English Teachers Conceptualize and Instruct Culture.* Unpublished MA Thesis. Taipei: NTNU.

Tsai, F. F., and Yang, W. H. (2005). *When NESTs Meet Non-NESTs: Competitive or Cooperative?* APAMALL & ROCMELIA 2005. 崑山大學: 台南.

University of Cambridge Local Examinations Syndicate (UCLES). (1998). *Syllabus and assessment guidelines for course tutors and assessors.* Cambridge: CUP.

Yang, W-H. (2003). *An interpretative analysis of teachers' perceptions of educational change in Taiwan.* Unpublished doctoral dissertation. Exeter, U.K.: University of Exeter.

Yang, W-H. (2004). CALL: Anxiety or Assistance for English Teachers? *The Programme of The 12th Korea TESOL International Conference,* (pp.241-244). Seoul, Korea.

Yang, W-H. (2005 a.). **台灣教師與學生對當前英語教學之態度研究-以南部地區為例**。實踐大學高雄校區 2005 管理與創意研討會，實踐大學：高雄。

Yang, W-H. (2005 b.). A Survey of INSET Needs and Provisions for English Language Teachers in Taiwan. **台北市立師範學院學報**，**36** ,**1**, 301-328。

Yang, W-H. (2005 c.). *An examination of the Introduction of teacher appraisal in primary and secondary schools in Taiwan: An analysis of new leadership based on societal culture.* 「學習與創造教育與創新」國際學術研討會，政治大學：台北。

APPENDIX

Questionnaire: (1= totally irrelevant; 2= of minor importance; 3= important; 4= very important; 5= absolutely important; NS= not sure) From Murdoch, G. (1997).

PART A : ELT COMPETENCIES

1. The teacher presents language points in clear and interesting ways.
2. The teacher employs a range of techniques to teach new

vocabulary.

3. The teacher tries to relate language forms, functions, and vocabulary to contexts relevant to students' interests.
4. The teacher employs a range of techniques for practicing grammatical forms.
5. The teacher sets up interactive pair/group activities appropriately.
6. The teacher employs a variety of activities for developing speaking/ listening/ reading/writing skills.
7. The teacher achieves a good balance between accuracy-focused, and integrative, content-focused activities.
8. The teacher uses games and puzzles effectively and appropriately.
9. The teacher gives students sufficient time to respond to questions.
10. The teacher encourages students to ask questions.
11. The teacher elicits language and background knowledge from students appropriately.
12. The teacher does not impede student learning via over-use of the mother tongue or attempts to learn the students' mother tongue.
13. The teacher is a good language model for the students.
14. Teacher talk time is appropriate for the language level of the class.
15. The teacher uses, and gets students to use, correct classroom language.
16. The teacher deals with errors systematically and effectively.

17. The teacher gets students to self-correct minor mistakes.
18. The teacher gets students to correct/comment on each other's written work.
19. The teacher makes students aware of the strategies they can use to learn English more effectively.
20. The teacher uses/develops appropriate quizzes and tests to evaluate students' progress and increase motivation.
21. The teacher gives students some say in the selection of classroom activities.
22. The teacher maintains a dialogue with students to gauge their reaction to the materials and his/her teaching methods/
23. The teacher makes students aware of the pedagogic purposes of classroom activities.
24. The teacher takes into account students' different style of language learning.

PART B : GENERAL TEACHING COMPETENCIES

1. The teacher has a good classroom presence and personality.
2. The teacher is patient, polite and enjoys helping students acquire new skills/knowledge.
3. The teacher positions himself/herself well at different stages of the class.
4. The teacher's style of dressing is an asset in the classroom.
5. The teacher communicates an enthusiasm for the subject.
6. The teacher establishes a good rapport with students.

The teacher has good strategies for dealing with inappropriate student behaviour.

1. The teacher does not intimidate shy students in the classroom.
2. The teacher recognizes student achievement and develops students' interests in learning.
3. The teacher attends to the learning needs of the various ability levels in the class.
4. The teacher gives appropriate feedback to students about their progress.
5. The teacher is able to adapt his/her teaching plan to respond to students' immediate needs and reactions to planned activities.
6. The teacher's lessons have sufficient variety and change of pace to sustain students' interest.
7. The teacher prepares classes adequately and has clear aims and objectives.
8. The teacher uses a variety of techniques to asks questions and elicit responses from students.
9. The teacher gives clear and sufficient instructions, examples or demonstrations before students begin activities.
10. The teacher organizes students well.
11. The teacher makes good use of the whiteboard.
12. The teacher makes good use of visuals and other media.
13. The teacher constantly checks to find out if students have understood teaching points or benefited from activities.

PART C : KNOWLEDGE AND ATTITUDES

1. The teacher believes that learning English is vitally

important for students' future success.

2. The teacher sees language learning as a part of a larger process of promoting international contacts and interest in other cultures.
3. The teacher believes that education has a vital role in determining the nature of societies.
4. The teacher is knowledgeable concerning the use of different varieties and styles of English in different societies/cultures.
5. The teacher considers students' cultural background to be of great importance when preparing an ELT course.
6. The teacher believes that he/she should empower students to become increasingly more responsible for their own progress in learning.
7. The teacher is prepared to experiment and carry out classroom research in order to further improve his/her teaching competencies.
8. The teacher makes constant efforts to maintain/develop his/her own English communication skills.
9. The teacher is aware of the value of professional development activities and makes full use of available professional support.
10. The teacher is enthusiastic about working with colleagues to raise the quality of ELT programs.

Source : Murdoch(1997)

Chapter 6

Portfolios for Assessing Pre-service English Teachers

INTRODUCTION

When the new teacher education policy was enacted in 1996, many universities in Taiwan were chartered to train elementary and high schools teachers. Thus, more and more student teachers island-wide do their practicum every year, which makes universities' supervision to ensure the quality of student teachers very vital. According to the law, in addition to university supervisors' periodical visiting, the formation of (practice) teaching portfolios is one of the very important criteria to assess these student teachers' performance during the practicum (教育部，民 95). Portfolio assessment, one kind of alternative assessments, different from traditional assessment, is usually used to assess learners' achievement in school subjects in the beginning, and indeed, has been proved to be effective. Nevertheless it, now, can also be adopted to assess or ensure (student) teachers' performance in schools for teachers' portfolios can help them reflect and then grow professionally (張德銳，民 89、92、93； Wolf, 1996; Wolfe-Quintero &

Brown, 1998). The portfolios are supposed to help them not only record the process of practicum but become reflective teachers eventually by reviewing and reflecting on them usually.

However, the issue that whether teacher portfolio can certainly promise a professional and reflective teacher without doubts and whether such educational innovation, i.e. teacher portfolios for evaluation in teacher education is truly a great idea or simply a waste of time is still researchable (Brown & Wolfe-Quintero, 1997). This chapter tries to examine the likely content of a student teacher's portfolio and his/her extent of agreement to the claimed benefits and flaws of a portfolio from a number of student teachers.

LITERATURE REVIEW

In this following section, a number correlated issues about teaching portfolios will be briefly reviewed; the topics include the meaning of teacher portfolios, the purposes, the functions, the modes, the formats, the evaluation of it, and a number of related empirical studies.

Portfolios contain personalised data which display ones' growth in professionalism. These data are purposefully collected and systematically organised about the teachers' performance, professional growth, and achievements, and they can facilitate self-/other- evaluation and reflections towards their professionalism (王金國，民 92；張德銳，民 89；羅綸新，民 90；台中市社會學習領域網頁，民 95；Wolf, 1996).

However, teaching portfolio is not simply a collection of teaching evidence; instead, it has a number of unique characteristics. Teaching portfolios are substantial and continuous for they include many dimensions of on-going both learning and teaching evidence. They are constructive and purposive because all evidence are selected, collected and constructed based on certain purposes. Portfolios are periodical, contextual, and reflective; furthermore, they are cooperative and interactive as well for not only teachers themselves but students, parents, teaching and administrative staff, institution and even community are likely involved. Besides, they come from multiple sources and the inclusion of them are various or virtually anything else, which, thus, can reflect their differentiated performance accordingly with different teaching qualities and in different teaching contexts (王金國，民 92；高雄師範大學，民 95；Brown & Wolfe-Quintero, 1997).

In terms of purposes or functions of teaching portfolios, there are, indeed, many in the literature. Wolf (1996) ,鄭宇樑(民 89),張德銳(民 91) believe that teaching portfolios can demonstrate teachers' achievement which can used to evaluate teachers' performance and then decide their future employment, promotion or awards. Printer (2001) and Antonek, Mccormick, and Donato (1997) assert that student teachers' portfolios can display their growth and reflection in professionalism, which allows them to join multiple experiences and influences in cohesive and coherent document and thus showcases abilities to a future employer. In short, teaching portfolios provide chances for teachers to select and record activities and behaviours in their classrooms, represent teachers' professional growth and changes in the teaching experience over time, and provided an alternative form to assess teachers' performances (Wade & Yarbrough, 1996; Antonek, *et al.* 1997; Tanner, Longayroux, Beijaard & Verloop, 2000). In teacher education programmes, portfolios assessment has become increasingly popular for first it reflects authentic and dynamic teaching-and-learning experiences in practice which cannot be easily achieved in any standardised assessment. Second, the developing of a teaching portfolio embedded (student) teachers with ownership and responsibilities and third it can strengthen pre-service teachers' belief of why portfolio assessment is desirable and useful when they will adopt it to their future students in the real teaching (Krause, 1996; Stowell, Rios, McDaniel & Kelly, 1993).

As discussed earlier, the sources of inclusion in a portfolio are multiple and this makes the content of it very personalised and different accordingly. There is no regulation about what should be definitely collected in a portfolio but this would, indeed, largely rely on the purposes, the readers, the institutions, or the applications. Nevertheless, it still has a basic framework i.e. emerging professionalism, teaching skill and classroom management, and community involvement (Frederick, McMahon, Shaw & Edward, 2000; 黃俊傑，民 92). 王金國（民 92）and 張德銳（民 92、93）assert that the following items are necessary no matter what type a portfolio would be: teaching plan, classroom management, interaction with students and parents, teaching evaluation, reflection and professional growth. However, for pre-service teachers, a portfolio should also contain practicum plan, lesson plans of demonstrating teaching, the practicum of being homeroom teachers, the practicum of administration job, reports of attending seminars or workshops, records of classroom observation, and meeting records of discussing student teachers' portfolios (高雄師範大學，民95). Yet, one feature of teaching portfolios is its teachers' decision i.e. personalised product; thus, it is argued that rather than making compulsory requirements, teacher educators should negotiate the likely content of a portfolio with student teachers in advance.

As discussed in the introductory section, portfolio is regarded as an alternative assessment different from traditional paper-and-pencil assessment, which would make evaluation of it become complicated and challenging. Though teaching portfolios claim that they have higher face and content validities for they look attractive at the first glance and precisely measure the complex variables which contribute to (student) teachers' real abilities (王金國，民 92；Barton & Collins, 1993), yet owing to the lack of objective and standardised evaluation procedure, this makes the evaluation of portfolios subjective and less reliable among different evaluators. Barton and Collins (1993) even claim that there is no decisive approach to evaluate portfolio materials.

However, to defend the critique of lacking validity, reliability, and subjectivity in alternative assessment like portfolios, Huerta-Macias (1995) provides a very comprehensive argument against the criticism. First, she adopts Guba and Lincoln's (1981) terms i.e. trustworthiness in credibility and auditability of qualitative research to replace traditional truth value and consistency respectively. "Alternative assessment represents the best of all the worlds in that it looks at actual performance on real-life tasks.... The procedure in and of themselves are, therefore, valid" (Huerta-Macias, 1995: 9). In terms of reliability, it can be assured though the establishment of clear descriptors and the sufficient training of experienced evaluators. In addition, the means of triangulation is often used to assure the reliability in alternative assessment; thus, teacher educators or school supervisors would use other sources to verify teachers' performance rather then depending on teaching portfolios only. For example, meeting, discussion, teaching observation, self-evaluation sheet, or learners' feedback can also provide data for evaluation. Furthermore, Huerta-Macias(1995) also argues that compared with traditional standardised tests, alternative assessment does not apparently have less objectivity. She pinpoints that the reason why those standardised tests can claim their high objectivity is not because there is absolutely no biased subjectivity in them but there are simply agreed biases shared collectively by a number of people who agree on scoring procedures, format and content for those specific tests. All humans have biases, including the standardised test designers.

Hence, assessment criteria for evaluating teaching portfolios would then focus on whether the purposes for a portfolio has been openly negotiated and clearly articulated. Barton and Collins (1993), and Johnson (1996) offer two approaches reflecting the assessment criteria. The first one is technical. For instance, "does the portfolio have a goal statement and a reflection statement? Does each piece of evidence have a caption?" (Barton & Collins 1993: 205). The second one is substantive; for example, "am I convinced that the student has met or made progress toward the established purposes? If the answer is no, the question then becomes: What should I need to see added to this portfolio in order to be convinced that the purposes have been met?" (Johnson, 1996: 14). For most teacher educators and school supervisors, they would often use a customised checklist to examine if the achievements have clearly reflected the agreed purposes of a portfolio.

Huerta-Macias' (1995) explanations about the issues of validity, reliability or objectively in portfolio assessment clearly direct the very likely research paradigm any researcher interested in gauging the relationship between teaching portfolios and professional growth should belong to i.e. interpretative paradigm or qualitative research. However, it is a pity that the filed studies researching the above issue are very limited. In 鄭宇樑's（民 89）case study, his participant involved, one elementary teacher, expresses his positive attitudes towards how developing his teaching portfolio facilitated his reflection and growth in professions. Furthermore, in Antonek's *et al.* (1997) research, by viewing developing portfolios as a process of constructing self identities, two student English language teachers show "the uniqueness and complexity of forming the self as a teacher and the differences that emerge when action and belief are united in reflective practice" (p. 23-24). Each portfolio is a personal story telling a rich and vivid story, and it offers opportunities for student teachers to think about and eventually affects their own professional development. Wade and Yarbrough (1996) use both qualitative and quantitative data from 212 student teachers in an elementary teacher education programme to assure us of the existence of reflective thinking in the process of constructing portfolios. They find abundant "evidence of students making sense of their community service-learning experience, developing new understandings and appreciations, recognising links between different aspects of their life experience, and formulating insights for future actions" (p.75-76). However, both of these two research does not clearly address the issue that whether there are promised correlations between portfolio construction and effective teaching, either. It is possibly because that (student) teachers can articulate easily if they have experienced reflective thinking or not in the process of portfolio construction, but comparatively they cannot ensure if these reflective thinking can assist or transform their classroom practice to be effective and efficient.

Most of the studies concerning the correlation between teaching portfolios and professional growth are, indeed, very qualitative-based i.e. case studies, interviews, or autobiographies with a very limited number of the participants involved. Thus, there is still absent research linking practice and theory. We do not argue that hereafter some large-scale studies with many participants should be conducted to investigate the topic that how developing teaching portfolios can ensure professional growth, which is, indeed, very unlikely in the qualitative-based studies, but perhaps it can be argued that without statistical data from field experiments a solid theoretical base about portfolio assessment is apparently insufficient to persuade student teachers to undoubtedly accept the claim that developing a teaching portfolio is definitely beneficial for their future career. This concern results from the problem that how teaching portfolios function as a significant tool in teacher development is still seriously lacking. Therefore, we may question whether teaching portfolios for evaluation is a great idea or simply a waste of time. These issues need further investigation.

RESEARCH METHODS

Instrument

The instrument used for this study is a self-designed close-ended questionnaire (see Appendix 1), composed of three major sections. The first part includes background information. The information about the content in teaching portfolios is in the second part, and the third section is about the respondents' extent of agreement to the claimed benefits and flaws of teaching portfolios. There are 51 questions in total. For the reason of easy administration and avoiding misunderstanding, the questionnaire is provided in Chinese version only. Before formally distributed to the respondents, the questionnaire was piloted by a number of colleagues and students, and some items were modified accordingly.

Analysis

The data were treated by using SPSS Chinese version 10.0, and the results were tabulated in the appendix 2.

Participants

The participants in this study were 22 student teachers from my teaching university. They were all practice English teachers either in junior or senior high schools, and each was supervised by a full-time subject teacher in schools and a university professor. Two of them were under the old teacher training programme i.e. they needed to do their practicum for one year while the rest were under the new programme i.e. they only practiced their teaching for half a year. These student teachers were required to finish the questionnaire after their six-month practicum and establishing a teacher/practicum portfolio was compulsory for them by the regulation.

Limitations

First, due to the limitations of a close-ended questionnaire, more thorough data were not available such as the reasons why they perceived some information was easy to be collected while others was not. The deeper understanding of these reasons may help supervisors or teacher trainers realise the likely difficulties in practice teachers' practicum. Second, the number of the participants was not large enough and all of them were trained to teach English from the same university. Thus, the identical background may make this study unrepresentative or applicable to other cases. Third, though the participants might already have a general idea of what teaching portfolios should look like, they were, indeed, not well trained for how to develop their teaching portfolios in any formal teacher preparation course for the training like this was not required by the educational authorities concerned. This would turn out that the content of portfolios would be much differentiated or personalised which made objective and standardised evaluation hard as discussed in the preceding sections.

DATA ANALYSIS & DISCUSSION

All the statistic results of the questionnaires are tabulated as seen in the Appendix 2. However, not all the items will be discussed in details here due to the limitation of space but only the significant ones will be.

First of all, the data in the part one reveal that the respondents would spend time collecting portfolio data but apparently do not take equal time to review or reflect on them. That means teachers seem not be lack of the ability of reflectivity (張德銳，民 93). One purpose of creating a teaching portfolio is to help teachers reflect on their teaching periodically by reviewing their portfolios for portfolios can clearly record what they intend to do, what they actually do and what they can improve next in classrooms. Continuous reflection on portfolios assists teachers in achieving professional growth. Without reflection, teaching portfolio is simply a file filled up with data and will never become an accelerator for professionalism. After all, portfolios are done "by" teachers, not "to" teachers (Brown, & Wolfe-Quintero, 1997).

Second, in the second part of the questionnaire, it reveals that most of these student teachers do not collect data for the portfolios periodically and the majority of their data collected are the end items about personal learning portfolios and evaluation portfolios in paper- or photo- formats. In other words, the portfolios are still of a very traditional style. It is surprising that data in multi-media/computer format are not obviously favoured by the student teachers of the E-age. The multi-media/computer format, indeed, has its own advantages as follows: it can offer much larger space for storing data, it is more eye-catching due to the use of sounds, video, and texts, and furthermore it provides an easier way to modify the data compared with the traditional ones.

In addition, the respondents also favour the finished products of data, i.e. the manuscripts or the process are not considered as appropriate data for portfolios as end items are. Indeed, teaching involves a series of action taken and decisions made consciously or sub-consciously by teachers and these action or decisions are closely associated. Only recording the final products in the portfolios hinders teachers from realising the thread of thoughts and establishing personal system of teaching. Teaching is a cycle of professional growth and any data before, while or after teaching can be equally important, and teaching portfolios help teacher coordinate, construct, and accumulate knowledge. Perhaps these student teachers regard teaching portfolios without 'flaws' as important evidences for prospective employers to review and thus any 'un-finished' or raw data should be withdrawn or not selected in it. This also reveals the concern that for student teachers portfolios seem to be established for school employers' review not for their profession growth.

Next, most of these student teachers did their practicum in junior high schools but very few of their portfolios include the information about one-though-nine curriculum, which is yet a very vital education reform in Taiwanese junior high schools in recent years. This shows that the student teachers are not well supervised about the one-through-nine curriculum in their practice schools. How to integrate curriculum in the language area from elementary school level to junior high level is not their major concern for practicing teaching but instead how to teach well following the textbooks is. This narrow focus not only restricts their vision but de-skills their future teaching. Besides, their response of effortless collection of students' evaluation also reveals the fact that 'testing' still plays an important role in English language teaching and is must learning for practice teachers. It cannot be denied that any teaching will lead to assessment or evaluation in the end; however, it argues that 'testing' students should not become their major concern in the practicum but trying different teaching methods instead are. Too much learning on how to test student's English proficiency should never become student teachers' major task in schools.

School is an organisation full of its particular culture i.e. school culture. For student teachers, school should not only serve the role as experiencing or refining teaching methods but learning from peers or students. Growing societies like reading groups are one kind of school organisation which helps teachers grow professionally and associate with colleagues or students; however, only half the respondents record the information about this. It is very likely that many practice teachers perceive that they are simply passing visitors of schools and they will leave soon. Thus, it is, perhaps, not 'worthy' to join any such group. It would be ironical if student teachers encourage learners to learn collaboratively in classrooms but they do not outside classrooms.

In the third part of the results, a majority of the respondents agree with the claimed benefits of creating teaching portfolios in facilitating professional growth. Nevertheless, they do not show equal favour to the items 5 through 8, and the item 9. Indeed, teaching portfolios can be used as a criterion by schools to hire, appraise, promote or dismiss a teacher for it is regarded as a good source for appraising teachers' performance in teaching; however, it also confronts many difficulties or opposition (張德銳，民 93). Yet, in this study the respondents show higher disagreement with this use of teaching portfolios. Indeed, this concern is not surprising at all. According to Yang's (2003) research, most of the teachers in Taiwan do not welcome any mechanism to appraise their teaching in order to be promoted, dismissed or even ladder classified. They hold a very cautious attitude towards any mechanism for it is difficult to convince them of the fairness and truthfulness of these mechanisms including teaching portfolios. Teachers nowadays are used to being guaranteed to be promoted to a higher level annually without any essential appraisal. This is also one of the reasons attracting many young people to become teachers in Taiwan i.e. the job is well and safely secured.

In the item 13, the respondents question the relationship between teaching portfolios and increasing the effectiveness of students' learning. Less than half of the participants assert the positive correlation between developing teaching portfolios and teaching effectively in classroom. Indeed, evidence showing the above correlation is still very limited. However, we can still assume that when teachers are developing their individual teaching portfolios they can accumulate and construct teaching knowledge by means of reflecting continuously on them, and the beneficiaries, thus, can be not only teachers themselves but students. It is argued that teaching and learning are a whole; teachers' growth can usually promise the effectiveness of students' learning.

Furthermore, the majority of the respondents also agree with the claimed flaws of teaching portfolios as shown in the items 16 to 19. They especially show a higher agreement to the item 16 i.e. it is difficult to evaluate portfolios with objective criteria. It is undeniable that teaching portfolio is fairly personalised and contextualised, and thus it is not easy to meet the requirements of validity, reliability, or objectivity in evaluation as discussed in the preceding section. The reason why portfolio assessment is termed as alternative assessment is mainly because it is largely distinct from the traditional assessment which is always pencil-and-paper-based, standardised, norm-referenced, product-oriented, summative, and test-giver-controlled. On the contrary, using teaching portfolio to assess teachers' performance is non-pencil-and-paper-based, personalised, criterion-referenced, process-oriented, formative, and test-taker-centred which is still less commonly seen or wildly accepted in Taiwan. Learners, including student teachers here have been used to standardised tests for long and objective score, indeed, means a lot for them. The score may affect their entrance of universities, the chances of being employed, and the promotion in the job; hence, portfolio assessment lacking agreed and fair evaluation criterion would be doubted by the respondents. Indeed, their worries also precisely echo to their disagreement of using portfolios to appraise teacher's performance in terms of hire, dismissal, promotion and ladder classification. In fact, it is a big challenge for the Taiwanese educational authorities concerned to appraise teachers at high school levels and it seems that there has been still no agreed solution to this situation so far (Yang, 2003). The reasons of opposing teacher appraisal or evaluation mechanisms can be various and complicated. Yet, they are beyond what this study aims for and can be further researched.

IMPLICATIONS

As Johnson (1996) asserts, portfolios in assessing language teacher education should ultimately be viewed as a process rather than a product, and reflect teachers' pedagogical reasoning instead of teaching behaviours. Most of the student teachers would rather believe that portfolios are required by the laws and regarded merely as a criterion to finish their teacher education programme. Thus, the first advice will be that student teachers should change their perception of their teaching portfolios. Portfolios should not be thought of as a record or product of their practicum simply but rather the process of reflecting and developing a professional identity (Antonek, Mccormick & Donato, 1997). In other words, portfolios are a means not an end for teachers. They provide "an opportunity for the students to think about and ultimately influence their own professional development" (p.24). Only by, firstly, modifying their concept of teacher portfolios, can student teachers realise how portfolios might help them during the practicum and then value them instead of viewing it as a duty merely.

Next, in terms of what content a student teacher's portfolio should include this should be determined in advance by students themselves and supervisors. It happened that many student teachers just collected what they have had in hand i.e. they collected the data passively not actively. Before their practicum, student teachers, teacher educators and school supervisors have to decide what they should concentrate during the practicum and then collect and select the relevant data; otherwise, the portfolio would become hodgepodge instead of organised, developmental and personal data.

Besides, it is advised that the application of portfolios should be negotiated in advance too. The purpose of it should also be decided by student teachers, teacher educators and school supervisors. If the portfolios are going to involve assessment, then the issues of validity, reliability, and objectivity should be catered carefully. A customised checklist usually can be developed to enable teacher educators to give student teachers feedback on their professional growth. Nevertheless, evaluators should bear in mind that this customised checklist is developed to assess student teachers' portfolios against their pre-set negotiated and individualised aims which have been formulated for themselves; besides, the feedback they give should help those student teachers concentrate on and formulate how they can develop individually, not to assess them against a set of fixed criteria (Tanner, *et al.* 2000). Furthermore, in terms of triangulation, teacher educators and school supervisors should not regard portfolio assessment as the only one means to evaluate student teachers' practicum. Other sources of evidence can be considered as well; for example, conference, periodical meeting, teaching observation, interview with peers, or students' feedback can provide other evidence of student teachers' performance for evaluators.

In addition, a number of training courses should be offered beforehand to student teachers and teacher evaluators respectively. As discussed in the earlier sections, students apparently are not sufficiently trained about how to develop teaching portfolios in their language teacher education programme which makes their portfolios less organised, less personalised, and disconnected from current education trends or polices. A workshop discussing the meaning of portfolio assessment and how to construct a portfolio may be needed, then. Furthermore, to meet the requirement of high reliability in portfolio assessment, portfolio evaluators including teacher educators and school supervisors should also be well trained about how to ensure that their evaluation is reliable among different scorers. The training courses can focus on helping evaluators develop clear descriptors and well understand what each descriptor stands for and training evaluators to design multiple tasks that lead to the same outcome. The teacher preparation institutions even can monitor periodically to ensure that evaluators use criteria and standards in a consistent manner (Wilde, Del Vecchio, & Gustke cited from Huerta-Macias, 1995).

In a word, the results imply that teacher educators or school supervisors should avoid assessing teaching portfolios as the product but the process instead. As discussed earlier, portfolios reflect teaching behaviours and pedagogical reasoning, and this implies that right answers to good teaching are multiple perspectives. Portfolios provide opportunities for student teachers to demonstrate their multiple competencies and experiment possibilities. Thus, external judgement seems less important than internal sense-making and self-analysis (Johnson, 1996). Certainly, to achieve the above internal sense-making and self-analysis relies much on student teachers' reflection on their portfolios periodically.

CONCLUSION

Portfolio assessment is classified as one type of alternative assessments for it is different from other tradition paper-and-pencil assessments in a large scale. The former one places test-takers in a central position i.e. they actively take up more responsibility for providing relevant information for assessment while the latter emphasises the importance of testers and the role of test-takers are very passive. However, portfolio construction can become very stereotyped if developers do not well understand the essential meaning of it. Portfolio assessment, indeed, realises the spirits of constructivism; "it means moving away from assuming there are right answers about teaching to accepting multiple perspectives, providing multiple opportunities for teachers to demonstrate their competencies, and carrying out assessment that is less like external judgement and more like internal sense-making and self-analysis" (Johnson, 1996: 14). For novice teachers, teaching portfolios provide opportunities to discover the thread of their action and decisions making before, while and after teaching, and then construct the personalised teaching knowledge and philosophy in the end. Indeed, a teaching portfolio is not simply a file filled up with abundant data but a tool, instead, assists teachers in reviewing and reflecting their teaching. It is argued that practice teachers in Taiwan should view teaching portfolios as a tool to facilitate professional growth, not simply a compulsory duty to comply with. Experiencing the developmental process of "collection, selection, reflection, and innovation", the construction of teaching portfolios helps student teachers make a clear sense of what they have already learnt during the practicum.

REFERENCES

王金國（民 92）。實習教師如何建立教學檔案。**靜宜大學地方輔導教育通訊，7**，1-7。

台中市社會學習領域網頁（無日期）。**教學檔案全說明**。民 95 年 6 月 22 日，取自：http://social.loxa.edu.tw/

高雄師範大學（無日期）。**實習教師教育實習成績之評量**。民 95 年 6 月 22 日，取自：http://www.nknu.edu.tw/~intern/teach/gr05.html

教育部 （無日期）。 **師資職前教育課程**。民 95 年 3 月 30 日，取自：http://www.edu.tw/EDU_WEB/EDU_MGT/HIGH-SCHOOL/EDU2890001/main/2_2.htm

黃俊傑（民 92）。教師教學檔案在教學評鑑的應用。**教育研究（高雄師大），11**，205-218。

張德銳（民 89）。教學檔案在國小師資培育教育實習課程應用之初探。**初等教育學刊**，8，219-240。

張德銳（民 91）。以教學檔案提升教師教學效能。**教育研究月刊，104**，25-31。

張德銳（民 92）。促進教師專業發展的教學檔案。**國教新知，49，4**，60-68。

張德銳（民 92）。工欲善其事—提升中小學實習輔導效能之三項利器。**中等教育，54，1**，110-123。

張德銳（民 93）。**教學檔案：促進教師專業發展**。台北市：高等教育。

鄭宇樑（民 89）。國小教師教學檔案經驗之個案研究。**國民教育研究**

集刊，**6**，183-225。

羅綸新（民 90）。教學檔案與教師專業成長。**教學科技與媒體，57**，12-21。

Antonek, J., Mccormick, D., & Donato, R. (1997). The Student Teacher Portfolio as Autobiography: Developing a Professional Identity. *The Modern Language Journal, 81*, 15-27.

Barton, J., & Collins, A. (1993). Portfolios in Teacher Education. *Journal of Teacher Education, 44* (3) , 200-210.

Brown, J. D., & Wolfe-Quintero, K. (1997). Teacher Portfolios for Evaluation: A Great Idea of a Waste of Time? Language Teacher, *21* (1), 28-30.

Frederick, L., McMahon, R., Shaw, J., & Edward, L. (2000). Pre-service Teacher Portfolio as Autobiographies. *Education, 120* (4), 634-639.

Guba, E. G., & Lincoln, Y. S. (1981). *Effective Evaluation: Improving* the *usefulness of evaluation results through responsive and naturalistic approaches.* San Francisco: Jossey-Bass.

Huerta-Macias, A. (1995). Alternative Assessment: Responses to Commonly Asked Questions. *TESOL Journal, Autumn,*8-11.

Johnson, K. (1996). Portfolio Assessment in Second Language Teacher Education. *TESOL Journal, Winter,*11-14.

Johnson, K. (1996). The vision versus the reality: The tensions of the TESOL practicum. In D. Freeman, & J. C. Richards (Eds.), *Teacher Learning in Language Teaching* (pp.30-49). New York: CUP.

Krause, S. (1996). Portfolios in Teacher Education: Effects of Instruction on Pre-service Teachers' Early Comprehension of the Portfolio Process. *Journal of Teacher Education, 47* (2), 130-138.

Printer, B. (2001). Using Teaching Portfolios. *Educational Leadership, 58* (5), 31-34.

Stowell, L. P., Rio, F. A., McDaniel, J. E. & Kelly, M. G. (1993). Casting wide the net; Portfolio assessment in teacher education. *Middle School Journal, Nov.*, 61-67.

Tanner, R., Longayroux, D., Beijaard, D., & Verloop, N. (2000). Piloting portfolios: using portfolios in pre-service teacher education. *ELT Journal, 54* (1), 20-30.

Wade, R. C., & Yarbrough, D. B. (1996). Portfolios: A Tool for Reflective Thinking in Teacher Education? *Teaching & Teacher Education, 12* (1), 63-79.

Wolf, K. (1996). Developing an Effective Teaching Portfolio. *Educational Leadership, March,* 34-37.

Wolfe-Quintero, K., & Brown, J. D. (1998). Teacher Portfolios. *TESOL Journal, Winter*, 24-27.

Yang, W. H. (2003). *An interpretative analysis of teachers' perceptions of educational change in Taiwan.* Unpublished doctoral dissertation. University of Exeter, Exeter, U.K.

APPENDIX

Appendix 1: 問卷

說明：本問卷旨在調查英語科實習老師對於其本身所建立之「教學檔案紀錄」（Teaching Portfolios）是否能提升英語教學專業的認知做一研究探討。本問卷共分三大部分、五十一題。請依據您的現況回答下列問題。感謝您的寶貴時間及幫忙。所有內容皆為保密。本問卷之回答完全無關教學實習成績之評定，請放心做答。

實踐大學 楊文賢

一、個人資料：

1. 姓名：______________________。
2. 性別：□男；□女。
3. 實習學校：□高雄市；□高雄縣。______________________（校名）。
4. 實習制度：□新制（半年）；□舊制（一年）。
5. 教學檔案收集所花的時間共：______年______月。
6. 檢核教學檔案以進行教學省思的頻率為：□總是、□經常、□有時、□很少、□從不。

＊實習總成績：______________（此欄位請不必填寫）。

二、個人教學檔案內容的整備：請在適當的空格裡打勾（√）。

1. 請問您收集教學檔案的習慣都是：□定期收集整理、□不定期收集整理。
2. 請問平均大約多久您會有新的收集資料加入您的教學檔案中：□每日、□每週、□每隔兩週、□每月、□其他________。
3. 請問您目前的教學檔案中是否有包含下列模式：□個人學習檔案、□評鑑檔案、□就業檔案、□學生學習檔案、□其他__________（可複選）。
4. 請問您目前的教學檔案中是否有包含下列形式：□書面資料、□錄音帶、□錄影帶、□著作、□圖表、□照片、□電腦多媒體、□其他_______（可複選）。
5. 請問您目前的教學檔案中是否有包含下列性質：□草稿、□過程、□成品、□其他_______（可複選）。

6. 請問您目前的教學檔案中是否有包含下列項目？（可複選）：□個人基本資料、□教學歷程檔案、□班級經營、□班群檔案規劃、□專業性資訊、□教學行動策略（指教學後的省思後轉化成實際教學行動）、□學生學習檔案、□行政實習歷程檔案、□九年一貫全紀錄、□實習教師檔案、□師生成長團體全紀錄、□教學檔案省思。（本題中各選項之內容可參考題 7~題 26）。
7. 在你的教學歷程檔案中包括了哪些資料？（可複選）1.□教學計畫。2.□教學活動設計、闖關評量、實作評量、真實評量、口語評量、教學活動照片。3.□主題統整、統整方式、統整舉例。 4.□課程統整、統整模組、統整舉例、九年一貫。 5.□學生學習資料。 6.□如何設計學習單、學習單設計模組。 7.□教學評量、各種評量法。 8.□各種檢核表。 9.□教學發表。
8. 在上列資料中較易收集的是（填編號）：_______；較難收集的是：_______。
9. 在你的班級經營檔案中包括了哪些資料？（可複選）1.□經營策略。2.□教室佈置。3.□戶外教學。4.□親師溝通。5.□班級班刊。6.□家長回饋。
10. 在上列資料中較易收集的是（填編號）：_______；較難收集的是：_______。
11. 在你的班群檔案規劃檔案中包括了哪些資料？（可複選）1.□主題活動。2.□統整課程教學。3.□親師合作。4.□班群行政。5.□教學活動。6.□會議紀錄。7.□多元評量。8.□進修研習。9.□學習角佈置。10.□教師手記。

12. 在上列資料中較易收集的是（填編號）：_______；較難收集的是：_______。
13. 在你的專業性資訊檔案中包括了哪些資料？（可複選）1.□研習、教師專業成長、研習一覽表、研習心得、進修證書。2.□著作。3.□專長資料。4.□得獎紀錄。5.□教學研究。
14. 在上列資料中較易收集的是（填編號）：_______；較難收集的是：_______。
15. 在你的學生學習檔案中包括了哪些資料？（可複選）1.□學習日誌。2.□小書製作。3.□闖關評量。4.□真實評量。5.□檔案評量。
16. 在上列資料中較易收集的是（填編號）：_______；較難收集的是：_______。
17. 在你的行政實習歷程檔案中包括了哪些資料？（可複選）1.□教學行政檔案的內涵。2.□行政職掌的內容。
18. 在上列資料中較易收集的是（填編號）：_______；較難收集的是：_______。
19. 在你的九年一貫全紀錄檔案中包括了哪些資料？（可複選）1.□九年一貫活動。2.□九年一貫課程空白表格。3.□各領域小組。4.□成果報告。5.□行政會議討論。6.□家長說明會。7.□教師填寫之空白表格。8.□會議紀錄通知等。9.□課程發展委員會組織架構。10.□課程節數計畫。11.□學校特色。12.□檢核表。13.□課程計畫。
20. 在上列資料中較易收集的是（填編號）：_______；較難收集的是：_______。

21. 在你的實習教師檔案中包括了哪些資料？(可復選)1.□研習資料。2.□教育實習計畫。3.□教學觀摩。4.□資訊應用。
22. 在上列資料中較易收集的是（填編號）：_______；較難收集的是：_______。
23. 在你的師生成長團體全紀錄檔案中包括了哪些資料？（可複選）1.□教師讀書會。2.□學生讀書會。
24. 在上列資料中較易收集的是（填編號）：_______；較難收集的是：_______。
25. 在你的教學檔案省思檔案中包括了哪些資料？(可複選)1.□教學檔案的省思。2.□教學檔案的回饋。3.□教學檔案的評鑑。
26. 在上列資料中較易收集的是（填編號）：_______；較難收集的是：_______。

三、教師對教學檔案的功能、目的和限制之態度：

在下列問題中，請依照您同意的程度在適當的空格裡打勾（√）。

（1. □非常同意、2. □同意、3. □沒意見、4. □不同意、5. □非常不同意）

1. 教學檔案能提升教師自我專業成長。

（1.□非常同意、2.□同意、3.□沒意見、4.□不同意、5.□非常不同意）

2. 教學檔案能共享教學心得、豐富教學經驗。

（1.□非常同意、2.□同意、3.□沒意見、4.□不同意、

5.□非常不同意）

3. 教學檔案能啟發教學新思想。

（1.□非常同意、2.□同意、3.□沒意見、4.□不同意、5.□非常不同意）

4. 教學檔案能作為指導學生建立其學習檔案的前置作業。

（1.□非常同意、2.□同意、3.□沒意見、4.□不同意、5.□非常不同意）

5. 教學檔案能促使師資培育機構與教師共同負起績效責任。

（1.□非常同意、2.□同意、3.□沒意見、4.□不同意、5.□非常不同意）

6. 教學檔案能作為將來教師分級、升等之依據。

（1.□非常同意、2.□同意、3.□沒意見、4.□不同意、5.□非常不同意）

7. 教學檔案能評量教師個人的教學績效，作為敘薪或敘獎之依據。

（1.□非常同意、2.□同意、3.□沒意見、4.□不同意、5.□非常不同意）

8. 教學檔案能作為學校徵選、或調動教師之依據。

（1.□非常同意、2.□同意、3.□沒意見、4.□不同意、5.□非常不同意）

9. 教學檔案在強調反思和自我導向學習。

（1.□非常同意、2.□同意、3.□沒意見、4.□不同意、5.□非常不同意）

10. 教學檔案能協助教師建立獨立、具批判性的思考模式。

（1.□非常同意、2.□同意、3.□沒意見、4.□不同意、

5.□非常不同意）

11. 教學檔案能促進教師同儕間的合作對話和互動。

（1.□非常同意、2.□同意、3.□沒意見、4.□不同意、5.□非常不同意）

12. 教學檔案能統整教師的教學經驗之多元性。

（1.□非常同意、2.□同意、3.□沒意見、4.□不同意、5.□非常不同意）

13. 教學檔案能提升學生的學習成效。

（1.□非常同意、2.□同意、3.□沒意見、4.□不同意、5.□非常不同意）

14. 教學檔案能協助教師建立本身的教學資料庫，以支援爾後之教學評鑑。

（1.□非常同意、2.□同意、3.□沒意見、4.□不同意、5.□非常不同意）

15. 教學檔案能幫助老師了解本身的教學脈絡。

（1.□非常同意、2.□同意、3.□沒意見、4.□不同意、5.□非常不同意）

16. 教學檔案的結論較難以客觀評鑑的標準去判斷。

（1.□非常同意、2.□同意、3.□沒意見、4.□不同意、5.□非常不同意）

17. 教學檔案的發展會花費教師更多、或更長的時間。

（1.□非常同意、2.□同意、3.□沒意見、4.□不同意、5.□非常不同意）

18. 教學檔案的內容選擇不易，較無法呈現專業。

（1.□非常同意、2.□同意、3.□沒意見、4.□不同意、

5.□非常不同意）

19. 教學檔案較難達成評鑑上所講求的信度與效度。

（1.□非常同意、2.□同意、3.□沒意見、4.□不同意、5.□非常不同意）

※問卷至此結束，再度感謝您寶貴的意見和時間。謝謝！！

實踐大學 楊文賢

Appendix 2: 問卷分析結果

第一部分

2.性別　男：2　女 20

3.實習學校　高雄市：17　高雄縣：5

4.實習制度　新制：20　舊制：2

5.時間

2 個月	4 個月	5 個月	6 個月	1 年	1 年 6 個月	無
3 人	1 人	2 人	11 人	1 人	1 人	3 人

6.教學檔案省思頻率：總是：1　經常：7　有時：12　很少：2

第二部分

1.

定期收集整理	不定期收集整理
2	20

2.

每日	每週	每隔兩週	每月	其他
1	6	4	9	2

3.

個人學習檔案	評鑑檔案	就業檔案	學生學習檔案	其他
17	14	3	11	3

4.

書面資料	錄音帶	錄影帶	著作	圖表	照片	電腦多媒體	其他
22	0	4	6	7	21	10	2

5.

草稿	過程	成品	其他
7	12	19	2

6.

個人基本資料	教學歷程檔案	班級經營	班群檔案規劃	專業性資訊
17	18	13	3	4
教學行動策略	學生學習檔案	行政實習檔案	九年一貫紀錄	實習教師檔案
6	7	12	2	15
師生成長團體全紀錄		教學檔案省思		
5		7		

7.

1	2	3	4	5	6	7	8	9
10	9	0	2	9	15	5	6	5

8.較易收集

1	2	5	6	8	9
6	11	3	2	1	2

較難收集

2	3	4	5	7	9
3	2	9	1	2	3

9.

1	2	3	4	5	6
12	6	6	6	3	1

10.較易收集

1	2	3	4	5
8	7	2	4	2

較難收集

3	4	5	6
4	2	5	9

11.

1	2	3	4	5	6	7	8	9	10
7	0	3	4	15	3	2	12	4	2

12.較易收集

1	3	4	5	8	9
2	2	2	8	6	2

較難收集

2	3	4	6	7	10
5	3	2	1	3	1

13.

1	2	3	4	5
21	2	5	10	1

14.較易收集

1	2	3	4
18	1	1	4

較難收集

2	3	5
7	1	10

15.

1	2	3	4	5
5	1	2	6	7

16. 較易收集

1	5	4	5
4	1	3	7

較難收集

2	3	5
6	3	3

17.

1	2
11	16

18. 較易收集

1	2
8	12

較難收集

1	2

8	4

19.

1	2	3	4	5	6	7	8	9	10	11	12	13
5	0	2	3	3	0	0	4	0	2	4	0	3

20. 較易收集

1	8	9	10	11	13
2	2	1	1	1	2

較難收集

4	5	6	11	12	13
2	1	1	1	1	1

21.

1	2	3	4
19	17	18	3

22. 較易收集

1	2	3	4
12	6	6	1

較難收集

2	4
3	12

23.

1
11

24. 較易收集

1
7

較難收集

2
6

25.

1	2	3
9	11	9

26. 較易收集

1	2	3
5	10	2

較難收集

1	3
3	10

第三部分

1.

非常同意	同意	沒意見	不同意	非常不同意
13.6 %	63.6 %	22.7 %	0 %	0 %

2.

非常同意	同意	沒意見	不同意	非常不同意
22.7 %	68.2 %	9.1 %	0 %	0 %

3.

非常同意	同意	沒意見	不同意	非常不同意
18.2 %	31.8 %	50.0 %	0 %	0 %

4.

非常同意	同意	沒意見	不同意	非常不同意
18.2 %	63.6 %	18.2 %	0 %	0 %

5.

非常同意	同意	沒意見	不同意	非常不同意
9.1 %	36.4 %	27.3 %	27.3 %	0 %

6.

非常同意	同意	沒意見	不同意	非常不同意
4.5 %	36.4 %	18.2 %	40.9 %	0 %

7.

非常同意	同意	沒意見	不同意	非常不同意
4.5 %	22.7 %	22.7 %	45.5 %	4.5 %

8.

非常同意	同意	沒意見	不同意	非常不同意
9.1 %	36.4 %	18.2 %	36.4 %	0 %

9.

非常同意	同意	沒意見	不同意	非常不同意
18.2 %	68.2 %	13.6 %	0 %	0 %

10.

非常同意	同意	沒意見	不同意	非常不同意
18.2 %	54.5 %	22.7 %	4.5 %	0 %

11.

非常同意	同意	沒意見	不同意	非常不同意
9.1 %	63.6 %	27.3 %	0 %	0 %

12.

非常同意	同意	沒意見	不同意	非常不同意
18.2 %	63.6 %	13.6 %	4.5 %	0 %

13.

非常同意	同意	沒意見	不同意	非常不同意
4.5 %	45.5 %	36.4 %	13.6 %	0 %

14.

非常同意	同意	沒意見	不同意	非常不同意
27.3 %	59.1 %	13.6 %	0 %	0 %

15.

非常同意	同意	沒意見	不同意	非常不同意
40.9 %	50.0 %	9.1 %	0 %	0 %

16.

非常同意	同意	沒意見	不同意	非常不同意
22.7 %	68.2 %	9.1 %	0 %	0 %

17.

非常同意	同意	沒意見	不同意	非常不同意
22.7 %	40.9 %	27.3 %	9.1 %	0 %

18.

非常同意	同意	沒意見	不同意	非常不同意
4.5 %	40.5 %	31.8 %	22.7 %	0 %

19.

非常同意	同意	沒意見	不同意	非常不同意
4.5 %	68.2 %	22.7 %	4.5 %	0 %

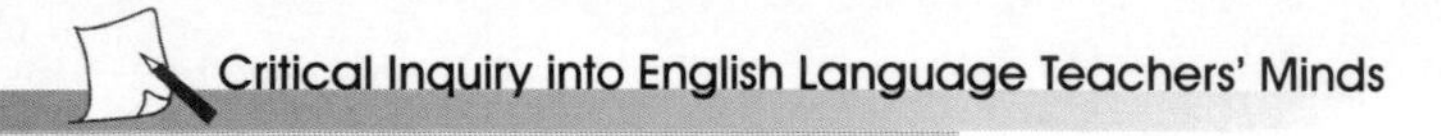

Chapter 7

Maximising Chances for Pre-service English Teachers- Creating A Blue Ocean for them

INTRODUCTION

Since 1995, the Ministry of Education (MOE) in Taiwan enforced the new Law for cultivating teachers, the demands and job-market of teachers has sprouted abruptly for the past few years, 'being teacher' seems to become one attractive career for many university graduates. According to the statistics, currently there are seventy-one centres for teacher education island-wide established by universities or colleges to educate secondary and primary teachers (MOE, 2004). Nevertheless, this excessive number of student teachers also has nearly half of them unemployed and thus leads to keen competitions in the job market (黃以敬與申慧媛，民 95；黃以敬，民 95). In order to obtain the limited jobs how to beat other competitions seemingly becomes student teachers' major concern before they enter the job market formally. Thus, it is very commonly to see rehearsed teaching demonstration embedded with various dramatisations, techniques or even 'exaggerations' in teaching interviews. However, it is argued that the factors determining what these prospective teachers demonstrate in teaching may be greatly influenced by how they perceive themselves as teachers and their beliefs about teaching. Besides, what really can help prospective teachers to secure the jobs, indeed, does not depend on 'value addition' but 'value innovation'. This means how to create personal uncontested values and to make other competitions irrelevant should turn into their prior task, and the strategic moves they can act on to reach the target are what blue ocean strategies (BOS) can inspire them. This chapter tries to first analyse pre-service teachers' perceived strengths, weakness, opportunities, and threats in terms of becoming capable teachers, i.e. teacher's belief about self and teaching, and second to establish an action framework to help them create irreplaceable values in the job market by applying the BOS.

LITERATURE REVIEW

In this section, the issues regarding with teachers' beliefs in being (English) teachers, a brief overview of the theories of the blue ocean strategy, and the examples of applying blue ocean strategies will be reviewed concisely.

Teacher beliefs

Teacher belief refers to an innate belief system which includes values and goals teacher hold towards their teaching.

This belief system will influence greatly how teachers perceive their roles as teachers, and accordingly make decisions and actions about their teaching based on their individual goals and values (Richards & Lockhart, 1996; 陳國泰，民 92; Richardson, 1996). Teacher's belief may be cultivated from three different sources, i.e. personal life experience, their experiences of being taught as students, and formal knowledge (周鳳美，民 91). Therefore, pre-service (English) teachers (PSETs), indeed, must have developed a belief system of how teaching should be like before they enter the teacher education programme. A number of educators assert that their former experiences of life and of being as learners take up a larger portion in determining these pre-service teachers' belief, and their perceptions of being teachers and teaching are reflective, practical and individualised (周鳳美，民 91； 陳國泰，民 92). Hence, we can assume that how PSETs see themselves and their roles as teachers will unavoidably affect their future performance in schools, and the stage of pre-service teacher education is apparently a very critical period to cultivate or reform their beliefs (李麗君，民 94).

However, undeniably due to the very personalised characteristic, teacher's belief is, indeed, fairly difficult to change or amend. Instead, it is always stable and sometimes serves as a gatekeeper to filter beneficial growth in professionalism (李麗君，民 94). For instance, PSETs regard "teaching" as "lecturing" and "learning" as "memorising" equally according to their previous learning experience, and thus may teach in the same way in the future. In Richards' survey (1996), it demonstrates how Chinese English teachers of Hong Kong perceive English and learning and how these perceptions form their beliefs about teaching. They believe English teachers are supposed to provide useful learning experiences, act as a model of correct language use, answer learners' questions, and correct their linguistic errors. Therefore, English teachers may accordingly believe owning proficient English ability is essential even strength in competing with other teachers. Another research (李麗君，民 91) even asserts that those PSETs studying in teacher education programmes (different from teacher universities) have greatly distinct teacher's belief for they hold very different life experience, educational backgrounds, expectations, and reasons of studying in the programmes. In addition, these PSETs tend to comparatively teach in a traditional 'teacher-centred' mode owing to their parents' expectations of them to be teachers. Consequently, these PSETs may largely emphasis the importance of 'teaching techniques', 'personal qualities', and 'learning experiences' but ignore the necessity of theories and knowledge. Hence, it can be presumed that PSETs would demand training courses about instant teaching 'tips' or 'techniques' rather than solid 'theories' or 'knowledge', and perceive that owning them is an opportunity and lacking them is a weakness when competing with other applicants. Thus, every PSET seemingly has the identical goals, requirements, and actions, which is obviously a red ocean where each competes bloodily and only saviours can reach the goal. How to create an uncontested market space and make the competition irrelevant, which is the spirits of applying the Blue Ocean Strategy and the key to ensure personal distinction and value, is completely neglected.

Blue Ocean Strategy (BOS)

When it comes to innovative blues ocean strategies, the competition-based red ocean strategies which have been executed for many years by businesses traditionally and lead to bloody competitions have to be discussed as well. The figure 1 concisely but clearly illustrates the significant differences between two strategies.

RED OCEAN STRATEGY	BLUE OCEAN STRATEGY
Compete in existing market space	Create uncontested market space
Beat the competition	Make the competition irrelevant
Exploit existing demand	Create and capture new demand
Make the value-cost trade-off	Break the value-cost trade-off
Align the whole system of a firm's activities with its strategic choices of differentiation *or* low cost	Align the whole system of a firm's activities in pursuit of differentiation *and* low cost

Figure 1: Red Ocean Strategy vs. Blue Ocean Strategy adopted from Kim & Mauborgne (2005 a.)

In a word, Blue Oceans rely on a "strategic move" i.e. "the set of managerial actions and decisions involved in making a major market-creating business offering" (Kim & Mauborgne, 2005 a.: 10), also the right unit of analysis for explaining the creation of blue oceans and sustained high performance. This move is realised through the approach that businesses or individuals create 'value innovation, not 'value addition'. The former, belonging to Blue Oceans, places equal emphasis on value and innovation. In the teaching job-market, this approach apparently implies that winners of PSETs are definitely not those who add values on their teaching which can be easily expected and thus duplicated by others but those who innovate their unique values which differentiate themselves from other job competitors and thus make them worthwhile (replacing the original low-cost in business) and irreplaceable for hiring schools.

In order to create their blue oceans, PSETs have to possess a tool to plan their strategic moves and reverse the traditional model. Kim and Mauborgne (2005 a.) provide a framework consisting of four actions. Indeed, these four questions (see the Figure 2) can help per-service teachers to challenge a competition-based model of what pre-service teachers are supposed to survive. In brief, asking these four questions continuously is very similar to the process of raising self critical thinking or reflection to enhance professionalism. The process of critical reflection helps pre-service teachers to distinct their value curve from typical ones, and this, indeed, confirms what many educators claim about how to ensure pre/in-service teachers' professional performance (李麗君，民 91; Richards & Lockhart, 1996; Tanner, Longayroux, Beijaard & Verloop, 2000).

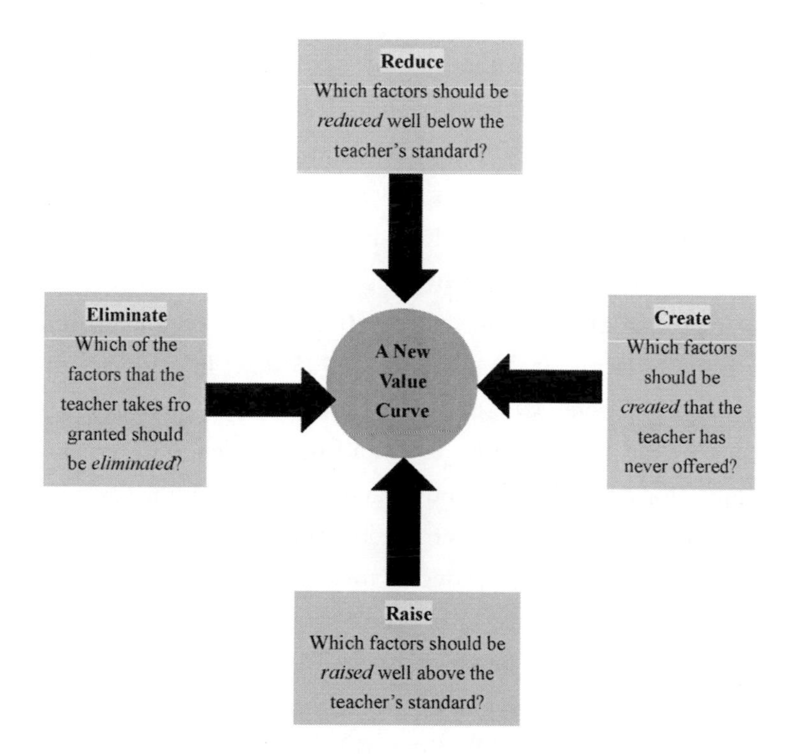

Figure 2: The Four Actions Framework adapted from Kim & Mauborgne (2005 a.)

Examples of BOS

BOS can be found in any business or industry provided that it meets any following principles: create a particular value curve, increase new needs, and provide effective barriers to imitation (Kim & Mauborgne: 2005 a.; 朱博湧，民 95). A renowned foreign case of applying BOS is the Cirque of Soleil from Canada. Within the four actions framework (see the

Figure 2), compared with any other traditional circus though it eliminates star performances, animal shows, aisle concession sales, and multiple show arenas, reduces fun, humour, thrill, and danger, raises, yet contrastively it raises a unique venue, and thus creates a specific theme, refined environment, theatrical story, and artistic music and dance, all of which make the Crique of Soleil unique, successful, innovative, and difficult to imitate (Kim & Mauborgne: 2005 a.). In Taiwan, the Taiwanese Opera Ming Hwa Yuan effectively creates new needs i.e. attracting both young and old audience by creating unique stories, enchanting music and lighting. Another example of BOS is the Taiwan Semiconductor Manufacturing Company, which adopts a strategic move in forwarding the manufacturing of crystal circle to many specialised small-scale but modern IC companies, and the needs generated from these IC design companies is what a typical BOS requires i.e. increasing new needs (朱博湧，民95). All of the successful cases simply follow the principle that "don't beat the competitions but make them irrelevant". This rule makes businesses unique and thus irreplaceable. Despite that any case discussed in either book does not embrace teaching job-market; yet it is assumed that PESTs can also create their own specific value curve to provide unique service and create new needs by applying the four actions framework of the BOS, and this is what the chapter tries to contribute.

RESEARCH METHODS

As discussed earlier, on the one hand there are many university graduates who intend to choose teachers as their careers and thus start to study the related courses in universities; however, on the other hand, the quantity of qualified teachers in the market at present outnumber by far the requirement of all schools. Even many of the newly-trained qualified teachers are still jobless; nevertheless, the heat-wave of becoming teaching does not cease. We need to understand why university students want to become teachers i.e. what external and internal reasons make them choose teaching as their careers, even if they realise that they may not be guaranteed a secured teaching job in the end. Furthermore, to establish a framework for prospective teachers to increase the chances of becoming English teachers is another main purpose of this study.

The research instrument is a self-designed open-ended questionnaire (see the Appendix) which was distributed to twenty-four students in my teaching university. These students were enrolled in the secondary teacher education module of English subject, and currently are taking a number of courses related to education and ELT. They are also supposed to become English teachers in the future. The participants come from different departments of the University, only two of whom are males.

The collected questionnaires were analysed by applying a grounded theory. This means that there are no set categories beforehand but contrarily all the categories (including main headings and sub-headings) encoded were generated from the properties of the data in this research. All of the participants' responses, firstly, were grouped into five main headings, which were termed by seeking the linkage between each response. Next, in order to achieve comprehensive understanding of these main headings, the respective sub-headings under each main theme were further coined according to their close link or similarity in meaning.

Then, the next step is to interpret these categorised data i.e. constructing meaning to the data. In the interpretation, inevitably person feelings, emotions, knowledge and opinions were involved. This kind of interpretation facilitated the development of the grounded patterns, theories or concepts in this study. Only after personal theoretical explanations of the data have been constructed can the interpretation be compared to the other existing theories or explanations, and then can the new concepts be formulated in line with the findings from field work (Denscombe, 1998; Randor, 2003).

Open-encoding helps the researcher discover, name and categorise the unique phenomenon and setting in this research (Strauss & Cobin, 1990). After peer checking of the encoding, the data were reflected on, interconnected, and interpreted with reference to the blue ocean strategies. In conclusion, the procedure of analysing the data of this research consisted of open reflection, flexible interpretation, analytic induction, BOS application, and constant comparison in order to generate particular patterns, frameworks, or concepts for this study.

DATA ANALYSIS & DISCUSSION

In this section, the data gathered from the open-ended questionnaires will be presented. The participants' responses can be categorised into five headings i.e. political guidance, socio-economic appeals, cultural heritages, career-long planning, and professionalism predominance. The sub-headings under each main heading are themed based on the interlinks of each responses.

Political Guidance

This refers to that the authorities' political decisions lead these respondents to engaging in the profession of teaching. These decisions can be categorised further as the followings:

Status Moulding: This category refers to that the government deliberately promotes the status of English in Taiwan. Examples of these are

(a) English language learning will begin from the second grade of elementary school,

(b) English will likely become the second official language in Taiwan, and

(c) university students are required to pass a threshold of English proficiency test before graduation, and

Handsome Incentives: This category means that the government provides a handsome package of benefits for teachers by laws. The examples of this include:

(a) the authority promises teachers a handsome package of

subsidies during their teaching such as tax-exemption, sponsorships for children education, and long vacations,

(b) the government provides teachers a well reliable pension after retirement such as monthly pension income equal to their previous salary, and

(c) the laws ensure teachers to benefit from a stable and job-guaranteed working environment.

Multiple Channels: This category suggests that the government amends the related laws to endow all universities with chances for training teachers, which was only possible in a number of teacher universities in the past. The examples are

(a) the new law of teacher cultivation was enforced in 1995, which terminated the monopolisation of teacher training within twelve teacher universities but provided each qualified university with an official charter to cultivate teachers, and furthermore

(b) the introduction of native English teachers in 2004 makes this profession more challengeable but attractive as well.

Socio-economic Appeals

This theme means that a number of societal and economic factors in Taiwan, usually positive ones, make these respondents more willing to become teachers. This main theme can be further divided into the following sub-headings.

Respected Status: This implies that the profession of being teachers enjoys a higher social status than most other professions in Taiwan. Examples of this are

(a) teachers has been long respected and valued in Taiwan society,
(b) teachers enjoy a very high social status ranking after one's parents,

Profitable Market: This means that English language teaching has become an enterprise and its profits seem much unlimited. Examples are
(a) the huge profitable market of running a English cram school attracts the participants' involvement, and
(b) the highly demands of language teachers training, curriculum design and materials writing also bring in unlimited profits.

Secured Job: This suggests that compared with other jobs, teaching is a more stable and beneficial job without worrying much about being fired. For example,
(a) due to the difficulty of finding a new job, teaching becomes a life-long job guarantee; too 'solid' as 'iron' to be broken,
(b) due to the economic recession, teaching still offers a reliable and stable income in spite of the de-salary and lay-off of other professions,
(c) in terms of welfares, teaching accompanies with many advantages such as long vacation, tax-exemption, sufficient pension, higher salaries, and other sponsorships for families.

Cultural Bounds

This category explains how the traditional culture, expectations, and values in Taiwan impact these respondents' decision. The following are the sub-headings of this.

Confucianism Influences: This indicates that teachers are viewed as models by the public and enjoy certain respect. For instance,

(a) teachers enjoy a high status ranking after Heave, Earth, Leader, and Parents as the fifth important one in the society, and

(b) teachers are supposed to be as pure as water, as noble as *Junzi* （君子）, as intelligent as mentor, and as perfect as model, and

(c) individual adoration to Confucius and his teaching theories results in personal commitment to teaching.

Clan Expectations: This refers to the belief that traditionally sons and daughters, especially females are expected by their families to get involved with teaching in any area of their life. Examples of this response are

(a) females are traditionally regarded to choose teaching as their life-long career in a family owing to the image of being 'tame' and 'well-educated', and

(b) the offspring's teaching job makes a family proud and brings honour to their ancestors

Foreign Appealing: This means that English accompanied with its Anglo-Saxon culture inspires and motivates a number of Taiwanese to teach English. Here are the examples:

(a) traditional Taiwanese cultures can be brighter if integrated with English cultures,

(b) learning English is not simply the acquisition of it but to achieve an understanding its own new cultures and ideas.

Lifelong & Career-long Planning

This category refers to that the respondents' decision of becoming a teacher involves with their lifelong and career-long plans. These concerns can be further classified into the following sub-headings.

Marriage of Convenience: This indicates that teachers have more chances to marry to a good husband or wife. This can be exemplified by these.

(a) Taiwanese people welcome teachers to become their future husbands or wives due to 'teacher' connoted with good reputation,

(b) to marry to a teacher implies no worry in their life in terms of stable income and reliable pension, and similarly

(c) teachers can have a wide range of choices about their partner due to their higher social status.

Childhood Dream: This means that teaching is the one and only job that a person can think of in his/her life while planning the career. Examples include

(a) being a teacher has always been the dream since one's childhood, and

(b) strong interest in learning English since the childhood make the respondents hope to teach English in the future.

Lifelong Handsome Benefits: This refers to that the attractive welfares during the teaching and after the retirement make teachers free from worries of their life. Examples like this are

(a) long vacation and stable off-days allow teachers to pursue further learning,
(b) stable incomes and subsidies make life less-worried, and
(c) reliable pension eases the worry of retirement life.

A Stepping Stone: This suggests that teaching is a temporary choice merely but it endows a person with good qualification and experience for the next job. For instance,
(a) teaching is temporary but beneficial for the further studies in graduate school,
(b) teaching experience can embellish one's resume for the next job, and
(c) teaching experience can be helpful in running an English cram school in the future.

Professionalism Predominance

This theme means that the reasons why the respondents choose teaching as their professions result from their strong belief in the high requirement of professionalism in English teaching. This can be further classified into the following sub-headings.

Non-replacement: This indicates that the profession of being English teachers cannot be replaced easily due to its requirement of skills. For instance,
(a) not everyone can become English teacher for this requires special training and certificates, and
(b) the status of its professionalism is very high and not easily replaced.

English-majors' Predestination: This suggests that English majors believe that their future career should be English teachers for there are supposed to be. Examples are like the followings.

(a) The heavy learning of courses related to English teaching leaves the respondents no choice but to teach English after graduation,
(b) the running of the educational courses for secondary school English teachers are largely tailor-made for English majors, and
(c) people commonly believe that the only career for the English undergraduates is being English teacher.

*Higher Capability:*This category refers to the respondents' belief that they are interested in the subject of English and can manipulate the better command of it, compared with other subjects. For example,

(a) Their comparatively high proficiency of language skills can turn them good English teachers than other majors,
(b) due to the long exposure to English language as English majors, they are more qualified to become English teachers, and
(c) owing to well-trained and proficient skills in materials design of English teaching, these majors are more confident of being a qualified English teacher.

S.W.O.T. Analysis

In this category, the participants state their strength, weaknesses, opportunities, and threats of becoming successful

English teachers. Their responses are divided into four sub-headings as the followings.

Inner Strength: This means that the respondents view a certain number of their inner characteristics as the potential advantages of becoming successful English teachers. These characteristics include passion, patience, friendly, sympathy, tameness, language proficiencies, optimistic, the bearing of hardships, care, and sensitivity.

External Opportunities: This subheading indicates that the participants also believe that a number of their outer qualities can be the bonus of becoming successful language teachers. These involve the characteristics of being conversable, proper-looking, solemn-looking, articulate, good performing, communicative, and active physical response.

Professional Weakness: This refers to the participants' conscious awareness of their likely deficiency in professional competency as language teachers. For example, the respondents are worried about that they do not know how to manage a class effectively, their English is still not proficient enough, they do not how to endure pressure and overcome occupational tiredness, they are less confident in active performance, and do not know how to teach students with different levels in a class.

Threshold Threats: This suggests the respondents' worries about the competitive and very limited entries of the job. These include limited vacancies for English teachers, difficult examination of obtaining teacher qualification, too many competitors, and threshold of English proficiency tests.

DISCUSSION & SUGGESTIONS

It is, in fact, very difficult to classify each response to a perfectly suitable category for a number of reasons of being English teachers are closely interwoven. For example, the response of 'having a high status' can contributes to both cultural perspective and societal perspective. Thus, inevitably a number of them will apparently overlap and reappear in other headings. Yet, the above analysis reveals the following findings and offer according suggestions.

First, pre-service teachers' belief about teacher and teaching does greatly affect their perception of becoming teachers. Their beliefs, as Chou asserts (周鳳美，民 91), mainly come from their personal life background and their experiences of being taught, instead very few of which are from teacher training courses. Though due to ethical concern it may not be very appropriate to correct teachers' individual beliefs (李麗君，民 94), yet this chapter argues that without proper emendation to passe or false beliefs pre-service teachers will face the situation of losing job opportunities and hindering their professional growth with trends. This relies much on teacher education programme providers' effort to put the situation right. These providers are suggested to offer training or education to help PSETs build up correct values of teaching and responsibilities, to endow them with fresh new attitudes, beliefs, global trends in (English) teaching, and to learn global and cross-cultural knowledge (陳憶芬，民 92；鄭玉疊，民 93). These measures help PSETs eliminate false beliefs, create new values and thus raise opportunities.

Second, from their perceived S.W.O.T. it is argued that the participants care much more about how to add extra values to them in order to increase the chance of being hired than how to innovate their existing or new-generated values to create an uncontested market. In other words, what the participants are concerned about is how to compete within competitors instead of how to create values across them. Believing the former principle, competitors would tend to follow the competition-based assumption and focus on being the best within it, to focus on the same target hiring bodies like schools, students or the stakeholders, to define the scope of efficient teachers offered by their competitors similarly, to accept stereotyped functions and emotions of being teachers, and thus to centre on current competitive threats in formulating strategic moves (Kim & Mauborgne, 2005 a.). All the above assumptions merely create a red sea for bloody competition. "The more that [PSETs] share this conventional wisdom about how they compete, the greater the competitive convergence among them" (p. 48).

Contrarily, PSETs are advised to "break out of the accepted boundaries that define how they compete" (p.48). Kim and Mauborgne (2005 a.; 金偉燦與莫柏尼，民 94) offer six basic paths to remaking the boundaries, which are based on looking at familiar data from a new perspective. In order to fit to the framework of PSETs, they are converted into as follows. (1) PSETs should look across alternative possibility. Teachers providing similar functions or utility will be substituted and ignored easily. Instead, dominant job seekers will reveal their different functions and efficiency even with the same purposes. (2) They should look across strategic groups within competitors. Rather than improving personal competitive position within a group, it is more important for PSETs to understand which factors will determine hiring school's decision to bow to or turn down one from another. (3) They are advised to look across the chain of employers. Instead of appealing in-service/interviewers teachers' attention, there are still other influential stakeholders' viewpoints which need to be catered as well. It is necessary to prepare for what parents, students, authorities or professors may expect from a PSET's performance. (4) PSETs need to look across complementary service teachers traditionally can offer. This service always involves hidden innovative value and a total solution by reflectively asking self: what context I am going to teach in, what the school expects me to do before, during, and after the employment, what pain points I can identify and how I can eliminate them through a complementary value I can offer. (5) Though PSETs have to look across functional or emotional appeal to recruiting schools, however it is, indeed, very difficult to clearly define whether "teaching job" should be classified as emotion-oriented or function-oriented. Thus, the key point here is to encourage PSETs to consider adding either extra emotional or functional appeals for hiring schools. It is because emotional or functional factors always can embed PSETs with creative attraction and thus generate new demand. The last path (6) requires PSETs to look across time. All qualities and conditions required by school to recruit new teachers are greatly influenced by trends, demands or polices. Thus, PESTs always need to take actions to adapt the possible future trends. This does not mean that PSETs should be able to predict what may happen in their future teaching but instead they have to be able to penetrate what trends have a high probability of impacting teaching, are irreversible and are evolving in a clear trajectory, how these changes may affect teaching, and how they can broaden unprecedented school utility (Kim & Mauborgne, 2005 b.). In a word, PSETs are suggested to look over the above six paths systematically in order to create blue oceans i.e. making them irreplaceable.

Third, the participants' motifs of becoming teachers mostly come from external factors rather than internal factors. No matter what the reasons of choosing to become a teacher, or their self analysis of strengths and weakness are, the participants are greatly influenced by external incentives such as the handsome benefit, family expectation, highly-respected status, a good command of English language proficiency or even the convenience of marriage. It cannot absolutely be concluded as simply as that the participants' beliefs about teaching are rather shallow but since teachers' decisions and actions in classroom are closely related to their beliefs, we do hope that most of their beliefs will be generated from internal reflection on the values of teaching profession. In other words, it is hoped that student teachers can develop their beliefs about teaching from different dimensions, i.e. beliefs about English, learning, teaching, the programme and the curriculum, and langue teaching as a profession. It is because teachers can learn much from the process of self-inquiry and critical reflection can trigger an understanding of teaching. It is assumed that if teachers, no matter pre-service or in-service, are actively involved in reflecting what is happening to teaching or in their classroom, they are in a position to discover whether there is a gap between realities and theories (Richards & Lockhart, 1996). Reflective teachers are greatly distinct from the traditional teachers, which would make their particular values revealed. Thus, training a reflective student teacher should become the concern of teacher preparation courses. Richards (1996) provides a constructivism view on this. That is teaching belief can be taught, discussed, and shared, which makes students teachers perceive themselves as in-service teachers. Even Raths (2001) suggests teaching belief be a criterion for selecting student teachers and courses clarifying values be taught. In addition, Gebbard, Gaitan and Oprandy recommend a multiple-activities approach to assist student teachers as investigators in equipping them with investigative and decision-making skills they require to act as responsible, autonomous, and reflective teachers. These activities may include "teaching a class, observing the teaching act, conducting investigative projects of teaching, and discussing teaching in several contexts" (1997: 24). All the above measures discussed aim at helping students teachers develop or re-shape their beliefs on teaching at a deeper level.

Finally, the capability of critical reflection only lies at a very superficial level. Though they can examine reflectively their beliefs and SWOT, but not critically enough. In other words, they are simply thinking how to add or duplicate the values they lack but others already had, which merely intrigues more competitions. Indeed, to be distinct from others critical thinking/ reflection on individual professionalism and values should become the major focus. Kim and Mauborgne's framework (2005 b.) for action can be beneficial for PSETs to draw their own unique value curves. Rather than concerning about adding teaching skills or techniques, PSETs are recommended to consider what factors below standards they should reduce, which factors as being teachers taken for granted should be eliminated, which factors no other has can be created, and what factors above standards can be raised. This is a process of self analysis similar to SWOT as well but more thorough, comprehensive, and critical. According to the results of the analysis, a number of strategic actions discussed earlier as the six approaches must be taken to form self value curve which then is very different from others'.

CONCLUSION

As discussed in the preceding sections, teacher's belief about teaching and teachers greatly influence what actions and decision they may act on teaching, and these beliefs can be very stable and difficult to revise. However, prospective teachers are going to still immerse in a bloody competition-based red ocean if without any radical change, i.e. creating personal value-curve in blue oceans. What makes them outstanding and thus picked is not how many different teaching techniques they can demonstrate in half an hour to beat other competitors but instead is whether they can possess critical thinking and reflective attitudes towards how to initiate an unexplored area where their values are distinct, innovative, and thus irreplaceable. It cannot be denied that one's value curve will be copied one day due to its success and a blue ocean will gradually turn into a red one. Then, it is time to think about creating another blue ocean, and this is certainly what reflective teachers are capable of.

This study is, indeed, a very initial try to apply the business-oriented blue ocean strategies to probe the issues of pre-service teacher education and thus a number of incompatible surfaces may inevitably occur. Thus, it is hoped that the future research can be conducted to investigate this issues from a deeper and broader scope. This chapter simply opens a window for researchers to examine the issues of teacher education from a different angle.

REFERENCES

朱博湧（民 95）。**藍海策略台灣版：15 個開創新市場的成功故事**。台北市：天下文化。

金偉燦與莫柏尼（民 94）。**藍海策略：開創無人競爭的全新市場**。（黃秀媛譯）。台北市：天下文化。（原著出版年：2005 年）

李麗君（民 94）。師資培育在改變師資生教學信念之意義及其困難與挑戰。**教育資料與研究**，62，134-144。

李麗君（民 91）。職前教師教學信念及其改變之研究。**中學教育學報，91**，1-26。

周鳳美（民 91）。教育改革下之師資培育教學改革：挑戰與導正師資生教學信念。**新時代師資培育的變革，0**，108-138。

陳國泰（民 92）。教師的實際知識及其對師資培育的啟示。**教育研究，11**，181-192。

陳憶芬（民 92）。全球化時代中小學師資培育之革新。**教育資料與研究，52**，29-35。

黃以敬（民 93 年 10 月 12 日）。教師供過於求。教育部：減招。**自由時報**，第 9 版。

黃以敬（民 95 年 2 月 8 日）。師培過剩逾 5 萬人。**自由時報**，第 9 版。

黃以敬與申慧媛（民 95 年 2 月 8 日）。師培就職率 長庚逾七成居冠。**自由時報**，第 9 版。

鄭玉疊（民 93）。培育優秀的新手教師─談實習機構如何落實實習教師之輔導。**國教新知，50，3**，30-45。

劉潛如（民 92 年 8 月 16 日）。師資培育過剩十萬人沒書教。**中央日報**。民 93 年 12 月 1 日，取自：http://www.cdn.com.tw/live/2003/08/16/text/920816e4.htm

Denscombe, M. (1998). *The Good Research Guide for Small-scale Social Research Projects.* Buckingham: Open University Press.

Gebbard, J., Gaitan, S., & Oprandy, R. (1997). Beyond prescription: the student teacher as investigator. In J. Richards & D. Nunan (Eds.), *Second Language Teacher Education* (pp.16-25). Cambridge: CUP..

Hockly, N. (2000). Modelling and 'cognitive apprenticeship' in teacher education. *ELT Journal, 54* (2), 118-125.

Kim, W. C., & Mauborgne, R. (2005 a.). *Blue Ocean Strategy: How to create uncontested market space and make the competition irrelevant*. Boston, M.A.: Harvard Business School Press.

Kim, W. C., & Mauborgne, R. (2005 b.). Blues Ocean Strategy: How to create uncontested market space and make the competition irrelevant. *KUULASAT, 13*(4), 1-8.

Ministry of Education (MOE). *Information for Centres of Teacher Education.* Retrieved December 1, 2004. from http://www.edu.tw/EDU_WEB/EDU_MGT/HIGH-SCHOOL/EDU7362001/main/teacher/teacher.htm

Radnor, H. (2002). *Research Your Professional Practice: doing interpretative research.* Buckingham: Open University Press.

Raths, J. (2001). *Teacher's beliefs and teaching beliefs.* Paper presented at a Symposium honouring ECRP. Champaign IL. (ERIC Document Reproduction Service No. ED452999).

Richards, J. C., & Lockhart, C. (1996). *Reflective Teachers in Second Language Classrooms*. Cambridge: CUP.

Richardson, V. (1996). The role of attitudes and beliefs in learning to teach. In Sikula, J.P., Butteru, T. J., & Guton, E. (Eds.), *Handbook of research on teacher education.* New York: Macmillian Library.

Strauss, A. T. J., & Corbin, J. (1990). *Basics of Qualitative Research: Grounded Theory Procedures and Techniques.* London: Sage.

Tanner, R., Longayroux, D., Beijaard, D., & Verloop, N. (2000). Piloting portfolios: using portfolios in pre-service teacher education. *ELT Journal, 54* (1), 20-30.

APPENDIX

Questionnaire

Instruction: This questionnaire is mainly to investigate your perceptions and beliefs of being an English teacher. Please write your responses in the space below. Please try to say as much as you can. Your responses will be treated anonymously and for research purpose only.

Name: ________________, Grade: ________________,

Dept.:__________________

Gender: □ Female; □ Male

壹、請問你為什麼會選擇就讀中等教育學程以便將來可成為一位英語老師？請就下面所提供的面向來思索。

1. 就政府政策層面而言：
2. 就社會、經濟層面而言：
3. 就傳統文化層面而言：
4. 就個人生涯規劃而言：
5. 就英語教師專業層面而言：
6. 其他任何原因:

貳、你認為你有何內在特質和外在條件能使你成為一個稱職的英語老師？

、你認為在未來有哪些挑戰是你在成為一位英語老師的過程中你必須克服的？

Chapter 8

English Teachers' Perceptions of Teacher Appraisal

INTRODUCTION

With the rapid booming of economics in East Asian countries for the past two decades, the governments within this region (Taiwan, Japan, South Korea, Hong Kong, Singapore and China) have started to focus their national development on education (Lee, 1991). Normally, these countries are usually categorised as a cultural group sharing the similar values i.e. the influence of Confucianism. The thinking of Confucianism has dominated the educational values and traditions within these countries for thousands of years (Walker & Dimmock, 2000).

However, after the successful economic revolution since 1980s, these governments have begun to consider adopting some educational reforms from the Western countries (mainly from the U.S. and the U.K.) to enable their education systems to be integrated with the main stream in the world. Thus, the most convenient shortcut is usually to borrow those educational reforms from the Western countries. These East Asian countries link economics and education. Globalisation, presumably the unity or one standardised pursuit of one issue without diversity throughout the world, has become a major concern in both economy and education within these countries. How to link school effectiveness with school improvement practically and precisely in order to keep up with the trend of educational globalisation has merged as a focus. (Fullan, 2001; Reynolds, Bollen, Creemers, Hopkins, Stoll & Lagerweij, 1996). However, during the process of the borrowing or improving, a crucial issue has been sometimes ignored by the authorities. That is the influence of societal culture.

Cultural factors can play an important part in the success or failure of an education reform, especially when this reform is adopted from a completely different culture. It cannot be denial that the cultures in Confucianism societies and Anglo-American societies obviously differ in a large scale (Dimmock & Walker, 2000 a.). Some potential problems may occur seriously if the cultural issues are not taken into consideration, especially if the reform originates from a totally different culture. Taiwan is a typical example facing these problems currently.

Before entering the millennium year, the educational authority in Taiwan had been trying to introduce a series of educational reforms from Western countries to Taiwanese education system, such as the teacher career ladder system, teacher appraisal, one-to-nine year curriculum, and the abolishment of Entrance Examinations (Ministry of Education, 2002). However, unfortunately, according to many news reports the former two reforms have resulted in much criticism and many doubts even before their implementation, while the latter two reforms have come across many problems after they were implemented (Liberty Times, 2002). Some TV news and the printed media have reported that many teachers, students and parents have started to urge the government to cease these reforms because of the pressure and uncertainty they have suffered, compared with before (Liberty Times, 2002).

The most likely significant reason accounting for the public's opposition and suspicion about educational changes may be that the authorities in Taiwan did not pay close attention to the cultural factors while implementing a Westernised educational change. Therefore, this chapter aims to investigate the potential problems of implementing an educational change, originating from Western countries, in Taiwan. The introduction of teacher appraisal in Taiwan will be used as a focus for this study to probe this understanding in the study.

Perhaps, globalisation in economy is what a developing country pursues eagerly in order to be one member of this global village. Nevertheless, as what Walker and Dimmock (2000) argue, is globalisation also suitable for education, especially for two completely different cultures? Does one size fit all? This issue needs to be researched from the perspective of cultural factors.

The chapter will be divided into several main sections. Section two will provide some basic information about educational background in Taiwan at present. Section three is the literature review of educational change, educational globalisation, cultural dimensions and cross-cultural examinations on changes, and teacher appraisal. The research methodology will be discussed in section four. In section five, I will analyse the results of this study and discuss them critically. Implications and conclusion will be put in section six as the final section.

BACKGROUND

This section introduces some background information about present education system in Taiwan, mainly focusing on teacher quality control. Regulations stated below are mainly based on the information provided by the Ministry of Education (MOE, 2002) in Taiwan on its website.

Teacher Appraisal in Taiwan

Each college or university can design its own appraisal system owing to the entitled power of university self-determination, while primary and secondary schools are still not empowered or required to carry out any official teacher appraisal island-wide, except for some schools which may have their own school-based appraisal. Hence, the Taiwanese Government currently is considering implementing an official evaluation system, borrowed from Western countries, into these schools. However, this adoption has not been approved yet legislatively. It means carrying out teacher appraisal in each school is still not officially required island-wide. Since this study mainly focuses on the teacher appraisal applied to primary schools and secondary schools teachers, the situation in higher education will not be discussed in this study.

Teacher Source and Quality Control

The main source of teachers in Taiwan comes from the graduates in nine teacher colleges and three teacher universities. A college graduate will teach in a primary school while a university graduate will enter a secondary (junior or senior high school) to teach. The length of studies normally combines four years of university-based learning and a one-year teaching practice in a school. Literally and officially, the more appropriate English translation of "teachers' colleges or universities" in Taiwan should be translated as "Normal College and Normal University"(*Shi-fan-xiao-yuan and Shi-fan-da-xiao*). Here, it can clearly be seen that traditionally and culturally, a teacher in Taiwan not only 'teaches' but also has to be the 'model' for students and the society. 'Normal' refers to a 'good model' (*mo-fan*) in Chinese. A teacher in Taiwan is not only supposed to only teach but also to be responsible for teaching students how to become good human beings in the society after their graduation. However, the premise is that unless the teacher can be a nearly perfect prototype as a sound human being, the above targets cannot be achieved easily. Owing to this cultural demand on teachers in Taiwan, these pre-service teachers in teacher's college will receive many lessons about how to become a good human being and how to make their future students become sound human beings as well.

In addition, moral education is highly emphasised not only during the cultivation of a teacher in Taiwan but also at each level of education. This can be attributed to the traditional influence of Confucianism. Confucius proposes that the highest level of a person is *'chuntze* (gentle man)', which can be achieved by continuous moral education through ones' life. Moreover, teachers enjoy a higher social status in Taiwan compared with other occupations. Traditionally, the importance of a teacher is only ranked after 'heaven, earth, ruler, parents' according to Analects of Confucius (Toyogahuen University, 2002). These five 'constitutions in universe' are termed as five cardinal virtues (*Wu-chang*) in Chinese (Toyogakuen University, 2002).

Once these pre-service teachers complete their school education, they have to choose a secondary or primary school to practice teaching for at least one year to obtain their certificates of qualified teachers. At present, any qualified teacher should be examined yearly by a committee of teacher's checking of his/her school by law. However, such kind of evaluation is different from teacher appraisal system. First of all, this checking focuses highly on teachers' behaviours rather than the quality of their teaching. For example, teachers' punctuality on class, good model for students, crime records, or mental condition (please refer to MOE 2002 for detailed regulations) are significant evaluation items. Usually unless a teacher commits a serious crime or has a severe mental disease, s/he is always entitled to keep his/her working right for the next years along with a salary increment. Hence, the assessment of teaching quality is not so highly profiled.

Secondly, such annual checking is done by a committee composed of teacher representatives and administration staff. Normally and usually, there is no obligatory classroom observation taken for assessing teachers before the committee meeting. Therefore, this present form of evaluation can be a type of teacher appraisal but not very thorough and serious. However, the quality of teaching is still always a school's major concern, especially in a highly competitive education society like Taiwan. Consequently, teachers in Taiwan still take most responsibilities in improving the quality of education for all in a school. Teachers thus have to ensure their teaching quality, enhance students' quality, realizing school's targets and cultures, and even show full cooperation with colleagues in order to bring effectiveness to schools, which unavoidably could cause much stress and pressure for teachers (Reynolds *et al.*, 1996).

Teacher Career Ladder System

To overcome the seeming contradiction between assessment and teaching quality, the educational authority in Taiwan proposed a teacher career ladder system in 2001. The policy tries to divide all the current teachers into four different ladders i.e. advisory teacher, advanced teacher, intermediate teacher and basic teacher according to their teaching years (eight years is a minimum for applying for an upgrade), INSET and research, and professional performance. It is the professional performance that plays an important part during the assessment. The assessment of teachers' professional performance is largely equal to teacher appraisal, which evaluates a teachers' counselling ability, teaching accountability, research results, and the promotion of educational service (Tsai & Cheng, 2001). This policy originated from and was adopted from the educational systems in the U.S. and the U.K., where the governments require that teachers should be able to "realise their full potential and to carry out their duties more effectively" in order to increase school-effectiveness (Gunter, 2001: 242).

What the policy-makers advocate is that if this new change can be adopted and implemented with success, then it can help teachers to increase teaching quality, enhance teacher's professional growth, build up a life career ladder system, and encourage teachers' life-long learning. Once the results of the assessment are satisfactory, then teachers may have salary promotion and are entitled to teach for fewer hours. However, so far there has still been no obvious empirical research proving that this ladder program had come up with the above merits either in the U.S. or in Taiwan.

However, the change is still under extensive discussion at the current stage though the education authority in Taiwan is trying to persuade teachers to accept this change. The policy has been made but it seems not so easy to carry it out immediately. Many teachers' opposition, rising from their uncertainty is the major reason along with other problems such as the time-consuming amendments of many related laws or the inadequacy of the national budget (Chang, 1999).

LITERATURE REVIEW

In this following section, I will review briefly the current literature about the five issues: (1) educational change, (2) educational globalisation, (3) cultural dimensions and cross-cultural examination on educational changes, and (4) the appraisal systems in other countries, including the U.K., the U.S., Japan, China, and Hong Kong, and their confronted difficulties in implementation.

Educational Change

We are now living in an era of change. We face changes in our life, our work and even in our values (Fullan, 2001). The pace of change is so fast, especially in economy when compared with the last few decades. To cope with the challenge of changes has become a crucial issue for many organisation leaders or participants (Hooper & Potter, 2000). In the 21st century, changes can emerge quickly from many directions and can influence our different aspects of life, which sometimes makes us fall behind the pace of changes (Fullan, 2001). In fact, organisations in the 21st century are largely market-driven and hence 'accountability in performance' becomes a very important component in an organisation. Since education and schools are often regarded as the solutions to societal phenomena, effectiveness and improvement in education are of concern (Reynolds *et al.*, 1996). However, schools seem to unsuccessfully fulfil their missions to satisfy pupils, parents or politicians, and one solution to coping with this is to review the educational systems to ensure quality of outcomes (Fullan & Stiegelbauer, 1991; Reynolds *et al.*, 1996).

There is often an assumption that any change or reform will bring some benefits to some extent no matter what. However, many changes in fact would easily fail to make progress even at their early stage of the implementation (Reynolds *et al.*, 1996). It is usually because the theories of these changes are usually faulty or unsuitable to another setting, and the people who are supposed to practice these changes are seldom given the chance to understand what the changes are for (Fullan & Stiegelbauer, 1991). Fullan (1993) concludes that a change will result in defensiveness, superficiality or short-lived success quite easily if many circumstances are neglected purposefully such as decision-making, organisational atmosphere, or the way educational hierarchy generates. A change will fail easily if a change is taken simply because we need some change. In other words, "change for the sake of change will not help at all" (Fullan & Steigelbauer, 1991: 15).

Changes may not happen in a linear way; on the contrary, it is usually full of surprises. "Productive educational change is full of paradoxes and components that are often not seen as going together" (Fullan, 1993 : 4). In order to implement educational changes successfully, it is very important to detect the sources of education changes, and understand what these educational changes mean to us. Too often, change will sometimes result in unexpected chaos or failure; however, it might be worth viewing change as a journey of complexity, full of non-linear feedback, instability, paradoxes, and dynamics (Fullan, 1999; Fullan, 2001; Reynolds *et al*., 1996)

Levin (1976) states that the pressure for educational policy may come from natural disasters, external forces e.g. imported values or technology, and internal contradictions such as "when one or more groups in a society perceive a discrepancy between educational values and outcomes affecting themselves or others in whom they have an interest" (Fullan & Steigelbauer, 1991:17). However, changes in Asian cultures may also partially be driven by another force. For example, many educational reforms, especially in Asian countries (like Japan, Taiwan, Hong Kong, Singapore, South Korea, China or some south-east Asian countries), may be attributed to the startling economic boom since the late 1970s as well (Lee, 1991). These countries have started to invest more money in education after they had become richer than before. For these countries, basically investment in educational change is regarded as necessary to enhance a nation's competition either in economy or human knowledge. To some degree, educational change can be very cultural and political. It can serve the function of not only transmitting or transforming its cultural values to its future generations but also maintaining its political order (Lee, 1991).

The sources of educational change are many but in what form does it occur? Educational change may be driven voluntarily or imposed either externally or internally. To put it differently, changes can happen at a surface level, as a transactional change, or at a deep level, as a transformational change (Middlehurst, 1993; Fullan & Stiegelbauer, 1991; Hooper & Potter, 2000). However, in either situation, the meaning of change is still vague (Fullan & Stiegelbauer, 1991). Therefore, Fullan & Stiegelbauer (1991) define the meaning of educational changes as two dimensions i.e. the subjective reality of educational change and the objective reality of educational change. The former refers to a change that only makes sense when it can meet a person's or a group's reality in implementing while the latter means that "individuals and groups interact to produce social phenomenon, which exists outside any given individual" (p.37). They propose that the objective reality enables us to recognise that new reforms are out there in existence, and the real practice can be implemented with success only when a change or reform can be embedded with the consideration of personal, organisational or national contexts culturally.

In addition, Fullan (2001) also mentions that in understanding the change process we should bear in mind that the goal is not simply to innovate something novel but to develop the capacity and commitment to solve complex problems. This means only having the best ideas for changes is not enough, but contrarily, innovative leadership for changes needs to contain authoritative, democratic, affiliative, and coaching characteristics (Fullan, 2001). Certainly, very often, a sense of uncertainty, fear or resistance would appear when a change is adopted. However, Fullan (2001) encourages the leaders to appreciate this implementation dip and to redefine resistance. He proposes that problems are our friends and they are usually inevitable. It is because resistance may be a good source for providing alternatives in a change, and successful implementation is built on valuing differences and appreciating problems (Fullan 1993; Fullan 2001). Furthermore, he (Fullan 2001) also advocates that changing the culture and the way people do things around them is crucial in making a change progress. "Leading in a culture of change means producing the capacity to seek, critically assess, and selectively incorporate new ideas and practices inside or outside the organisation" (Fullan, 2001: 44). Finally, he reminds us that change is a journey not a blueprint (Fullan, 1993). Change is not a checklist, a step-by-step process. On the contrary, it is loaded with uncertainty, complexity, and excitement and sometimes perverse. Hence, leadership in a complex change may begin with coercive actions in order to be rescued from chaos but then may alter to a democratic style to welcome differences in communication (Fullan, 2001). In a word, not only is change itself full of complexity but so is leadership.

In conclusion, an educational reform or change cannot be viewed as an educational progress equally. Sometimes, "resisting certain changes may be more progressive than adopting them" (Fullan & Stiegelbauer, 1991: 4). To ensure the success in changing, it is quite fundamental to understand what the meaning of a change is, what it is for, and how it precedes under a personal or a group's contexts.

Educational Globalisation

As discussed earlier, a change may have multi-dimensional influence in our daily life and may lead us to a more 'standardised' life-style globally. There seems a plausible belief that each global issue may be settled more easily and successfully if dealt within one standardised regulation. This is the case when many East Asian countries at economic-developing or nearly economic-developed stages have made efforts either voluntarily or forcibly to reach their compromises in economy, commerce, human rights, and manufacturing with so-called Western countries i.e. the U.S., the U.K., Canada, the European countries, and Australia. In Taiwan, the government has successfully linked its economic situation with the globalised regulations in WTO (World Trade Organisation) in 2002. However, it seems not enough for Taiwanese government. The authority also tries to implement many globalised educational reforms in Taiwan currently such as teacher career ladder program, teacher appraisal, or accountability. However, we need to question that is globalisation in education really unavoidable and will it certainly bring some merits to each peculiar context?

The power of media accelerates the prevailing of globalisation (Hallinger, 1998). Information, communication, and transformation between East and West have been made much easier with the network of media. This implies that now a more dominant cultural with its values can be introduced or transmitted to another without too many difficulties. Besides, the globalisation is also strengthened by the growing influence of international agencies (Dimmock & Walker, 2000 b.). Organizations such as UN (United Nations), World Bank, or WTO have been trying to dominate and determine issues under their standardised global structures and regulations. It can be seen that the broader boundaries between countries are blurring. Cooperation is a tendency from economics to trade, commerce, human rights, politics and education (Fullan, 2001). Thus, 'union' becomes the product of this phenomenon; European Union and Free Trade Agreement are two typical examples of this trend.

However, globalisation without considering individual societal context would definitely result in chaos (Huh, 2001; Dimmock & Walker, 2000 b.). According to Maclean (2001: 190-191), many Asian countries are facing a dilemma when implementing an educational change, which originated from Western countries. These are

> *the tension between the global and the local, the tension between tradition and modernity, the tension between long-term and short-term considerations, the tension between the need for competition and the concern for equality of opportunity, the tension between the extraordinary expansion of knowledge and human capacity, and the tension between the spiritual and the material in a world (Maclean, 2001: 190-191).*

Maclean (2001) argues that these tensions may result from an adopted policy or a change that is hugely distinguished from what its original cultural values root in.

Many educational reforms failed because cultural factors were not taken into careful consideration before or during their implementing. Huh (2001) looks at educational changes in South Korea for examples, claiming that these reforms i.e. 'ability grouping', 'school governing body system' and 'Seven curriculum in Korea' cannot be successfully adopted in economic-developing countries like South Korea. He states that "any policy in one country, including an educational one, cannot be transferred directly to another without some kind of transformation that will include severe distortion or result in a totally different outcome" (Huh, 2001: 257). Therefore, he makes a strong claim that educational changes, as part of social product, cannot be transferred with any success if these changes will be separated from their own peculiar and unique place and time (Huh, 2001). Besides, Dimmock and Walker's (2000 a. b.) studies on a series of educational changes in Hong Kong also reveal that cultural factors really play an important role in the adoption of some Western reforms, and these factors will definitely determine their success and failure eventually. Indeed, Huh's concern supports the arguments that "the tensions exist between globalisation and societal culture and that globalisation makes the recognition of societal culture and cross-cultural similarities and differences more, not less, important" (Dimmock & Walker, 2000 b.: 307). Therefore, the influence of societal culture should be taken into account during the process of globalisation in educational change.

There is a strong need for us to look at both globalisation and local societal contexts based on a cross-cultural examination of educational change if there are expectations about this change, and this is what the following section will discuss.

Cultural-dimensions and Cross-cultural Examination of Educational Changes

In this section, I will discuss what kinds of effects the individual cultural values may have on the adoption of imported educational changes. To begin with, it is necessary to know what the dimensions of a culture may consist of.

With regard to cultural dimensions in a society, usually Hofstede's (1991) typology will be referred to firstly. He tries (Hofsteds, 1985; 1991) to categorise cultures in dichotomy, which results in being criticised as likely simplifying the complexity of a culture. Firstly, he talks about power-distance (PD), referring to the degree an individual can agree to the unequal power distribution in an organization. High PD culture can accept the differences between superiors and subordinates while low PD culture would prefer democratic participation in power allocation (Lu, Rose & Blodgett, 1999). Secondly, Hofstede (1985: 347) mentions "uncertainty avoidance" (UA), which means "the degree to which members of a society feel uncomfortable with uncertainty and ambiguity, leading them to support beliefs promising certainty and to maintain institutions protecting conformity." A culture with high UA would prefer security by following explicit regulations while one with low UA could be tolerant of uncertainty.

Next, he (Hofstede, 1985) distinguishes between a culture with collectivism and a culture with individualism. The former would advocate personal time, freedom, independence and skills (Lu, Rose & Blodgett, 1999) while the latter would view group interests as the priority rather than personal interests. Besides, masculinity/feminity is another dimension of a culture, which means that a culture of masculinity will be characterised as "assertive, aggressive, ambitious, competitive, and materialistic"; on the contrary, a feminity culture will be more "interpersonally- oriented, benevolent, less interested in recognition in terms of close human relationships" (Lu, Rose & Blodgett, 1999: 94).

Finally, the fifth dimension Hofstede includes in his taxonomy of a culture is Confucian dynamism (Lu, Rose & Blodgett, 1999). By this, he means a culture emphasising Confucian dynamism will follow Confucius' teachings modified by social norms. They stress "thrift, persistence, and ordering relationships, along with a sense of shame" (Lu, Rose & Blodgett, 1999: 94). Hence, values such as politeness, obedience, self-discipline, and honouring parents and elders are hugely emphasised in a culture with high Confucian dynamism.

Although Hofstede has tried to encompass the whole dimensions of culture into his five terminologies, some researchers still create their own terms based on the combinations of what Hofstede has proposed and what they have found in their studies. Dimmock and Walker (2000 a.; b.) list their six dimensions of societal culture as follows. They use power-distributed/power-concentrated to replace Hofstede's Power Distance (PD) construct. Masculinity/Femininity has been replaced by consideration/aggression. Proactivism/Fatalism has taken the place of 'Uncertainty Avoidance (UA)'. Furthermore, Dimmock and Walker replace Hofstede's Indivifualism/Collectivism with Group-oriented/Self-oriented. These different terminologies in fact share the same meaning largely.

Dimmock and Walker (2000 a.; 2000 b.) create another two dimensions. The dimension, Generative/Replication, acknowledges that some cultures "predispose to innovation or the generation of new ideas and methods while other cultures tend to replicate or adopt ideas and approaches from elsewhere" (Dimmock & Walker, 2000 b.). In addition, they use the dimension, 'Limited relationship/Holistic Relationship', to measure the characteristics and importance of interpersonal relationships. In culture with limited relationship, interactions and relationships are greatly determined by 'rules' and these rules are applied to everyone equally. Contrarily, in culture with holistic relationship, interpersonal relationships can largely be constituted of some invisible obligations such as kinship, patronage and friendship.

In our view, it seems that Dimmock and Walker's six dimensions are more suitable to investigate what cultural influences will have on the implementation of a change between two countries with two different cultures. However, we would like to re-name those above Western categorisations by using our own Eastern terminologies to make my analysis more sensible to me. (Please refer to diagram 1 in the appendix for the process of this conceptualised change)

At first, instead of saying power distributed/concentrated, the way of distributing power can be classified into power-shared and power-focused. A culture may centralise its power to particular people and operationalise it from a top-to-down hierarchy, while another culture may release its power to be shared by all people based on a flat hierarchy. Accordingly, a power-shared culture will also allocate the responsibilities to all the stakeholders; however, in a power-focused culture, most responsibilities will only fall on those superiors/heads who enjoy the most power. This phase also determines if stakeholders' opinions will be valued or not while a change is formulated or adopted.

Next, a culture can be said to have self-centred interest or group-centred interest rather than consideration/aggression. A self-centred culture will put personal interests as the priority while a group-centred society will place group interests in the first place such as family, organisation, and nation. This dimension will influence teachers' perceived priority in personal accountability or the whole school effectiveness.

Furthermore, in the dimension of target-achieving, we conceptualise it as performance-preferential or harmony-preferential culture. In the former culture, targets-achievement is highly stressed through fierce competition but in a harmony-preferential culture, harmony is more important than the target-achieving. In other words, during the process of finishing a task, any aggressive climate will be depressed in order to maintain a harmonious atmosphere. The sense of competition will be discouraged (Dimmock & Walker, 2000 b.; Walker & Dimmock, 2000). Perhaps, the validity of appraisal feedback will be questioned if feedback is made in the premise of keeping harmonious. In fact, this dimension is similar to transformational leadership because leaders and followers are fused together to maintain their values together, while in self-centred interest group leadership is separate from its other members as a transactional style (Middlehurst, 1993).

In the belief of relationships between human beings and the nature/environment, some cultures believe in human-control, which means human beings believe they can conquer or control each difficulty if they want to. However, some cultures believe in destiny-control (Cheong, 2000). This means people in a destiny-controlled culture believe that human's power cannot exceed the power of the great nature/environment. Everything has been fated at the beginning and it is difficult to change the rules of destiny. "What is meant to be, will be" (Dimmock & Walker, 2000 a.: 155). Thus, it can be suggested that appraisees under different cultures may attribute their success or failure in appraisal to obvious different reasons.

Furthermore, due to the belief of 'human-control', some cultures believe humans not only can create the world but also everything. This is known as a 'creativity-originated' dimension. Inventions or innovations of new ideas and methods are encouraged highly in such culture. However, a culture may also tend to be 'replication-originated', owing to its fear of violating the natural laws, making errors and bringing shame to human beings. Therefore, a culture like this is inclined to rely on what it has already had in hand or borrow something directly from elsewhere (Dimmock & Walker, 2000 b.; Walker & Dimmock 2002). This dimension may account for the reason why some countries will mainly adopt foreign educational reforms directly in terms of changing its education system.

Finally, in the dimension of interpersonal relationships, some cultures advocate linear-relationships between people. "One way in and one way out." The rules or laws control the line tightly and impartially. However, in a culture with network-relationships, people's interactions will largely and flexibly depend on the kinship, bloodline, closeness, or familiarity rather then fixed rules. Many appraisees would suspect the reliability of the appraisal results if these results are influenced and finalised based on any other un-professional factor during appraisal.

In fact, it is difficult to gauge the diversity of different cultures in dichotomy but it will become crucial and obligatory to take cultural dimensions into consideration if we hope to cope with an educational change smoothly, especially if this change is imported from a totally different culture such as the Westernalised teacher appraisal being implemented in East Asian (Confucianism) countries.

It cannot be denied that sometimes we may need or borrow some changes to make education better, but in fact many current educational theories, policies and changes are tailor-made and closely relate to its environment (Reynolds, Bollen, Creemers, Hopkins, Stoll & Lagerweij, 1996) to suit

Anglo-American contexts and these newly-generating ideas "make little to bound or limit their work geographically or culturally" (Dimmock & Walker, 2000 b.: 304). In other words, we have to consider clearly and carefully whether an imported change will definitely suit our needs and contexts, and what impacts this change may bring to us before carrying it out immediately. Therefore, we need to take different contexts, dimensions of a culture, and its histories into consideration cautiously when we are talking about the formulation and adoption of a borrowed educational reform.

Teacher Appraisal: When East Meets West

In this section, we will talk about the difficulties both some Western countries (mainly the U.K. and the U.S.) and some East Asian countries have confronted in implementing an Anglo-Americanised reform i.e. teacher appraisal in their education systems.

Teacher appraisal may originate from the idea of performance management in the business world. 'Accountability' and 'personal performance' are highly demanded in a culture full of competitive individualism and "performance appraisal may be the most valuable tools in managing human resources and productivity" (Chow, 1995: 67) from the Anglo-American view. It cannot be denied that teacher appraisal was tailor made to suit the Anglo-American cultures, which hold strong beliefs in power-shared, self-centred, performance-referential, human-controlling, creativity-originated, and linear-relationship dimensions. According to Chow (1995), this Westernised appraisal system puts great emphasis on valid measuring criteria and instruments, good relationship between the appraiser and the appraisee, mutual respect and trust, frequent and open communication, clearly set standards, and feedback. In other words, this Westernised appraisal demands components of transformational leadership such as attention, communication, trust, and positive recognition (Midlehurst, 1993).

Like the performance appraisal in managerism, the purposes of teacher appraisal are (1) to improve teaching, and (2) to ensure accountability and this performance appraisal system has been practiced for a long period of time, ranging from over 30 years in the U.S. and nearly 12 years in the U.K. (Fullan & Hargreaves, 1992; Yang, 2000). It could include formative and summative evaluation. The results of the former are mainly used to help teachers to detect the merits and shortcomings in their teaching in order to achieve professional growth, while those of the latter are used to select or promote teachers (Tunner & Clift, 1988).

The forms of teacher appraisal are various. They could be teacher's self-appraisal, peer appraisal, superordinate's appraisal, students' appraisal, outsiders' appraisal (referring to teachers, principals or administration staff from another school), and non-educational professionals' appraisal (referring to parents, PTA or others) (Wragg, 1987). Besides, the tools used for evaluation are also in varieties. These may include teaching demonstration, classroom observation, videotaping, students' academic performance, teaching diary, teaching portfolios, questionnaire, or interviews. (McColskey & Egelson, 1993). Usually, at least two different kinds of the above tools will be adopted for implementing teacher appraisal.

In addition, the U.S. government started to offer teachers extra 'merit pay' according to their teaching performance from the 1970s. However, such incentive was criticised and opposed greatly by many teacher unions and therefore it is still not widely accepted throughout the whole nation so far. At present, each state in the U.S. has its own appraisal system to evaluate teachers' working performance (Yang, 2000).

In the U.K. teacher appraisal became a legal requirement in 1986, but not until 1991 was the detailed practice published (Gunter, 2002). LEAs (Local Educational Administration) are entitled to take full responsibilities for running and monitoring the appraisal of its schools. Effective school management is what this system aims for, and the relationship between teachers' salaries and their performance are highly emphasised (Mo, Conners & Mccormick, 1998; BBC, 2002). The main reason why the U.K. government links teachers' pay to performance is to provide teachers with improved incentives for excellence; however, school-effectiveness depends not only on teachers' performance but also learners' motivation. National expenditure spent on teachers cannot necessarily ensure the positive outcome of school-effectiveness (Reynolds *et al.*, 1996). While the link between pay and performance has almost failed and been opposed greatly in the U.S. in the 1970s, ironically the U.K. government is considering re-linking them (Yang, 2000).

So far, evidence shows that this appraisal still needs more improvements to make it better (Gunter, 2000). The difficulties the U.K. faces are the problems of time and budget spending in the appraisal, extra working loads, using the outcomes, LEA's financial supports, linking personal performance with staff development plan, and confidentiality of protecting appraisees (Wragg, Wikeley, Wragg, & Haynes, 1996; Fidler, 1995; Bartlett 2000; Gunter, 2002). In fact, during the process of change, emotions would frequently rise from both leaders and followers, which refers to the differences in opinion. Under this circumstance, emotional leadership is then desirable (Hooper & Potter, 2000). It means negotiation, communication, respect, and empathy could be characteristics for a leader to maintain good relationships with his/her followers i.e. so called emotional intelligence or Emotional Quotient (EQ). In a word, emotional leadership can help a leader to transform his/her behaviour to arrive at a higher level of performance. (Goleman, 1995; Hooper & Potter, 2000; Fullan, 2001)

In East Asian countries, China has developed its own system to appraise teachers' performance; however, the criterion of evaluation has a large portion on assessing teachers' political positions i.e. if they are loyal to Communism. Besides, teachers will be classified into four different ranks based on their performance. The teachers in the highest rank can enjoy renowned reputation and higher pay but very few achieve this rank. In addition, due to the extreme pressure to maintain this reputation, teachers with the highest position would prefer to stay in a lower rank to avoid this extreme pressure (Yang, 2000).

In Japan, teachers are offered different certificates of qualifications, and each level of certificate has to be renewed within a period of time if a teacher can obtain enough credits in his/her INSET. Therefore, in fact, Japan does not have a clear system evaluating teachers' performance in work but it does encourage teachers to join INSET in order to renew the teaching certificates (Tsai & Cheng, 2001).

Hong Kong, highly influenced by British culture due to its colonial status before 1997, carries out a career ladder system for secondary school teachers, according to which teacher's pay is based on their ranks. A teacher in Hong Kong will be appraised if s/he is nominated for a senior post in school but due to the limited number of these posts in a school, quite surprisingly most teachers have never been appraised officially in their entire teaching career (Mo, Conners & Mccormick, 1998). Furthermore, in Cheng's (1992) study, it shows that only 24.7% of the 241 schools has a clear appraisal system. Many teachers doubt the completeness and objectiveness of the appraisal system, and thus can seldom believe the judgements the head made about their performance. Some people strongly question the suitability of teacher appraisal policy and its approaches, invented in Western cultures, to be applied in Hong Kong schools with predominantly Chinese culture. This results in that many schools in Hong Kong think of the implementation of teacher appraisal as the most problematic aspect of educational change (Walker & Dimmock, 2000).

In Taiwan, there is no official teacher appraisal in secondary and primary school. However, the government is trying to implement a teacher career ladder system and a large part of this system will depend on teachers' performance in work including teaching, servicing, researching and counselling (Tsai & Cheng, 2001). Though this new reform is still under discussion, some schools have begun their own appraisal systems and some local governments request their schools to implement an unofficial trial appraisal system. Take Kaohsiung City for example, in 2001 schools were only given some major guidelines to the trail appraisal system, but each school was empowered to design its own evaluation items. Due to these diversities and its temporary trial, no evidence so far can show the likely effectiveness this new change may cause.

After examining the difficulties the above countries have confronted in implementing teacher appraisal either in the West or East, we need to re-consider the plausibility of it in Taiwan cautiously because

> *the appropriateness of different approaches to appraisal and their associated processes has been largely restricted to English-speaking Western setting and little has been written about teacher appraisal outside these confines, and in particular, the influence of societal culture on teacher appraisal in Asian educational contexts (Walker & Dimmock, 2000).*

The Taiwanese government should seriously take the cultural dimensions into account if it wants to adopt an imported educational reform e.g. teacher appraisal successfully in Taiwan. What do teachers think about the system? What are their expectations of this system and what kinds of role does societal culture in Taiwan play in influencing its effectiveness? This is the main purpose of conducting this study to probe the possible answers.

RESEARCH METHODOLOGY

The following section will discuss the research aim, the methods, the participants, and the limitations of this study.

The research aim was to examine the introduction of teacher appraisal in secondary schools in Taiwan by referring to the influences of its societal cultures. We decided to conduct a study to probe the concerns, issues, and opinions of the core stakeholders, influenced greatly by this change (Guba & Lincoln, 1989). This meant that the teachers in elementary and secondary schools in Taiwan would be the major participants in this study. The major two research questions in this study are:

(1) What do Taiwanese secondary teachers of English think of teacher appraisal?
(2) What roles does culture play in administering teacher appraisal?

Based on what we believe in epistemology about educational research, knowledge is meaningful when each stakeholder makes sense of it by constructing or reconstructing his/her own existing knowledge. As Radnor (2002) suggests, each human in society is a meaning-attributor and knowledge is possible through the interpretive process by interacting with the participants of my inquiry. Knowledge is generated through a series of interactions with the knower. This belief within the interpretive paradigm played an important role in my adoption of the research methods for this study.

The study was divided into two stages and each stage applied a different research method respectively i.e. open-ended questionnaire and semi-structured interview. At the first stage, there were 23 Taiwanese English teachers in total involved in the study island-wide. All of them teach the English subject in secondary schools in Taiwan. Their teaching experience varies enormously, ranging from three-year-experience to 20-year-experience.

At the very beginning, 23 completed questionnaires were returned to me by e-mail, and all of them were English teachers. The strategy we used was 'snowball/network sampling' namely, which refers to "a process of selecting a sample using networks" (Kumar, 1999: 162). We believe this sampling could be quite efficient and helpful especially when it is nearly impossible to ask for the participants' help to join the research face to face. However, the disadvantage could be that participants selected through a network may belong to a particular party with strong fixed viewpoints (Kumar, 1999). However, in this study, the participants' responses to the questions show a moderate attitude towards the topic i.e. no seemingly significant bias or strong fixed viewpoints found.

The questionnaire was designed in ten open-ended questions in order to investigate the participants' opinions in a deeper way. Before we distributed it to my colleagues, the form had been examined and piloted carefully by two Taiwanese English teachers. Thus, some amendments were made accordingly to make it more understandable for other English teachers, especially that these teachers have minimum knowledge about teacher appraisal. Considering that these participants' English proficiency may vary a little we provided both Chinese and English versions for them, and similarly the teachers were also allowed to use any of the two languages to complete the questionnaire. All the returned questionnaires were treated anonymously except for tracing some basic background information i.e. gender, teaching subject, school, and experience. Here are the ten items asked.

1. What is the purpose of implementing teacher appraisal?
2. Overall to what extent do you accept and support teacher appraisal?
3. What sort of qualifications/qualities must an appraiser possess?
4. What kind of relationship should there be between appraiser and appraisee during the appraisal?
5. How often should teacher appraisal be carried out?
6. What aspects of you and your teaching should be appraised?
7. What factors do you think will influence your performance during your appraisal?
8. What should the atmosphere be like during the

appraisal?

9. What feedback will you expect from the appraisal?
10. How do you think the feedback should be given?

Items 1, 2, 5, 6, and 9 were mainly asked to answer research question one i.e. the understanding of teacher appraisal, while the rest (items 3, 4, 7, 8, and 10) were asked to answer research question two i.e. the cultural influences on teacher appraisal. However, this dichotomy is not absolute because some responses in question one may be influenced by participants' perceptions based on a cultural level.

After collecting the questionnaires, we tried to analyse the responses immediately by categorising all the answers of each question into several sub-groups. In other words, the categorisations within each main question were grounded, not applying any existing classifications. After that, we tried to interpret what the data meant to us on the basis on our knowledge and the literature. These results will be presented in section 5, results and discussion. However, during the process of analysing the data, some questions still kept emerging in our mind like 'why they said that?' or 'what situation s/he had experienced before to make her/him think so?' These questions were related a lot to cultural thinking or values, which were not easily probed. Therefore, we decided to take the second stage i.e. semi-structured interview. Due to the limitations of distance, time and budget, we interviewed two participants by telephone for 30 minutes each. We believed this procedure could be worthwhile for we may probe the participants' deeper understanding about the issue. Yet, only two interviews took place and they may be insufficient for evidence.

Except for making some clarifications of general opinions, the interview questions mainly focused on cultural factors that might affect the participants' attitude towards this educational change i.e. teacher appraisal system. These factors could contain cultural philosophy, thinking, values or traditions.

During the process of the phone interviews, we noted down the main ideas of each interview on the paper and these opinions were confirmed by both interviewees. These interviews offered us a chance to listen to the stakeholders' concerns more directly; besides, it also served the function of making up for the shortcomings of a questionnaire i.e. the opinions at a surface level only or the reliability of responses. The results of the interviews were used mainly to supplement or support the statements of stage one.

The strengths and weaknesses of this study may be the following. Firstly, because of our stance in interpretive paradigm in this study, the major strength of this study is that participants were offered chances to construct their reality or knowledge about this issue by an open-ended questionnaire and a semi-structured interview, and moreover the participants' responses were categorized by open-coding. We, coming from the interpretive paradigm, also benefited from this process of knowledge-construction. However, some may argue that our interpretation and implications might be only applicable to this peculiar setting and thus in lack of 'generalisability'.

Secondly, with regard to the sample size, though the participants can be generally representative of other teachers in Taiwan, the opinions from our participants still cannot represent all the other teachers in Taiwan owing to the small number of the participants. Moreover, all of the participants are English teachers in senior high schools in Taiwan, it means these English teachers' responses would inevitably dominate and then influence the results claimed. Teachers teaching the same subject at the same level of school may share similar attitudes and beliefs towards one educational issue; however, this same sharing may be different from other teachers teaching different subjects at different levels. Thirdly, in the research method, the open-ended questionnaire helped us to probe the respondents' understanding of the issue at a deeper level; however, as a common drawback of it, some respondents complained that they were not willing to spend too much time completing a ten open-question questionnaire like taking an essay examination; hence, some of the responses were really too short to be analysed. Finally, in the sampling method, network sampling saved us much time in looking for the participants, yet some problems might occur as well. For example, when few responses were completely blank or unrelated to the questions, it was difficult for us to figure out why these answers were left blank because we nearly had no single chance to re-ask the participants again in person.

RESULTS AND DISCUSSION

In this section, the results from the study will be presented and discussed. First, we will show each research question and then analyse its related questionnaire items, followed by their categorized responses. Finally, we will discuss what these results mean with reference to the existing literature.

Research Question One: What do Taiwanese secondary teachers of English think of teacher appraisal?

To answer this question, items 1, 2, 5, 6, and 9 in the questionnaire were asked.

Item 1: What is the purpose of implementing teacher appraisal?

Except for two respondents did not answer this question, all the others expressed their opinions about this as follows.

(a) Fig.: 1 External Control: (times mentioned)

(1) to monitor teaching quality	10
(2) to filter out/dismiss unsuitable teachers	3
(3) to provide reference for the current annual report on teachers	3
(4) to rank teachers' positions	2
(5) to maintain teaching as a professionalism	2
(6) to experiment on the plausibility of a new educational policy	1

(b) Fig. 2: Internal Control: (times mentioned)

(1) to provide teachers with teaching feedback	9
(2) to make teaching a reflective process	2
(3) to strengthen personal beliefs in education	1
to encourage teacher self-growth	1

Most teachers view the purpose of teacher appraisal as one of the government's tool to demand educational accountability; besides, teacher appraisal also provides teachers with feedback in their teaching. These two aims have been confirmed in the literature about teacher appraisal (Fullan & Hargreaves, 1992). However, it is interesting to notice that teachers' perception about the purpose of teacher appraisal is quite different from the educational authority's. In the government's view, the system is supposed to increase teaching quality, promote professional growth and encourage life-long learning; however, from the responses, most teachers would regard this appraisal as an outer instrument to control them in teaching. Not so many participants said that it could be helpful in facilitating their professional growth in teaching. In Taiwan, the exercising of power and the right of decision-making in education are still tightly held in the highest authority. Usually, teachers at the basic level have no chance at all to share the power or even 'opinions' in the decision of implementing an educational change. It is not surprising that every change the authority proposes will be viewed as a tighter control on teachers for the viewpoints of each 'stakeholder' of a reform are always ignored or unattended purposefully.

In fact, many respondents both in the questionnaire and the interview stressed that increasing teaching quality is more desirable and reputed for the school or the organisation i.e. school effectiveness rather than individual teacher effectiveness. One interviewee said, *"The whole school is composed of all teachers and each teacher has to try his/her best to teach students well. We are building good reputation for the whole school, not for individual teacher."* Indeed, a collective culture always places the group interests as the priority rather than personal achievements.

In addition, some teachers stated that teacher appraisal can help filter out unsuitable teachers. The reason why they said so is possibly because the current annual evaluation of each teacher cannot effectively filter out unsuitable teachers. In fact, it is not unusual for the evaluation committee in each school to have each colleague pass the evaluation annually in order to keep a good relationship with these colleagues. The suitability of being a teacher professionally and physically is seldom taken into account in the meeting. However, whether the new reform in teacher appraisal can avoid such phenomenon is still highly questionable based on the Taiwanese societal culture.

Item 2: Overall to what extent do you accept and support for teacher appraisal? Why?

The question was asked to express two different responses: one was the degree of acceptance and the other was the degree of support; however, most respondents mixed these two together and only gave one overall percentage. In this case, the single percentage in each response was treated as representatives of both degree of acceptance and degree of support. Here are the results.

Fig. 3: Percentages of acceptance & support

The overall degree of acceptance on average	61.8%
The overall degree of support on average	59.0%

Their reasons can be classified as (a) supportive reasons and (b) suspecting reasons.

(a)Supportive Reasons:

(1) It can make teachers believe teaching is professional.
(2) It can provide teaching feedback.
(3) It can monitor teacher's daily behaviour.
(4) It can offer excitement and challenges in life.
(5) It can be like other professionals in the society i.e. all professionals should be appraised.

(b)Suspecting Reasons:

(1) It may make teaching become a well-rehearsed play
(2) It may be in lack of suitable criteria for assessing

performance.

(3) It may be difficult to evaluate each aspect of teaching.

(4) It may be difficult to 'standarise' and 'quantify' teaching.

(5) It may not be easy to be fair enough on each appraisee.

(6) It may increase teacher's workloads and thus be time and labour consuming.

(7) It may pose too much extra pressure and restrictions on teachers.

(8) It may become a matter of formality finally.

(9) It may have different values existing between the appraiser and the appraisee.

(10) It may result in peers' aggressive competition.

From the statistics, we can know that nearly half of the teachers do not accept or support teacher appraisal. There are two main reasons accounting for this. One is that not many teachers have a clear idea of what is teacher appraisal and this reform aims for. An educational reform will likely be less successful if only a small portion of 'stakeholders' know about it (Fullan, 1992). In fact, teacher appraisal would definitely influence or change what teachers do in the classroom and behave in school, and it is necessary to cater for these 'stakeholders' concerns about this issue (Guba & Lincoln, 1989). The second reason is that a majority still doubt that the change is suitable or helpful for them. Teachers are worried that there will be many outside factors such as superior's pressure, relationship, bribery or lobby that may influence the objectiveness and fairness of the appraisal results. Furthermore, *"the appraisal results will become negotiable in order to keep harmonious relationship with other colleagues; then in this way, the system will lack merit"*, an interviewee said.

In addition, due to low effectiveness and the unpleasant experiences from many previous educational reforms since 2000 such as multi-directional school entrance or one-to-nine curriculum, *"teachers are suspicious that teacher appraisal will become a form of acting or formality for the government's determination in reforming is always weak"*, an interviewee said. A reform/change may sometimes be necessary for improving the education but too many reforms within a short period of time may lead to chaos, emotional reactions or even no progress (Fullan 2001; Reynolds *et al.*, 1996).

Item 5. How often should teacher appraisal be carried out?

Seven out of 23 teachers stated that teacher appraisal should be carried out once every semester, which was ranked at the first place. The detailed responses are showed as follows. The teacher appraisal should be carried out once every

Fig. 4: The frequency of administrating appraisal

semester	7	3 academic years	6
1 academic year	5	more than 4 years	1
2 academic years	2	fewer, better	1

One teacher mentioned "fewer, better", while another participant said there should be no fixed schedule for appraisal because teachers should be appraised all the time.

There is no particular pattern about the actual frequency of teacher appraisal; nevertheless, very interestingly, 'once every semester' is the highest choice compared with others. This means teacher appraisal will be carried out twice a year; in the U.K. the formal teacher appraisal is taken once only every three years. This response seems slightly contradictory to that of item 2. Theoretically speaking, the less teachers accept and support the reform, the less frequently teachers hope the reform will take place. Ms. S said in the interview, *"Actually, I do not fully understand the content of teacher appraisal because it is totally new for me. I thought it only got involved with completing some questionnaires and it was quite reasonable for me to fill in a questionnaire each semester."* In fact, appraisal is not a simple and easy task. After our explaining the complete procedure an appraisal needs to include, Ms S expressed her wish to change the original answer in her questionnaire. Normally, most other teachers state that appraisal should take place once within one year or longer than one year.

Item 6. What aspects of you and your teaching should be appraised?

The responses of this question vary in a large scale and they can be broadly classified into five major categories.

(a)Box 1: Teaching Performance (including pre-teaching, teaching, and post-teaching stages)

teaching accountability, material application, activity design, ways of evaluating students, body language and oral expressions, classroom interactions with students, subject knowledge, the presentation of curriculum, teaching methods, timing, and teaching prompts.

(b) Box 2: Professional Competence:

classroom management, in-service education, administrative ability, research ability, the ability of being a homeroom teacher or a subject chairman, the ability of organising an extra-curriculum activity, the ability of processing data, and counselling ability.

(c) Box 3: Professional Attitudes:

cooperation with the school, commitment to education, motivation, thinking process, and reflective teaching.

(d) Box 4: Student-related Items:

students' feedback/reactions on teaching, students' acceptance of a teacher, students' autonomous learning, and students' academic performance.

(e) Box 5: Teacher's Behaviour:

personal characteristics of being a teacher, and relationship/interactions with students and colleagues in school.

From the responses of these teachers, we can foresee a huge gap between what aspects should be appraised the government perceives and what aspects should be appraised the teachers believe. In fact, the official policy will assess teachers' abilities in teaching (50%), counselling (20%), researching (15%) and servicing (15%) (Tsai & Cheng, 2001); however, most responses only focus on the assessment of teaching accountability. In other words, seldom do they mention the evaluation of their counselling, researching, and serving ability. The reasons may be these: first all the teachers in this study come from state-run schools and they need not worry about the recruitment of students or the promoting of schools, and second the job of doing research mainly belongs to the professors in the university level; on the contrary, teaching competency is highly demanded by students and parents in secondary schools rather then doing research. Besides, doing research well is not considered equal to teaching well. Usually, what parents and students or even principals think of a good teacher in Taiwan depends on how many students s/he teaches can enter senior high schools or universities instead of how much research s/he has presented. Third, as both interviewees said, a teacher in secondary school in Taiwan usually has five periods each day on average and it is nearly impossible for them to spend extra time on doing research or school service.

Besides, the hours or credits of joining INSET for in-service teachers were only mentioned by five respondents, while INSET is a highly requested and obligatory criterion in this official appraisal. Contrarily, the teachers express that 'relationship' with peers, staff, and students should be appraised, which is not clearly included at all in the official version. We can still see that teachers hope to maintain a friendly and harmonious working relationship with everyone in school. Furthermore, a sense of commitment/loyalty to school/organisation and off-job behaviours should also be appraised according to the participants (Chow, 1995; Fullan, 2001). These requests can be deemed very culturalised in Taiwanese society.

Item 9. What feedback will you expect from the appraisal?

Fig. 5: The inclusions of feedback

(a)what are the shortcomings of my teaching, how to make my teaching better, and the useful concrete suggestions or teaching demonstrations,	22
(b)what are the merits of my teaching,	8
(c)students' responses to my teaching,	2
(d)and experienced teachers' teaching experience.	1

In general, most of the respondents stated that they hope the feedback of the appraisal can clearly tell them "what, why and how?'. Where did I go wrong in my teaching, what may be the possible reasons, and how can I avoid this next time?

According to Western literature, "feedback provides the opportunity to recognise an employ's outstanding performance and highlights areas of improvement" (Chow, 1985: 77). For school, feedback can lead teachers' performance towards its setting target; for teachers, feedback can serve to examine whether personal requirements about teaching is met or not. In fact, feedback should contain both praise and criticism However, from the responses of this question, not so many teachers look forward to being praised in their feedback. Teachers are more desirable to know where they went wrong in teaching and how to change it from the feedback at harmonious atmosphere. Actually, being appraised from the appraiser is still needed but being humble is more important for the appraisee culturally. However, the appraiser will try to save face for the appraisee at the same time in giving feedback, thus it would usually result in that the comments are always 'harmless' and 'neutral' without losing anyone's face. Then, how can the feedback in appraisal still be valid and reliable, and how can teacher appraisal achieve its goal under these cultural values (Chow, 1995)? Currently, the annual evaluation of teachers in Taiwan confronts this problem, too.

Research Question Two: What roles does culture play in administering teacher appraisal?

To answer this question, items 3, 4, 7, 8, and 10 in the questionnaire were asked.

Item 3. What professional and personal qualities must an appraiser possess?

This question mainly focuses on who the teachers think are qualified to appraise them and what kinds of personalities these appraisers should have. These appraisers could be

Fig. 6: External Appraisers:/ times mentioned

Professors/ Professionals	13	Educational Authorities	2
Outside Teachers	2	Parents	3

Fig. 7: Internal Appraisers:/ times mentioned

Peers/ Teaching Colleague	12	Students	6
School Committee	3	Administrative Staff	3

Fig. 8: Professional qualities of the appraisers

(a)experts in teaching with real teaching experiences,	15
(b)experienced/ senior school teachers with successful teaching,	7
(c) and fully understand the procedure of the appraisal system.	2

Fig. 9: Personal qualities of the appraisers

(a)fair, or impartial in characters,	7
(b)flexible,	1
(c)empathetic,	1
(d)supportive,	1
(e)and easy to communicate with.	1

Most teachers strongly expressed that an appraiser must have a profound knowledge about their teaching subject with real teaching experience. Ms L. said, *"it is quite difficult to convince me of the appraisal results if my appraiser is simply a university professor or expert without similar teaching experience like mine."* Too often, a university professor in Taiwan rarely has teaching experience in secondary school and it is always s/he that designs the educational policy for the teachers to obey the change (Hargreaves & Fullan, 1992). In addition, the majority still believe that those who are senior or superior than them are more suitable to be their appraisers. This is due to the Confucian precept of obedience (Chow, 1995). Junior teachers would generally feel uncomfortable or embarrassed to criticize their senior colleagues (Walker & Dimmock, 2000). Indeed, this phenomenon is easily seen in a harmony-preferential culture for 'harmonious relationship' is the priority for each member in an organization.

12 teachers accepted the peer appraisal but they also expressed the fear that peer appraisal would disrupt the harmony between colleagues and thus not every one would take such risk. Just as one interviewee said, *"It is not ideal to be competitive among teachers for the competition or appraisal will easily ruin my good relationship or friendship with my peers. It is too risky to carry out peer appraisal for me."*

About personal qualities of an appraiser, justice or fairness is still what most teachers are concerned about or 'suspect'. It may be because that the judgement or the result will be influenced unfairly due to the external relationship or pressure.

Item 4. What kind of relationship should there between appraiser and appraisee during the appraisal?

Fig. 10: Relationships with the appraisals

(a) trust/honesty	9	(b) cooperation/partnership	7
(c) fairness/objectiveness	3	(d) respect	3
(e) equality	2	(f) communication	2
(g) harmony	1	(h) support/help	1

Previous studies show that the subordinate's trust and confidence in the superior is significantly correlated with the fairness and accuracy of the appraisal (Fulk, Brief, & Barr, 1985; Landy, Barnes & Murphy, 1978; Chow, 1995). Not surprisingly, the quality of being fair is still demanded by the participants in this study. Furthermore, in fact, a relationship of being cooperative, respectful and equal between appraiser and appraisee can culturally mean the same thing. Here, 'equality' does not refer to the same position between two sides, but means both two sides should enjoy mutual respect from each other. This can be seen as an issue of 'saving face' in Chinese culture. Saving face means no shame in public and this is extremely crucial in maintaining a mutual-respect (Walker & Dimmock, 2000). Therefore, no public negative criticism in order to keep face is important and thus the appraiser's constructive advice is more desirable. However, in fact, we can also argue that these respondents prefer a flat-hierarchy leadership from their heads for in this leading style each member within an organization has an equal opportunity to share his/her needs, aims, opinions. They cooperate with each other in order to achieve the final target (Jones, 2002).

"Equal respect" in Chinese culture means that the superior protects and cares for the subordinates, and subordinates respect and obey the superior. If any educational reform does not take this cultural dimension into consideration, then the plausibility of it perhaps will be very low. In a word, before implementing teacher appraisal, the education authority should ensure that from the reform teachers could still feel trustful, respectable, and cooperative without losing their face.

Item 7. What factors do you think will influence your performance during your appraisal?

This question is asked to investigate what factors the participants perceive may influence their performance or results during the appraisal. The responses can be divided into two major categories i.e. influences from outside and those from inside. Interestingly, the former one takes up 79% of all responses largely while the latter only occupies 21%.

(a)Fig. 11: Outside influences

(a) pupils' academic performance, daily behaviour, IQ levels, learning attitude, and cooperation/ interactions/ relationship with teachers,	10
(b) the appraiser's qualities or qualifications,	7
(c) the observer's negative or positive interferences,	4
(d) the relationship with the administrative staff in school,	4

(e) time for conducting the appraisal,	3
(f) the contents of the appraisal system,	2
(g) curriculum,	1
(h) workloads, and	1
(i) the unnatural setting during the observation.	1

(b) Fig. 12: Inside influences

(a) psychological condition e.g. nervous, shy, stressful,	5
(b) physical condition e.g. exhausted, sick,	1
teaching competence,	1
commitment to teaching, and	1
(c) other.	1

Fig. 13: The percentages of factors influencing appraisal results

	Responses	Percentage
Outside	34	79%
Inside	9	21%
Total	43	100%

It is very interesting to notice that nearly 80% of the attributions come from extrinsic factors, which are regarded as beyond the control of teachers themselves. There are also some likely reasons accounting for this. Firstly, in a collectivism culture, a task is not achieved mainly by individuals but instead by a group of people; this notion is very similar to the leadership in a flat hierarchy. Each one within a group is responsible for the success or failure of a task, thus when this task results in some negative effects, there should be many external reasons to blame for this. Secondly, 'saving face' is still greatly crucial even when one cannot achieve a satisfied appraisal result. Hence, it is better and more comfortable to attribute these negative performances to outer uncontrollable influences. Finally, Chinese culture teaches us that 'everything is destined in its origin' and "what is meant to be, will be" (Dimmock & Walker, 2000 b.: 309). No matter what the result will be like, positive or negative, it has been destined already. The appraisal result is out of personal power to be changed, and has been decided by an unknown outsider.

As the official teacher appraisal proposes, teachers' achieving their professional development is one of its final purposes. However, short-term solutions to teaching problems may not be enough to reach this goal eventually. It could be suggested that teachers need to think reflectively about personal factors that influence their professional performance rather than attributing much to external factors.

Item 8. What should the atmosphere be like during the appraisal?

Fig. 14: The atmosphere during appraisal

(a) natural, relaxing without pressure,	12	(b) harmonious with mutual respect,	5
(c) friendly,	3	(d) open and impartial,	2
(e) non-hypocritical,	1	(f) rational.	1

In Western culture, the whole process of performance appraisal should be carried out in an open and trustworthy atmosphere (Chow, 1995) and this climate of communication and trust is also requested for transformational leadership (Middlehurst, 1993). However, these two important factors are much less mentioned in the above statistics. Culturally, being too open or too direct to persons is regarded impolite. Contrarily, being humble, respectful, and saving face for others are thought of as virtues in Chinese culture. Hence, a direct and open atmosphere may not be so welcomed by a Taiwanese teacher for fear that it will ruin the harmony between peers and lose their face inappropriately.

Item 10. How do you think the feedback should be given? Why?

This question aims to know in what way the teachers hope to obtain their appraisal feedback. The responses can be categorised into two groups: public means and private methods.

(a)Fig. 15: Public ways

an appraisal committee, or	2	a teacher workshop/seminar.	2

(b)Fig. 16: Private ways

a private meeting,	8	a paper report,	8
a personal letter,	2	an e-mail, or	1
at a tea time break.	1		

The reasons why those teachers prefer to have the feedback in a public way are that

(1) it is better to put several heads together to optimise a scheme,
(2) it is a chance to share with other's experience,
(3) it can develop a sense of cooperative learning with others,
(4) and it fosters teachers' trust in the appraisal system.

However, the participants also mentioned that 'harmony' should be the crucial premise of the above four merits.

Next, the reasons why the teachers hope to obtain their feedback in a private form are because

(1) a private paper report can provide sufficient advice, reduce embarrassment, save time, make reference to teacher's annual report, and avoid suspicion,
(2) it can maintain a harmonious atmosphere without any harm,
(3) it can keep teacher's self-esteem respectfully,
(4) it decreases pressure of the public,
(5) it helps to clarify, negotiate and communicate mutually,
(6) it is more likely to be open and honest to each other,
(7) and it establishes a sense of equality between two.

From the above, we can see that most teachers would prefer to receive their feedback in a very private situation. Undeniably, feedback is important for both school and teachers, and how to give feedback is more crucial in Chinese culture

(Chow, 1995). It is very embarrassing to be criticised in public or even face-to-face in a 'face-saving' culture like Taiwan. Chow's study (1995) shows that even in a private way, over 70% of superiors still have difficulty in giving their subordinates negative feedback in terms of age and seniority. Therefore, it is not too surprising to know that most respondents prefer a private way to receive their feedback under the influence of 'face-saving' culture.

In conclusion, these ten questions were asked to study teachers' perception of the introduction of teacher appraisal under a Chinese culture in Taiwan. It is found that teachers' responses are highly linked with the influences of cultural dimensions in Taiwan, and some implications derived from these results along with the conclusion will be presented in the next section.

IMPLICATIONS, SUGGESTIONS & CONCLUSION

This section consists of two parts discussing what the results of this research may imply and what can be concluded for this chapter.

Implications and Suggestions

The following are the likely implications and suggestions generating from the results. Firstly, it is important to recognise that educational changes or reforms cannot necessarily be regarded as being equal to educational progress if we cannot recognise the complexity of a change such as types of leadership, destabilisation, or uncertainty (Fullan, 2001; Reynolds *et al.*, 1996). Sometimes, an educational change is introduced in order to keep up with the advancing of a society; however, it is naïve to believe any change would certainly result in some positive effects. As Fullan (1993: 4) points out, "productive education is full of paradoxes and components that are often not seen as going together." Change itself is definitely not a blueprint for us to simply follow the designation step by step; contrarily, it is more like a journey full of uncertainty and problems. A change will seldom lead to great success without considering many potential factors around the issue i.e. the internal and external environment of the change should be both catered carefully.

In this study, many participants expressed opinions that actually they did not fully realise what teacher appraisal is about; in addition, what the teachers perceived was quite different from what the government advocated. Very ironically, in this study the idea of changing was seemingly passed down as a top-to-down hierarchy instead of a flat hierarchy. The basic stakeholders i.e. these secondary teachers seem unable to be effective changing agents at all for their concerns, opinions, and issues were not considered seriously. The government should not be afraid of listening to teachers' opinions, for these viewpoints, or sometimes can be resistances, can always provide possible alternatives to make the change more acceptable and plausible (Fullan, 1993; 1999). Only when the opinions of all agents within a change can be taken into account

seriously can the change possibly-make it progress. In other words, the leader or the government should act as a "communication agent", especially in continuous change. The leaders should co-ordinate and align different opinions, and listen to different voices in order to win the hearts and minds of its employees, here the teachers (Hooper & Potter, 2000). This emotional leadership or skills is particularly necessary in dealing with the diversity.

Furthermore, in fact, the idea of 'globalisation' mainly comes from economy or commerce, and there are some dangers if we simply transfer and apply business management to varied educational contexts in a less than critical shape (Bottery, 1999). We cannot deny that globalisation seems to have been a world trend in many areas such as trade, human rights, commerce or environmental issues. However, when talking about the globalisation of education, we should seriously consider about the factors of cultural dimensions. Education is the productivity of human thoughts and these thoughts could be deeply influenced or led by their societal cultures. Will it be well compatible, suitable or appropriate for a policy, change or reform to be implemented in another different country with distinguished cultural values if this change was originally tailor-made for its peculiar context? Even a tailor-made change will very likely confront much complexity and uncertainty (Fullan, 2001), not to mention this change will be transferred to another different context. For example, the participants' responses to the item ten did not clearly show what Western teacher appraisal looks for i.e. 'openness'. Another example is the participants' responses to the item six. Some expressed that relationships with peer or students, and commitments to the school should be appraised as well; however, these evaluation criteria might be seldom seen in Western teacher appraisal.

Rooting a foreign change is not simply like following a blueprint step by step and naively expecting its final success (Fullan, 1993; 1999). It will stir more resistance, uncertainty, or turbulence, and we need to think about seriously which type of leadership can be more helpful to deal with this situation. In this case, we urge that during the process of transferring a theory, policy, or reform, it would be much more desirable to be culture sensitive to this change. In fact, if an imported reform is supposed to be a filter or mediator for some education phenomena, then it should be at the stage of formulation of this change that cultural issues are considered seriously rather then at the stage of its implementation (Dimmock & Walker: 2000 b.).

Next, though it cannot be denial that teacher appraisal may be one of the good instruments to assess teachers' teaching performance, yet the assumptions behind performance appraisal in Anglo-American cultures could possibly make it difficult to carry out in non-Western cultures, like Taiwan (Chow, 1995). To begin with, as the responses show, 'fairness' is always the major concern, which most teachers are worried about during teacher appraisal. In a society of viewing human relationship as a network like Taiwan, it is quite possible that the appraisal results will be greatly influenced by outer forces such as kinship, friendship, or close bloodline instead of pure teaching performance as what the participants and interviewees expressed these concerns in the study. In this way, then the results may not reflect the real situation of teachers' performance.

In addition, though the results in the item nine show that the majority of the respondents expect some 'weakness in teaching' in their appraisal feedback, yet 'harmony' and 'keeping face' are still highly emphasised during the whole process, too. As a result, the appraiser will be reluctant to give critical feedback to the appraisee, especially negative feedback to the senior or elder colleagues. Therefore, the Western performance appraisal system stressing open and direct confrontation between appraiser and appraisee may not be suitable for the Chinese culture (Chow, 1985). In the end, the feedback will likely be very neutral without losing anyone's face on both sides. This will lead to that feedback provided for the appraisees will not be effective at all. However, it can be encouraged that the appraiser can try to transform the appraisees to reach a mutual understanding between two parties i.e. help appraisees to view themselves as appraisers, too. By increasing appraisees' confidence, motivation, self-esteem, and aspiration of their teaching performance, the leader, i.e. the appraiser, can be integrated with these appraisees to reach a mutual understanding and this is exactly what transformational leadership aims for (Middlehurst, 1993).

Furthermore, from the Western view about performance assessment, the final target of appraisal is to help appraisees reach the stage of self-growth as a professional. However, in a group-oriented culture an individual is only one member within a group and the group interest is always the priority than any personal interest. Thus, the short-term solutions to solve the teaching problems immediately to make school effective will be more urgent and necessary than the demand for long-term professional self-growth. Therefore, many responses in the study show that teachers eagerly expect that the results of appraisal will tell them where they went wrong and how to 'cure' it. Contrarily, rarely did teachers ask for helps on planning their long-term professional growth. Again, the leader, the moral agent, could help these teachers transform to be empowered leaders too (Middlehurst, 1993), making teachers realise that group interest is reached by mutual understanding and communication. The meaning of teaching is not only to achieve school-effectiveness but also to help teachers re-gain their self-esteem, affiliation, and self-actualisation in professional teaching.

Finally, to be more practical, the government should compare what are the gaps existing in the educational systems between Western countries and Taiwan before it implements a borrowed educational change. We have to consider the types of leadership we need, teachers' working loads, teaching resources, teaching targets, school size, class size, human and financial resources for appraising. In practice, many problems may occur and lead to chaos if the government ignores to compare the crucial differences in education between two sides or if a leader applies the wrong leadership in the time of change (Fullan, 2001). Therefore, it could be argued that cross-cultural approach should be taken into consideration during the formulation and adoption of an educational reform if the change will unavoidably result in the questions of cultural suitability and new leadership. In fact, this cross-cultural comparison is fairly necessary and important, especially when the change only has limited existing comparative studies, and will relate to the globalisation of policy and practice (Dimmock & Walker, 2000 a.).

Conclusion

The main purpose of this chapter is to examine the introduction of teacher appraisal in Taiwanese societal culture from the perspective of educational globalisation or borrowing. An open-ended questionnaire and semi-structured interview were used to investigate 23 Taiwanese English teachers' perceptions and attitudes towards teacher appraisal. Their responses were analysed on the basis of the influences from societal cultures in Taiwan to raise the issue that if it is perfectly appropriate or suitable to implement teacher appraisal, which was designed originally to fit its peculiar Anglo-American cultures. Many factors from Taiwanese cultural dimensions were taken into serious consideration in discussing the plausibility of teacher appraisal. Finally, the study finds that many traditional culture values will inevitably play an important role in the success or failure of an educational change such as teacher appraisal if this change is developed and then transferred from the Western cultures.

In conclusion, we argue that no body intends to resist the change if any change is definitely necessary and will cause positive effects. However, what we have to stress is that during the formulation and adoption of a Western educational theory, policy or reform, we have to ask if we are totally ready for the change already, what kinds of new leadership we need to deal with this problem and, what management can we take to make it plausible. In fact, during the process of globalisation, an educational change needs to be more culture-sensitive, and the work of cross-cultural examination of this change should not be ignored before its formulation and implementation. Therefore, teacher performance appraisal must be re-considered or modified in order to fit the Taiwanese/Chinese cultural values if the educational authority in Taiwan still insists upon carrying it out at present or in the near future.

REFERENCES

Barlette, S. (2000). The Development of Teacher Appraisal: a recent history. *British Journal of Educational Studies, 48* (1), 24-37.

BBC. http://news.bbc.co.uk/1/hi/education/2165787.stm Retrieved on 01/08/2002.

Bottery, M. (1999). Global Force, national medications and the management of educational institutions. *Educational Management and Administration, 27* (3), 299-312.

Chang, D. R. (1999). The Problems We Face in the Implementation of Teacher Career Ladder and their Solutions. *Education Forum, 31*, 27-30.

Cheng, Y. C. (1992). A Preliminary Study of School Management Initiative: Responses to induction and implementation of management reforms. *Educational Research Journal, 7*, 21-32.

Cheong, Y. C. (2000). Cultural Factors in Educational Effectiveness: a framework for comparative research. *School Leadership and Management, 20* (2), 207-225.

Chow, H. S. (1995). An Opinion Survey of Performance Appraisal Practices in Hong Kong and the People's Republic of China. *Asia Pacific Journal of Human Resources, 32* (3), 67-79.

David, R., Bollen, R., Creemers, B., Hopkins, D., Stoll, L., & Lagerweij, N. (1996). *Making Good Schools.* London: Routledge.

Dimmock, C., & Walker, A. (2000 a.). Developing Comparative and International Educational Leadership and Management: a cross-cultural model. *School Leadership and Management, 20* (2), 43-160.

Dimmock, C., & Walker, A. (2000 b.). Globalisation and Societal Culture: reflecting schooling and school leadership in the twenty-first century. *Compare, 30* (3), 303-312.

Fidler, B. (1995). Staff Appraisal and the Statutory Scheme in England. *School Organisation, 15* (2), 95-107.

Fulk, L., Brief, A. P., & Barr, S. H. (1985). Trust-in-supervisor and perceived fairness and accuracy of performance appraisal systems. *Journal of Business Research, 13*, 301-313.

Fullan, M. (1993). *Change Forces: probing the depths of educational reform.* London: Falmer Press.

Fullan, M. (1999). *Change Forces: the sequel. London*: Falmer Press.

Fullan, M. (2001). *Leading in a Culture of Change: being effective in complex times.* San Francisco: Jossey-Bass.

Fullan, M., & Hargreaves, A. (1992). *Teacher Development and Educational Change.* London: Falmer Press.

Fullan, M. & Stiegelbauer, S. (1992). *The New Meaning of Educational Change.* London: Cassell.

Goleman, D. (1995). *Emotional Intelligence.* New York: Bantam Books.

Guba, E. G., & Lincoln, Y. S. (1989). *The Fourth Generation Evaluation.* London: Sage.

Gunter, H. M. (2002). Teacher Appraisal 1988-1998: a case study. School *Leadership and Management, 22* (1), 61-72.

Hallinger, P. (1998). Educational change is Southwest Asia: The challenge of creating learning systems. *Journal of Educational Administration, 36* (5), 492-509.

Hargreaves, A., & Fullan, M. (1992). *Understanding Teacher Development.* London: Cassell.

Hofstede, G. H. (1985). The Interaction Between National and Organizational Value System. *Journal of Management Studies, 22* (4), 347-357.

Hofstede, G. H. (1991). *Cultures and Organizations: software of the mind.* London: McGraw Hill.

Hooper, A., & Potter, J. (2000). *Intelligent Leadership.* London: Random House.

Huh, K. C. (2001). Big Change Questions: is finding the right balance with regard to educational change possible, given the tensions that occur between global influences and local traditions, in countries in Asia-Pacific? *Journal of Educational Change, 2,* 257-260.

Jackson, T. (2001). Cultural values and management ethics: A 10-nation study. *Human Relations, 54* (10), 1267-1302.

Jones, G. (2002). *Leadership and Management.* Unpublished Class Notes:

Exeter University.

Kumar, R. (1996). *Research Methodology: A step-by-step guide for beginners.* London: Sage.

Landy, F. J., Barnes, J. L., & Murphy, K. R. (1978). Correlated of perceived fairness and accuracy of performance evaluation. *Journal of Applied Psychology, 63,* 751-754.

Lee, W. O. (1991). *Social Change and Educational Problems in Japan, Singapore and Hong Kong.* London: Macmillan.

Levin, H. (1976). Educational Reform: Its meaning. In M. Carnoy & H. Levin (Eds.) *The Limits of Educational Reform.* New York: McKay.

Liberty Times. (2002). www.libertytimes.com.tw Retrieved on 28.07.2002.

Lowe, A. C-T., & Corkindale, D. R. (1998). Differences in "cultural values" and their effects on responses to marketing stimuli: A cross-cultural study between Australians and Chinese from the People's Republic of China. *European Journal of Marketing, 9* (10), 843-867.

Lu, L. C., Rose, G. M., & Blodgett, J. G. (1999). The Effects of Cultural Dimensions on Ethical Decision Making in Marketing: An Exploratory Study. *Journal of Business Ethics, 18*, 91-105.

Maclean, R. (2001). Educational Change in Asia: An Overview. *Journal of Educational Change, 2*, 189-192.

McColskey, W., & Egelson, P. (1993). *Designing Teacher Evaluation Systems that Support Professional Growth.* Washington, DC.: Office of Educational Research and Improvement.

Middlehurst, R. (1993). *Vision, Values and Leadership.* Buckingham: Open University Press.

Ministry of Education (MOE), http://www2.edu.tw Retrieved on

28.07.2002.

Ministry of Education (MOE). http://www.edu.tw/human-affair/rules/r7f.htm Retrieved on 28.07.2002.

Mo, K. M., Conners, R., & Mccormick, J. (1998). Teacher Appraisal in Hong Kong Self-Managing Secondary Schools: Factors fro Effective Practices. *Journal of Personal Evaluation in Edcation, 12* (1), 19-42.

Radnor, H. (2002). *Researching Your Professional Practice: doing qualitative research.* Buckingham: Open University.

Reynolds, D., Bollen, R., Creemers, B., Hopkins, D., Still, L., & Lagerweij, N. (1996). *Making Good Schools: Linking school effectiveness and school improvement.* London: Routledge.

Toyogakuen University, http://www.human.toyogakuen-u.ac.jp/~acmuller/contao/analects.htm Retrieved on 25.07.2002.

Tsai, P-T, & Cheng, T-F. (2001). *The Report on Teacher Career Ladder System in Taiwan.* Taipei: MOE.

Tunner, G., & Clift, P. (1988). *Studies in Teacher Appraisal.* London: Falmer.

Walker, A., & Dimmock, C. (2000). One Size Fits All? Teacher Appraisal in Chinese Culture. *Journal of Personal Evaluation in Education, 14* (2), 155-178.

Wragg, E. C. (1987). *Teacher Appraisal: A Practical Guide.* London: Macmuilan.

Wragg, E.C., Wikeley, F. J., Wragg, C. M., & Haynes, G. S. (1996). *Teacher Appraisal Observed*. London: Routledge.

Yang, C. L. (2000). *A Study on the Plausibility of the School-based*

Teacher Career Ladder System in Primary Schools in Taiwan. Unpublished PhD. Dissertation. Taipei: NCU.

APPENDIX

Appendix 1.

Diagram 1. Three Terminologies about Culture Dimensions

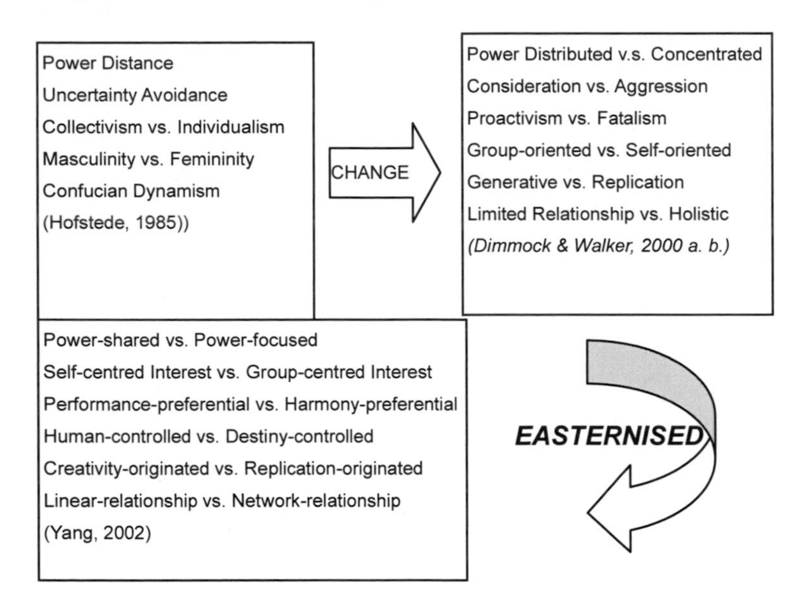

Appendix 2.

English Questionnaire

Instruction: Teacher Appraisal may include three major

stages: (1) pre-appraisal stage, including target-setting or observation-arranging, (2) official appraisal stage, including classroom observation, teaching demonstration, questionnaire, or interview etc. (3) post-appraisal stage, including following-up meeting for feedback or plans for future professional performance.

Please express your opinions about the following ten questions.

1. What is the purpose of implementing teacher appraisal?
2. Overall to what extent do you accept and support for teacher appraisal?
3. What professional and personal qualities must an appraiser possess?
4. What kind of relationship should there be between appraiser and appraisee during the appraisal?
5. How often should teacher appraisal be carried out?
6. What aspects of you and your teaching should be appraised?
7. What factors do you think will influence your performance during your appraisal?
8. What should the atmosphere be like during the appraisal?
9. What feedback will you expect from the appraisal?
10. How do you think the feedback should be given?

Appendix 3.

中文問卷

說明：本問卷的"教師評鑑"實施方式單指由他人透過行為／教學觀察方式對你的教學表現作出的評量；"評鑑過程"包含 (1) 觀察前的相互協商，目標設定，觀察安排 (2) 現場正式的行為觀察，教學觀摩，訪談，問卷等 和 (3) 觀察後的檢討改進會議和專業成長計畫的擬定。

一、你認為教師評鑑的實施目的為何？

二、整體而言，你對教師評鑑的接受度和支持度有多少（以0~100%表示）？為什麼？

三、你認為應該由哪些人來評鑑你的專業表現？他們應該具備什麼資格或特質？為什麼?

四、你認為評鑑者和被評鑑者在評鑑過程中應該建立什麼樣的關係？

五、你認為教師評鑑應該多久實施一次？

六、你認為教師評鑑應該評定哪些項目？

七、你認為在評鑑過程中有哪些因素會影響到你的教師專業表現？

八、你認為評鑑過程應該在什麼樣的氣氛下進行？

九、你希望你的評鑑結果內容會告訴你什麼？

十、你希望在什麼場合和氣氛下知道你的評鑑結果？為什麼？

個人資料：

性別： ____男，_____女

任教科目：___________

任教年資：_________年

實踐大學數位出版合作系列
社會科學類　AF0057

Critical Inquiry into English Language Teachers' Minds

解構英語教師

作　　者　楊文賢
統籌策劃　葉立誠
文字編輯　王雯珊
視覺設計　賴怡勳
執行編輯　詹靚秋　林世玲
圖文排版　郭雅雯
數位轉譯　徐真玉　沈裕閔
圖書銷售　林怡君
網路服務　徐國晉
法律顧問　毛國樑律師
發 行 人　宋政坤
出版印製　秀威資訊科技股份有限公司
台北市內湖區瑞光路583巷25號1樓
電話：(02) 2657-9211
傳真：(02) 2657-9106
E-mail：service@showwe.com.tw
經 銷 商　紅螞蟻圖書有限公司
台北市內湖區舊宗路二段121巷28、32號4樓
電話：(02) 2795-3656
傳真：(02) 2795-4100
http://www.e-redant.com

2006 年 9 月
BOD 一版
定價：340元

讀　者　回　函　卡

感謝您購買本書，為提升服務品質，煩請填寫以下問卷，收到您的寶貴意見後，我們會仔細收藏記錄並回贈紀念品，謝謝！

1.您購買的書名：____________________

2.您從何得知本書的消息？

☐網路書店　☐部落格　☐資料庫搜尋　☐書訊　☐電子報　☐書店

☐平面媒體　☐ 朋友推薦　☐網站推薦　☐其他__________

3.您對本書的評價：(請填代號　1.非常滿意 2.滿意 3.尚可 4.再改進)

封面設計____　版面編排____　內容____　文/譯筆____　價格____

4.讀完書後您覺得：

☐很有收獲　☐有收獲　☐收獲不多　☐沒收獲

5.您會推薦本書給朋友嗎？

☐會　☐不會，為什麼？____________________

6.其他寶貴的意見：____________________

____

____

____

讀者基本資料

姓名：____________________　年齡：______　性別：☐女　☐男

聯絡電話：____________________　E-mail：____________________

地址：____________________

學歷：☐高中(含)以下　☐高中　☐專科學校　☐大學

☐研究所(含)以上　☐其他______________

職業：☐製造業　☐金融業　☐資訊業　☐軍警　☐傳播業　☐自由業

☐服務業　☐公務員　☐教職　☐學生　☐其他__________

請貼
郵票

To：114

台北市內湖區瑞光路 583 巷 25 號 1 樓

秀威資訊科技股份有限公司　　　收

寄件人姓名：

寄件人地址：□□□

(請沿線對摺寄回,謝謝!)

秀威與 BOD

BOD（Books On Demand）是數位出版的大趨勢，秀威資訊率先運用 POD 數位印刷設備來生產書籍，並提供作者全程數位出版服務，致使書籍產銷零庫存，知識傳承不絕版，目前已開闢以下書系：

一、BOD 學術著作—專業論述的閱讀延伸
二、BOD 個人著作—分享生命的心路歷程
三、BOD 旅遊著作—個人深度旅遊文學創作
四、BOD 大陸學者—大陸專業學者學術出版
五、POD 獨家經銷—數位產製的代發行書籍

BOD 秀威網路書店：www.showwe.com.tw
政府出版品網路書店：www.*gov*books.com.tw

永不絕版的故事・自己寫・永不休止的音符・自己唱